IT'S KIND OF
A BAD IDEA

By the Author

Emma by the Sea

It's Kind of a Bad Idea

Visit us at www.boldstrokesbooks.com

It's Kind of a Bad Idea

by

Sarah G. Levine

2025

IT'S KIND OF A BAD IDEA

ISBN 13: 978-1-63679-920-9

This Trade Paperback Original Is Published By
Bold Strokes Books, Inc.
P.O. Box 249
Valley Falls, NY 12185

First Edition: October 2025

Credits
Editor: Ruth Sternglantz
Production Design: Stacia Seaman
Cover Design by Inkspiral Design

Acknowledgments

Here we go, book two!

As before, a huge and heartfelt thank you to Sandy Lowe and Ruth Sternglantz for all you do. It's terrifying to put your precious book child into the hands of others. You both, and everyone at Bold Strokes Books, make it that much easier.

To everyone who supported *Emma by the Sea*—thank you for making my lifelong dream come true. I can't wait for you to read this book and to see where this journey leads me. If I met you at a con, event, or signing this year, you have my endless gratitude.

Big love in particular to: Caroline Salis, for sharing your social media expertise and being my loudest fan; Mel Whitehouse and Liza Henowitz, for cheering me on and always being there over text; Rachelle Kredentser, for the in-person support and for always understanding; Allie Frosina, for your hospitality; Nancy, Melissa, and Laura Epstein, for the dog content and daily laughs.

To my Northshore community of friends and family, thank you for spreading the word about my book and supporting our local indie bookstores at the same time.

As always, nothing in my life would be possible without my family. Mom, Dad, Hannah, Winnie, Zach, Liza, Harrison, and Elias. Harrison, thank you for telling all the adults at your school to read *Emma by the Sea*. I'm sure they were very confused if they looked it up. Mom and Hannah, the characters in this book are NOT based on you. Nothing makes you more aware of your connection to your family than planning a wedding, and how lucky am I mine wanted to be involved in planning ours?

Carol, thank you for welcoming me into your family with open arms and for giving birth to the best girl in the world. Jasmine, by the time this book is officially published, you will be my wife. The profound sense of love and happiness typing that sentence gave me is more than I could ever have hoped for. Thank you for holding my hand as I follow my dreams.

And to you, reader of queer books, the biggest thank you of all. For celebrating queer joy and for making it so I can write more stories about it.

For my wife, Jasmine.
Here's hoping neither of us need to plan a wedding ever again.

PART ONE

The Engagement Party

September

CHAPTER ONE

Annika Silberberg hated weddings.

She did truly believe in celebrating and highlighting other people's romantic love. She teared up at every wedding ceremony she'd ever gone to and loved a good rom-com as much as the next girl.

What she didn't love—in fact, what she might even a little bit *hate*—was all of the extra shit that seemed to go along with a marriage these days.

The showers and brunches and presents, whole weekend you needed to block off, multiple outfit changes of it all. The thousands of dollars you could spend on vacations or buying property or having kids splashed on trips to Savannah and dresses you'd wear once, spill a vodka cranberry on, relegate to the back of some closet, and never think about again.

"It's just the spectacle of it all," she said as she sat at her mother's well-used kitchen table and dug her nail into the same groove she'd been wearing at for twenty-eight years. "I mean the wedding-industrial complex has spawned this, like, hodgepodge Franken-event that spans four months to a year."

"Oop," her sister Maia said and pointed a light pink gel manicured finger at her from across the table, "you said the words. Pay up."

"Seriously?" Annika whined.

Maia pointed to her face and said, "Does this look like I'm joking?"

Annika rolled her eyes and searched her pockets for her wallet.

"I can't believe you're making me do this," she said. Annika reluctantly pulled out a thin black leather wallet with leaves tooled on the front from her jeans and slowly plucked a wrinkled dollar bill between the short fingernails of her right hand.

Maia waved a plastic tub that had once held a Costco amount of peanut butter pretzels in front of her face. Ten dollar bills already sloshed around its depths, and Maia had only been engaged for a month. Maia said nothing as Annika dropped the money into the tub, just shook it ominously at her, her sleek high pony swaying with the movement.

"Mom," Annika whined at her mother as she bustled back to the table carrying a bottle of sparkling white wine and three glasses, "I'm already going to be spending a fortune on this shit anyway."

"You did agree to it, Niki," their mother said.

Annika huffed and sat back so forcefully in her chair the old wood creaked. She crossed her arms over her chest, the black lines of the tattoos beginning on her right biceps peeking out of the soft green cotton sleeve of her T-shirt.

"I'm going to be broke by the time you actually get married," she grumbled.

"You're already broke," Maia said as she took a dainty sip of wine and crossed one thin thigh over the other.

Annika kicked her under the table, and Maia kicked her back.

"Honestly, you two are grown women, and you still act like you're tweens," their mother said with a sigh. She settled herself in her chair. The motion caused her long braid to swing over her left shoulder. It was as dark and thick and unruly as Annika's but shot through with gray, like quartz in dark rock.

Annika stuck her tongue out at Maia before she picked up her own wine and flicked her bangs off her forehead as she slouched down in her chair.

"Can you at least pretend to be happy for me, Niki?" Maia asked, and a dash of hurt flashed through her dark eyes beneath the teasing tone.

"I *am* happy for you and Jonnie," Annika said emphatically.

She really was, too. She didn't hate the concept of marriage. Didn't believe that the whole institution was inherently sexist and should be abolished. Although maybe she did, just a little.

And being two years younger than Maia meant she'd seen her sister wallow and cry over subpar dudes since the age of twelve.

Annika liked to joke it was what turned her into a lesbian. But Jonnie, her sister's dependable veterinarian fiancé, was nothing like those other boys.

"You know I love Jonnie. He's the sweetest, kindest man around. I'm happy you're locking him down. I just don't get why you need all of"—she gestured expansively at the scene before her: the big calendar her mom kept hung on the kitchen wall, which now sprawled like an art model across the table, the glossy magazines and printouts and laptops filled with tabs to venues and tasting menus and table linen options joining it before them—"this."

"Because there's a certain expectation people have when you host one of these," Maia said haughtily. Annika could practically hear the tilt of her nose in her voice.

"Okay, Edith Wharton. You're not a fucking socialite in the Gilded Age, Mai." Annika snorted, then continued, "All you need is a marriage license, a rabbi, Dad, us"—she gestured between her mother and herself—"and two witnesses to sign your ketubah, and then boom, you're married. Maybe some dancing, maybe some drinking, but no passed apps, or roast station, or bridal shower, or engagement party, or any of that meshugas. Save yourself seventy-five thousand dollars."

"Are you done with your diatribe now?" Maia asked, her eye roll audible in her voice, "because I believe you now owe Portland Paw Patrol two dollars."

"Sweetie," their mom said to Annika placatingly, "maybe you'll understand when you have a wedding—"

"Oh, here we go," Annika grumbled. She slumped farther down in her chair and took a big gulp of wine, wiped away a dribble from her chin. Her mother kept finding ways to sneak in not-so-subtle hints about Annika's fluid love life since Maia's engagement.

"Oh my God, Mom, could you be any more heavy-handed?" Maia retorted, switching sides rapidly.

Their mother put her hands up in defense and shrugged.

"I'm just saying, maybe if you let your girlfriends stick around for more than a few months, you might understand the desire for a big celebration to show off your love," their mother said.

"I'm busy with the boutique," Annika replied, her usual response when this topic came up. She could feel her shoulders rising around her ears defensively. "You know this time of year is crazy for me, all the last-minute fittings and customer demands, I don't have time or energy to seriously commit right now."

"Yeah, lay off her," Maia said, jumping to her defense. "She's in the first few years of getting a business off the ground. You know that's when most of them fold."

"Plus, how am I going to have any time for dating when I'm planning and attending a billion events for this one's wedding?" Annika added with a jab of her thumb at Maia.

"Alright, alright," their mother replied and relented with a wave of her hand.

But as they turned to other topics, it wasn't lost on Annika that she and Maia had gone from bickering to teammates in about three seconds. She caught her mom's eye, and she winked at Annika over her wineglass.

Classic mom diversion tactic.

"At least you have one decision down for this wedding," their mother said a little while later as she flipped through a back issue of *The Knot*.

"Oh?" Maia inquired, one perfectly threaded and filled eyebrow raised in question.

"Where you're getting your dress from," their mother supplied.

They both turned to look at Annika.

The irony of all ironies in Annika's life was that despite hating the pageantry of early twenty-first-century weddings, she did in fact own and operate a wedding dress boutique.

It was a full-service boutique where she sold a handful of other small designers, tailored the dresses herself, and, *very* occasionally, did custom orders where she'd design and sew a dress or suit from scratch. Her mentor Anusha had sold the business to her when her rheumatoid arthritis made sewing too difficult. She was still a part owner and helped Annika with design and business questions. But for all intents and purposes, the shop was Annika's.

"That reminds me, what are you doing on December third?" Maia asked her.

"Uh, over two months from now?" Annika asked and shrugged. It was rare for her to know what she was doing the next week, let alone two months from now. "Probably cleaning snow off my car and praying I don't get frostbite on my tits before I get to work."

"Save that day for me," Maia stated.

A big sister command, not a request.

"Why don't you and Jonnie decide on a wedding date before we start thinking about a dress," Annika replied, not saying yes, but not saying no either.

Not that Annika needed to wait. She'd already started designing the dress three years ago when Maia had first met Jonnie. Listening to her older sister gush about their first few dates, seeing the sparkle in Maia's eyes as she'd described the way Jonnie's quiet presence made her feel more grounded, Annika had known. This was the one that would stick.

Maia waved her hand, and the perfect facets of the oval solitaire diamond on a thin platinum band on her left ring finger glinted in the kitchen light. Elegantly understated and modern, just like Maia.

"Fine, fine we'll settle on a date first. Speaking of dates," Maia said, leaning across the table when their mom got up to go get the snacks she'd prepared for them, "are you bringing that cute potter you brought to Jonnie's birthday last month to the engagement party this Saturday?"

"Lana," Annika supplied, "and no, I'm not."

"Why not?" Maia's eyes narrowed as she asked the question.

Annika shifted in her seat and looked into her wineglass to avoid meeting her sister's eyes.

"You fucking didn't," Maia said. "Niki, she was cute and sweet and offered to give me a free pottery lesson."

"She wanted to spend the whole weekend together and hold my hand when we walked out in public." Annika shivered, like she'd just said Lana'd wanted them to perform a ritual where they painted each other naked with their period blood.

"How awful, the woman you'd been seeing for two months wanted to do couple things with you," Maia said dryly. "I thought you were all excited about her when we met her."

"I know, I know, she seemed so cool and hot and perfect in the beginning, but then I just felt like she wanted too much from me, you know?" Annika said. She toyed with one of the thin silver hoops hanging through her earlobes.

"*Too much*," Maia repeated blankly. "Like holding your hand in public?"

Annika shrugged. "Holding hands is a gateway drug to other stuff. Like wanting to call you *babe*, know your middle name, and ask you about your deepest fears and shit. I liked her a lot at the beginning, but I asked myself the farmers market question, and my answer was no."

"Your fucking farmers market test," Maia said, and her whole head went with her eyes when she rolled them this time, sleek pony flying. "You know, one of these days someone is going to pass your test. And you better hope their answer about you is yes, too."

Annika just rolled her own eyes in response.

Fat chance, she thought and sipped her wine.

Chapter Two

Gabi could tell she wasn't in her apartment before she even opened her eyes.

For one thing, no one else was in bed with her. She reached her right arm out and encountered only cool sheets rather than Matt's radiator-like heat.

For a second, the sun slanted in the windows at the wrong angle. Her and Matt's bedroom in the apartment they'd been renting was south facing and only got light for a small sliver of the afternoon.

Sun already streamed in through the blinds, lighting up the darkness behind her eyelids.

For a third, there were small feet pitter-pattering outside the door. She heard her friend Rachel's voice call through the hallways after her two-year-old, Celia, as she raced away from her mother, apparently refusing to put her pants on.

Gabi sat up in bed, pushed her disheveled curls out of her face, and sighed. Her head hurt from lack of sleep, her back hurt from the hard mattress in Rachel's guest room—her thirties were proving to be fun—and her heart hurt for Matt and the life he'd dreamed they'd have together.

After a moment where she rethought every decision she'd ever made in her life, starting with ever agreeing to put on pants—stand your ground, Celia!—to applying for residency in Portland, she finally convinced her body to move. She got up and staggered toward the smell of coffee in her sleep shorts and a big baggy crewneck sweatshirt.

It led her to the kitchen, where she found Aaron, Rachel's husband, cleaning up the breakfast disaster his daughter had wrought.

"Morning," she croaked as she wound her long curly hair into a bun on the top of her head and secured it with the elastic on her wrist, "I see tornado Celia touched down in here."

"Hey, Gab," Aaron said. He was bent over the circular wooden table in their sunlit kitchen. He stood, his right hand cupping the remains of his daughter's breakfast and his left hand brushing against his black joggers. His dark brown hair was already thinning near his forehead, so he wore it short, showcasing a deep widow's peak over thick eyebrows and a short scruffy beard.

"There's coffee still if you want some," he said, "or you can have some of that fancy pod espresso Rach's mom insists on buying us."

"Thanks, man," Gabi said.

She padded over to the counter and poured herself a cup of coffee in a big blue ceramic mug. She saw that Rachel, despite having spent her morning wrangling a toddler, had also foamed oat milk in the frother Gabi and Matt had bought the couple for their wedding three years previously.

"How was your night?" Aaron asked when she sat down at the table.

Gabi tucked her legs up under her on the artfully weathered antique dining chair. Aaron and Rachel's small house was nestled on a tree-lined street in South Portland not far from Casco Bay. Every room was tastefully done, clean and comfortable and currently toddler-proofed within an inch of its life. It was the home of two successful middle-class people in established careers and a healthy relationship.

The type of home Matt wanted them to be in in a year or two, before Gabi blew up their life. Baby mess included.

"It was fine, just had work," Gabi said with a shrug and took a sip of her coffee.

"You're going to that engagement party tonight, right?" Aaron asked. "For your camp friend Maia?"

Gabi nodded.

"Is that going to be weird for you, going to an event without Matt?" he asked.

He gave her a look that she read as trying to be sympathetic to the possible pain being in a romantic setting might give her when she was only days removed from ending a relationship she'd been in for the last eight years.

It made her shift uncomfortably in her seat. Not because he was right, but because she felt guilty about how wrong he was.

"I think it will be okay," Gabi said with a shrug, "The only person I know that will be there is her sister, Annika, so it's not like I'm going to be explaining his absence constantly."

So far, she'd only told Rachel, who had known her and Matt since they'd met in college, about the breakup. They used to be a foursome in their early and mid-twenties, but then Aaron and Rachel had had Celia. And since Gabi had started her residency, she'd seen less of, well, everyone who wasn't at the hospital.

But when she'd called Rachel immediately after that last conversation with Matt ended, Rachel had answered. Unlike some of Gabi's other friends would have, Rachel hadn't asked too many questions when Gabi asked to stay with her and Aaron until she could find a place of her own.

She would have told Maia, at least, the truth. She had been counting on crashing with her the last few days, but then Maia and Jonnie seemed like they were in this little love bubble, and whatever Gabi's feelings about ending her relationship might be, intruding on that seemed a bridge too far.

Plus, Maia would have been *full* of questions that Gabi wasn't quite ready to answer.

Rachel came into the kitchen with a now fully clothed Celia balanced on her hip and shot Gabi a pitying look, as if the fact that Matt would no longer be attending the party with her was some great tragedy, and Gabi was being just so brave for soldiering on without him.

Never mind that she was the one who had dumped him.

Maybe she was being a little too defensive.

"Annika, she's the one who owns that fancy dress shop down on Commerce Ave?" Rachel said as she sat down at the table next to Aaron.

"Yeah. She designs and makes clothes, too," Gabi replied. She grabbed one of Celia's pudgy bare feet in her hand and shook it gently, sticking her tongue out at Celia until she giggled. "She'll probably be making all the dresses for the wedding."

"Did Maia officially ask you to be her bridesmaid yet?" Rachel asked as she bounced a squirming Celia, who did not want to be restrained, on her knee.

"Not yet, but I'm getting dinner with her later this week, so I think that's when the offish asking will occur," Gabi replied.

"And how are you feeling about being asked?" Rachel asked. Celia was now trying to climb her mom's torso. She grabbed a handful of Rachel's shoulder-length brown locks to use as leverage in her bid for escape.

"Hey, Aar, can you take her?" Rachel said calmly. She pried her daughter's sticky fingers from her hair without looking away from Gabi.

"Sure, babe. Hey, Celi-beli, want to build some blocks with Daddy?" Aaron said.

He freed Celia from Rachel and carried his wriggling child out of the room.

"I still can't believe you guys are parents even though I was at her baby naming and both her birthday parties," Gabi said. She turned back to Rachel as Aaron and Celia's chatter faded down the hall.

"Oh my God, girl, I know. Can you even?" Rachel said, and her whole body sagged against the high back of her chair. "Aaron has been just amazing, though. Doesn't put up any hassle about watching her at all."

She smiled fondly after her husband, and Gabi felt the tiniest of twinges deep in her chest at the look.

"But back to you, babe," Rachel said, and she turned her face to Gabi. Gabi noticed a half-chewed Cheerio stuck to Rachel's shoulder and picked it off.

"How are we feeling about potentially being a part of a wedding party so soon after breaking up with Matt?" Rachel asked.

Gabi sighed and took a big swig of coffee.

How the fuck *did* she feel about it?

"I think fine? I mean, part of why I broke up with him was that I didn't want to get married, and he did. So the whole being around a wedding and romantic commitment part isn't that painful because it's not really what I want for myself right now," Gabi said.

"Part of the reason," Rachel echoed, eyes intent on Gabi's face. Rachel had apparently decided four days was the limit on letting Gabi go without talking about the details of the breakup.

"Mm-hmm," Gabi replied. She finished her coffee in one big

heartburn-inducing gulp and got up to pull a Greek yogurt from the fridge, buying herself some time.

"But not the whole reason," Rachel pressed.

"Yeah…" Gabi said to the neat stack of toddler smoothie packs in the fridge. The chill air felt nice on her heated cheeks.

It's now or never, Gab, she thought. You can totally do this.

One deep breath of refrigerated air, and then she returned to the table, placed her carton of yogurt and spoon on the wooden surface, and took her seat, motions deliberate as she continued to pump herself up.

She opened her mouth to speak, and then an avalanche of thoughts flooded her brain.

What if Rachel didn't believe her? What if she asked her how she couldn't have known she was gay for thirty years? And was she sure she wasn't bi? Because eight years was a really long time to be in a relationship, to be having sex with someone, without realizing maybe you weren't really into it. What if Rachel asked her why she stayed with Matt for so long?

And what if Rachel didn't think the truth was good enough?

The truth was, it was just easy: being with Matt, having him navigate all the parts of their lives she couldn't pay attention to because she was training to be a doctor, not questioning why she never really wanted to have sex with him, chalking it all up to the sheer exhausting effort required of her job.

She'd taken it for granted that this was what she was supposed to be doing. People always said to marry your best friend, and that was what Matt had been, her best friend. Forget that she had found herself dreaming about faceless women touching her more frequently than ever, woke panting and aching between her thighs more mornings than she cared to remember.

"There are some parts I'm still sorting through myself," Gabi said in a rush, chickening out at the last second, "but, more or less, it boiled down to Matt having our whole future planned out and just, like, letting us roll toward it like we were on fucking train tracks," Gabi explained. She swept her right arm out in front of her in emphasis.

"And you didn't like that," Rachel stated.

"No, I mean," Gabi said and sighed, "I feel like I've been coasting by for the last eight years, my focus and energy on med school and my residency, and then I just looked around one day and was like, is this my life now, you know?"

"You looked around and you didn't like what you saw," Rachel clarified.

Gabi looked out the kitchen window at the sunlight streaming through the branches of the maple tree in Aaron and Rachel's front lawn.

"It was more I wanted what I didn't see," she said.

"Uh-huh," Rachel said.

Gabi knew Rachel was waiting for her to supply more details. But she wasn't sure she was ready to supply them yet. She needed more time to come to terms with what she had done, with what this all meant for her future, before she started sharing that part of herself with other people.

As if sensing her thoughts, Rachel reached across the table and rested her hand, warm and soft and well moisturized from diaper paste, on Gabi's and squeezed, the metal of her wedding band cool against Gabi's skin.

"Listen, if you're not ready, you don't have to tell me now. But know I'm here when you are," Rachel said with a smile.

Gabi smiled back and felt her chest loosen.

They shared a peaceful moment of morning quiet, watched the leaves of the maple tree sway in the early autumn breeze. Then a high-pitched shriek accompanied by the sound of stampeding feet and Aaron's voice calling for Celia sounded in the distance. A look of weariness passed over Rachel's face.

"Well, babe, what are you going to do? Because as much as I love having you here, you can see we're not really equipped for long-term guests right now," Rachel said.

There was a thud, a male groan, and a peal of Celia's giggles from down the hall.

Rachel grimaced and Gabi laughed.

"You want to check on that?" Gabi asked dryly.

Rachel waved her hand and took a sip of her coffee before she said, "Aaron seems like he's got it under control."

Gabi smirked, then said, "An intern gave me a lead on a one-bedroom for rent downtown, which, thank God, I can afford, so I'm going to check it out before my shift tomorrow."

"Good luck, girl," Rachel said.

They clinked coffee mugs moments before Celia, stripped to her diaper and covered in marker, barged into the room squealing with glee.

CHAPTER THREE

As she walked into Forage and Trawl, the recently opened farm and sea to table restaurant where Maia and Jonnie were having their engagement party, on a chilly Saturday night at the end of September, Annika almost wished she hadn't dumped Lana the potter two weeks ago.

She had been fun and would have looked banging in a cocktail dress, but she had started hinting at wanting to see more of each other, and Annika had coincidentally noticed that her front two teeth were crooked, and that she had an unsettling obsession with teacup pigs, and any feelings Annika had had for her were immediately extinguished.

"Niki, there you are!" her mother cried as she rushed up to her. She looked regal in a flowing blue silk dress with a cowl neck. Her long curls hung loose around her, and a thick strand of coral beads was strung around her neck. Despite being sixty, she was wiry and strong, thanks to being a daily practitioner of yoga for the last two decades, and it showed in the visibly toned muscles of her arms.

"Hi, Mom," Annika replied with a smile. She embraced her mother and breathed in her clean, citrusy scent deeply.

"You look lovely," her mom exclaimed as she held her arms out to take in the polyester crepe jumpsuit Annika wore. It was sage green and strapless with a structured bodice and left her tattooed right arm on full display. The jumpsuit's wide legs slid silkily over her round hips, accentuated her narrower waist, and made her slight bust look full.

She had dusted gold powder over her lids, which brought out the gold flecks in her brown eyes, and her natural waves hung over her left shoulder, revealing the right side of her undercut. Gold earrings like three links of chain dangled from her ears as her only additional ornament.

"Did you make this?" her mother asked.

"I do sometimes go shopping," Annika teased. Although she had, in fact, made the jumpsuit. "Where's Maia?" Annika asked, looking around the room for her sister.

"Over by the bar with Gabi and Jonnie," her mother said and waved vaguely behind her.

Someone called her mother's name, and she gave Annika a kiss on the cheek before rushing off to play hostess.

Annika left to find alcohol and her sister.

"Niki!" Maia called when she spotted her as she came through the crowd.

Maia was dressed in a white—of course—one shoulder tea-length dress with chunky pink heels that boosted her up a good four inches. Her long light brown hair was curled and brushed into effortless waves that Annika knew took her sister at least an hour to achieve. Restrained wings lined her upper lids, and a pink gloss shone on her lips. She looked classic and put together in that goyisha way that screamed J.Crew and clambakes.

Maia had inherited their mother's body, naturally slim and slight, while Annika favored their father, a touch broader in the shoulders, a dash taller, and with hips and an ass that had attracted comments, some wanted and many, many unwanted, since she was thirteen. She'd learned to love her body, but it had taken time to feel like hers.

They could be so different it was a wonder they came from the same womb, Annika thought as she hugged her sister tightly, rocked her back and forth before releasing her.

"Hey, Annika," a soft male voice said from her right.

"Well, if it isn't my favorite future bro-in-law," Annika said as Jonnie reached to hug her, his blue linen suit a perfect complement to Maia's restrained beauty, his pocket square and tie the exact shade of pink as her shoes.

Annika ruffled his sandy curls affectionately, freeing them from the gelled look Maia had no doubt created.

Her sister grabbed her arm to stop her, just as Annika had predicted she would.

"Stop it, it took me, like, twenty minutes to get it to look like that," Maia sniped.

"God forbid Jonnie's hair should look anything other than the *exact* right type of curly on this most special of nights," said Gabi Mendon, Maia's oldest friend.

"Hey, Gabi," Annika said in greeting.

She leaned in to give Gabi a brief one-armed hug and got a whiff of her perfume, something light and floral that made Annika picture an early spring garden wet with rain.

"Hi, Annika." Gabi smiled at her as she pulled away and handed her a glass of champagne. "I saw you over here and figured you'd need this before these two start spewing their love all over us."

Annika laughed, while Maia rolled her eyes.

Annika had always liked Gabi. She and Maia had been close since they were ten and shared a pair of bunk beds their first summer at sleepaway camp. Twenty years later, they were still best friends.

"Probably best we get proper protection before that happens." Annika nodded solemnly before she took a big gulp of her champagne, the bubbles burning up her nose.

"Yeah, yeah, get it all out now," Maia said, and she waved her hands in a bring-it-on motion.

"No, but seriously," Annika said, turning to Jonnie, "I know you've technically been around for the last four years, but it'll be wicked cool to be able to call you my brother-in-law officially."

Jonnie smiled down at her and gave her another hug.

"Aw, babe, you can't cry yet. We haven't taken any pictures," Maia exclaimed, as Jonnie pulled away from Annika and wiped at his eyes.

"Mazel tov, you big softy," Annika said.

She rose up to kiss his cheek.

"Oh, looks like Mom needs us for something," Maia said. She grabbed Jonnie's hand and all but yanked him through the growing crowd.

Annika grinned after them, shaking her head at her sister's antics. When she looked back, she found Gabi surveying her from head to toe.

"You look good—did you make this?" Gabi asked.

"Uh, yeah, I did, thanks," she said, fighting a blush.

No matter how many beautiful women complimented her in her life, it would still leave her flustered every time.

And Gabi was plenty beautiful.

She was shorter than both Maia and Annika, but drawn in sweeping curvy lines from head to toe. Even her hair was curvy—long and thick and coiled in tight, corkscrew curls that sprang loosely around her shoulders, the dark brown still highlighted from the summer sun.

"You look good, too. Did you also make your outfit?" Annika asked, gesturing to the ocher satin spaghetti strap A-line dress and tan backless heels Gabi wore.

"No, I actually got it at this place called a store," Gabi said. "It's this crazy invention where you can buy ready-made clothes and wear them without ever having to know how to sew."

Annika grinned down at her and said, "No sewing at all? That's the most ludicrous thing I've ever heard. Where's your shadow, by the way? I can see the scenery directly behind you for once."

Annika waved the hand not holding the glass of champagne at the space around a foot above Gabi's shoulder.

If there was anything constant about Gabi, it was her eight-year relationship with Matt, her college boyfriend. Annika thought Matt was nice enough. With his auburn scruff and dark-rimmed glasses, he had that nerdy professor thing that women who were into men seemed to enjoy.

Gabi glanced down into her glass, the smile on her lips slipping for a moment.

"He couldn't make it tonight," she said, glancing off somewhere behind Annika's right shoulder. "A, uh, work thing came up."

Matt was a high school science teacher at a school in a Portland suburb, so this excuse seemed a little suspicious to Annika. But Gabi seemed uncomfortable, so she didn't press.

Gabi sighed. "Haven't had an excuse to dress up in a minute, feels nice to be out of scrubs."

"How's your residency going?" Annika asked as she took a sip of her champagne.

"Oh, you know," Gabi said with a dismissive flick of her unpainted fingers, "people have vaginas, I examine them, they leave. Sometimes they're gross, mostly they're not. Occasionally a baby comes out of them."

"That's what I've been trying to tell straight women for years,"

Annika quipped and was rewarded by a small upward tug of Gabi's lips, the funk the mention of Matt brought dispelled.

"I'm on a labor and delivery rotation, so getting to hang out with the infants has been a nice perk. How's business?" Gabi asked.

"It's pretty good, store's still open, so that's something," Annika said with a shrug.

"Hey, that's huge, Niki," Gabi said. She gave Annika's arm an encouraging squeeze, her small hand a bit dry, but warm. "I'm assuming you're making the dresses for this shindig. You better make me look hot in my bridesmaid dress."

Wouldn't have to do much, Annika thought, and then mentally shook herself.

Gabi was, unfortunately, her sister's best friend, not to mention straight as far as she knew and in a steady, monogamous relationship.

Lusting after her would be typical for Annika. Fall for the unavailable ones, ditch the ones who wanted her.

"Presumptuous of you, assuming you'll be a bridesmaid," Annika said. She raised her eyebrow as she took another drink.

Before Gabi could respond, Annika's mother tapped her knife against her glass and directed everyone to take a seat.

Annika spent the rest of the evening in conversation with her cousins and various other family members and friends of her mother's, and she lost track of Gabi in the crowd.

Around ten, most of the older guests had filtered out, leaving Annika, Maia, Jonnie, and their friends crammed around one long table, getting progressively louder and more drunk.

When the general manager, a very pretty woman named Dina who happened to be an ex of Annika's, came to kick them out with a teasing grin, they tumbled into the night.

After a few minutes of meandering, they found themselves gathered in a trendy place near Jonnie's vet practice, the walls bottle-green glass tiles and the fixtures brass, the floor a polished reflective black.

Annika sat in a corner booth, drinking a beer and trying to avoid Jonnie's drunk college friends, who didn't quite understand that she wasn't interested in them.

She watched Maia and Jonnie at the bar. Maia stood leaning back against his chest, head lolling as she laughed loosely at something a friend of hers said, Jonnie's arm wrapped around her waist, stabilizing and safe.

"I still can't believe Maia is getting married," Gabi said. She slid into the booth across from Annika and followed her line of sight.

Gabi had piled her curls in a thick bun on top of her head, the heat of the bar making the skin revealed by the neckline of her dress glisten.

Annika briefly wondered what her skin would taste like if she ran her tongue up the length of her neck and knew she was drunk.

"I can't believe people get married, period," Annika said. She crossed her arms over her chest and slumped back against the wooden booth. "Having to consult with someone else about the way you live your life? No, thank you."

"Oh man, I so get that," Gabi replied and nodded emphatically. Annika watched a stray curl fall from Gabi's bun and brush against her bare shoulder as she turned to watch Maia and Jonnie, drunk on alcohol and each other, lean in to share a sloppy kiss.

Annika nearly leaned across the table to brush that curl off Gabi's neck and let her fingers trail against Gabi's skin when her words registered.

"What the fuck are you talking about?" Annika scoffed. "You and Matt are basically old married people. You're the type of couple that probably shares a toothbrush and knows exactly how many kids they're going to have and when. I bet you guys have a neighborhood picked out in a quiet suburb a respectable distance from the city, but still close enough to enjoy the culture. I bet you've already researched the school system."

"Matt certainly has," Gabi muttered darkly. Her brow furrowed slightly, eyes focused on her fingers as they picked at the label of her beer bottle.

Annika watched her, decided it wasn't her business, then asked anyway. "Trouble in paradise?"

Gabi forced a smile and took a slug from her beer, shaking her head.

She said, "Nah, it's nothing. I'm just tired and drunk and in my feels. How's your love life, by the way? Maia mentioned something about a potter a few weeks ago?"

"Dumped her," Annika said bluntly. She took a swig of her own beer and wiped a stray drip of liquid from her chin before she said, "Wasn't feeling it."

Gabi nodded sagely and said, "Ah, the elusive *it*."

"Yup," Annika said, popping the *p*, "seems more slippery for some of us than others."

They sat in comfortable silence for a beat, punctuated by the drunken laughter of Maia and Jonnie's friends around them.

"I'm getting married!" Maia said. She slurred her speech and waved her left hand around like an interpretive dancer as she swayed her way over to their booth. She plopped down heavily next to Annika, her sleek hair now tossed up in a high ponytail.

"Hey, girl," Gabi said, "you had any water recently?"

Maia ignored her and turned to Annika.

"Niki, my beautiful baby sister"—she smushed Annika's cheeks together in the claw of her right hand, shaking her face gently from side to side—"I know you *hate* marriage, but you're happy for me, right? Like, really, deep down, right in that secretly soft heart of yours, you're happy for me?"

She poked Annika in the center of her left breast, her drunken approximation of her heart, and her arm dropped to rest in Annika's lap, limp as a rag doll, her head against Annika's bare shoulder.

"Of course I'm happy for you, Mai," Annika said, and she rested her head atop Maia's as her older sister snuggled into her. She grinned at Gabi, who smiled back at her, her round cheeks plumping up with the stretch of her lips.

"And Gab, I can't wait for when you and Matt *finally* get married. I'm going to be, like, the best maid of honor for your ass," Maia slurred at Gabi, and Annika watched that soft smile slip off her sister's friend's face.

Gabi opened her mouth, but then Jonnie appeared.

"Jonnie!" Maia sang. She flung her arms out wide and smacked Annika's cheek lightly with the motion. "It's my *fiancé*." She drew the word out to about fifteen syllables.

"Hey, babe," Jonnie said, calm and cool and only slightly flushed, his white button-down open at the collar and rolled up to the elbows. He bent down to let Maia wrap her arms around his neck, and said, "I think it's probably time we get you to bed with about a gallon of water."

Maia pulled back and pouted but let him tug her to her feet.

"Bye, my ladies," Maia called, finger waving with her left hand at Gabi and Annika as Jonnie herded her to the door of the bar. She let out one last whoop of excitement, her group of friends echoing it back to her from the bar, before Jonnie managed to pour her out onto the sidewalk.

What a ridiculous woman her sister was, Annika thought, smiling ruefully as she shook her head.

"I should probably go, too." Gabi sighed. "I've got night shifts this week, and I need to get my life together tomorrow."

"God, being a doctor sounds fucking awful," Annika replied, and she followed Gabi as she stood from the booth.

Annika noticed that her feet were beginning to ache in her heels. She couldn't wait to get her jumpsuit off, smoke some weed in her underwear and a giant T-shirt, and snuggle with Vera Wang, her British shorthair cat, on the couch. Oh, and some pizza wouldn't hurt matters either.

"We can't all have essential, important jobs like boutique dressmaker," Gabi said, teasing her. "Some of us must settle for being humble medical professionals."

Annika rolled her eyes and looked back at Gabi as they strolled out of the bar. She thought she saw Gabi's eyes glance away from her ass, but it must have been wishful thinking.

"I'm going to head out, too, before one of Jonnie's friends realizes I'm gay and starts asking for tips on women. Or worse, asks me how I know if I've *never tried sausage before*," Annika said with a grimace.

"Gross," Gabi said and made a gagging noise. "Does that happen to you often?"

Annika took out a prerolled joint from her purse and lit it. She breathed in deeply, taking a long drag from the end before she let out a thick plume of white smoke. Immediately, her joints hung more loosely. She felt the last dregs of power slip from her social battery and thought fondly of the quiet apartment with only her cat in it waiting for her at the end of the fifteen minute ride home.

"Not that often," she told Gabi, and her voice came out scratchy with smoke, "but you never know. Put enough alcohol in any man that heterosexual and there's a high chance something offensive comes out of his mouth."

She offered the lit joint to Gabi, who eyed it, hesitated, and then waved it away.

"That fucking sucks," Gabi said, her voice sounding oddly resigned as she hugged herself against the early autumn chill.

Annika shrugged and took another drag.

"Hazards of the job, as they say," she replied. "The benefits more than make up for it, though."

Annika couldn't help herself from grinning cheekily at Gabi as she said it, just to tease. Life was too short not to flirt with a beautiful woman. Even if that woman was straight, in a relationship, and your sister's best friend.

Gabi's round cheeks flushed red, but she seemed to contemplate Annika's words as Annika took another drag off her joint.

After a beat, Gabi turned to her with purpose, and said, "Hey, Niki?"

Annika turned to face her, but just then a black sedan pulled up, the front passenger side window rolling down.

"For Annika?" the driver said from inside the car. He leaned across the console to see through the window.

"That's me," Annika said. She stubbed out her joint on the brick wall of the building and put it back in her clutch before she stepped off the curb. She paused with her hand on the car door. "Night, Gabi."

There was a distant sheen to Gabi's eyes as she said, "See you later."

Annika got in the car and rolled down her window to wave.

She watched as Gabi turned back to the street, something about her striking Annika as lost.

Chapter Four

A week later, Gabi, in an old college sweatshirt and faded jeans, walked into the Thai restaurant she'd arranged to meet Maia at, only to find both Silberberg sisters already seated.

Maia, long hair slicked back in her habitual perfect ponytail and dressed in a cotton knit sweater, talked animatedly to Annika, her hair up in a messy bun that revealed the shaved back and sides of her hair, her bangs looking newly trimmed. Annika wore a dark gray T-shirt with several thin silver chains slung around her neck, the tattoos twining up her right arm on full display, and an exasperated look on her face at whatever it was Maia was saying.

"Come on, Niki," Gabi could hear Maia practically whine as she made her way over to their table, "just admit that you do it."

"I'm not admitting anything," Annika said. She leaned back in her chair and crossed her arms over her chest stubbornly.

"What are you trying to get her to admit to?" Gabi asked as she dropped down into her own chair. She was exhausted. She'd assisted on five births today. The screams of the newborns, little miracles of course, still echoed shrilly through her head.

She was surprised to see Annika there but was too tired to get into her presence at their friend dinner now.

Maia bumped Gabi with her shoulder affectionately in greeting.

She said, "I'm trying to get Niki to admit that she wears the dresses in her store when no one is there. I mean, how could you not at least try them on?"

"Some of us aren't enamored with the wedding-industrial complex or the heteronormative ritual of it all." Annika shrugged, one corner of her mouth tipping up as she glanced at Gabi.

She's goading her, Gabi realized. An answering smile curved over her own lips before she realized it.

She loved Maia like a sister, but damn, could she be stubborn. And it looked like Annika knew how frustrating Maia found it when you didn't let her have her way.

"You own a wedding dress store," Maia exclaimed as she tossed her hands into the air.

"I sell other things, too," Annika said dryly.

"Two-thirds of your inventory and your sales are bridal related," Maia shot back. She crossed her arms to mimic Annika's pose unconsciously. "I've seen your books."

"Hi, Gabi, how was your day," Gabi said as she decided to interject herself between them.

"Sorry, girl," Maia said, and she shot a final glare at her sister before she turned to face her friend, "it just gets me heated."

"Blatant hypocrisy will do that to you," Gabi added and nodded sagely.

"Wow, you, too?" Annika said. She sent Gabi a betrayed look.

Gabi shrugged and said, "I helped deliver five babies today, my brain is fried. Be happy I'm here at all."

"You've been elusive lately, period," Maia said. She slung her arm around the back of Gabi's chair. "I feel like I've barely spoken to you since the engagement party."

"I've been working nights," Gabi replied. "And…"

She took a deep breath. So far, the only people she'd told about her breakup with Matt had been her parents, Rachel and Aaron, and her brothers. Once she told Maia, though, Maia who had known her since before Matt had entered her life, since before romance had yet to enter her life, it would be real.

Here went nothing.

"I broke up with Matt," she said in a rush.

They stared at her in silence for one second, two.

And then Maia erupted.

"You what?" she shrieked.

Annika, on the other hand, went silent. She and Annika had a friendly relationship, seeing more of each other in the last years since she and Matt had moved to Portland for her residency, but she hadn't planned on telling Annika personally. Hadn't planned on her being at this dinner at all. The sisters were close, but by no means a package deal.

"When, where, *why*, what?" Maia continued squawking.

"About two weeks ago, a few days before your engagement party," Gabi said. This was why she hadn't gone to Maia in the first place. She loved her to the ends of the earth, but Maia had to process her response, loudly, before she could handle others' emotions.

"Two fucking weeks," Maia yelled.

"Mai," Annika said, voice soft but firm, eyes gentle on Gabi's face, "let her talk."

"Sorry, sorry," Maia conceded. "I'm just…I'm shook by this news."

"I know, I'm sorry I didn't tell you sooner. I just needed some time to sort things out," Gabi said sighing, and her shoulders slumped.

"Wait, but where the fuck have you been living? Or did Matt move out? Did he break up with you? Did he cheat on you? That fucking asshole. I'll nail his hairy, lopsided balls to the wall for this," Maia went on, voice still at top volume.

And here come the questions, Gabi thought, already filled with regret for bringing this up.

"Woah, woah, Maia, slow down. He didn't cheat. I stayed at Rachel's for a bit and then someone at work hooked me up with a sublet that I've been crashing at for the last week or so. I…I broke up with him," Gabi clarified and swallowed, her mouth suddenly filled with saliva and her armpits prickled with sweat.

"But why?" Maia asked, voice returning to a normal volume now she was convinced she didn't have to seek vengeance on Gabi's behalf. Her face was open and curious and questioning, a look that reminded Gabi of the scrawny tween Maia she'd met so long ago. "I thought you guys were so solid."

"It was just…time, I guess. I realized that when he talked about the future, Matt had this crystal clear plan. Where we'd be in five years, how many kids we'd have, where they'd go to school," Gabi listed out. "When I think about the future, all I can imagine is the end of residency, maybe a fellowship. I realized I've barely been living outside of residency. The truth is, I don't think I've been in love with him for a long time. I just never slowed down long enough to see it," she concluded with a shrug.

I don't think I ever was, Gabi added internally.

"Oh, Gab," Maia said. She grabbed Gabi's hand where it rested on the tabletop just like Rachel had.

"I don't think he was really in love with me either, not by the end. He was just in love with this idea of settling down and making Jewish babies and being a dad. And I was the means to that end." Gabi added, "But we're good. No resentment or anything there."

Maia and Annika gave her the same sympathetic head tilt, the same soft smile playing on their lips.

It wasn't the full truth, Gabi thought, and she felt the words unsaid squirm around in the pit of her stomach. But it was as much of the truth as she could manage to give them right now. Let them, Maia especially, adjust to this news before she sprang the rest of it on them.

"Sounds like you made the right choice for yourself, then," Annika said, boiling down all the turmoil of the last several months to its essence.

A huge weight Gabi didn't even realize she carried lifted from her shoulders at her words.

She let out a long breath and laughed. "Yeah, it does, doesn't it?" She nodded at Annika.

"It does," Maia agreed. "And I'm happy that you're choosing you rather than what's easiest. That's so big and brave of you, Gab. Not everyone can do that."

Gabi felt her heart swell.

They got it.

She nodded.

It *would* have been easy, that was the thing, so easy, to just go along with Matt's plan. To coast into that forever after. To never look at herself too deeply. To think maybe she just didn't have the capacity for passion other people did, wasn't born with that same longing for sex and physical intimacy.

"Well, not to change the subject too wildly," Maia said, and she gave Gabi's hand a final squeeze before she released it, "but I invited both of you to dinner to ask you something, something I hope might raise your spirits, Gab."

"I was wondering why I was here," Annika said with a raise of her eyebrows.

"I wanted to give you both a little gift," Maia said.

Her body practically vibrated with suppressed delight as she reached into her leather purse and pulled out two lilac boxes tied with stiff sheer ribbon the color of sparkling wine. She handed one to Gabi and one to Annika with a flourish.

Annika stared down at the box in her hands like it might slime her. Gabi took hers with a sneaking suspicion of what might be inside.

"Oh my God, Niki, stop looking at it like it's going to explode and just open it," Maia said with a roll of her eyes and toss of her high pony.

Gabi smiled as Annika gingerly pulled the ribbon off the box and turned to open her own. Inside, nestled in white crepe paper, was a gold bangle, the metal twisted into the shape of a knot. On the upper lid of the box written in swirling golden script was the message *I couldn't tie the knot without you. Will you be my co–maid of honor?*

"Seriously, Mai?" Annika's voice was a groan of barely disguised disgust.

"Yes, seriously," Maia hollered at her sister. She chucked the discarded ribbon at Annika's face. "You're my best and only sister, and for some meshugana reason I actually really like and love you and want you to be a big part of my wedding, you idiot!"

Annika looked back down at the box in her hands, and mumbled, "I love you, too."

Gabi lifted the delicate bangle out of the box and slipped it on her wrist, feeling tears well. "Of course I'll be your co–maid of honor," she exclaimed. She threw her arms around her oldest friend and squeezed her tightly. "I love you so, so much, Maia!"

She pulled back to see Annika shake her head at her but noticed the matching gold bangle dangling on her wrist.

"Guess you and I will be spending a lot of time together this year," Annika said, a grin creeping through the cynicism.

For some reason, the thought made Gabi's heart race.

PART TWO

Initial Dress Consultation

October–November

CHAPTER FIVE

Annika's boutique, Something New—an inherited name, Annika thought it was a tad too on the nose, but Anusha loved it—was located in the shopping district that lined the narrow winding streets of the old port.

When the door was open, a salt breeze and the cawing of gulls wafted in, along with the sound of shoppers and tourists and the general hubbub of the waterfront.

Annika sat in the workshop in the back of the boutique, where she tailored and altered and took care of the administrative shit she hated. All she could hear now was the perky chatter of her only employee, Vanessa, as she assisted with the current appointment.

"What are our feelings about lace?" Vanessa asked the client.

Annika could picture her, taking a step back and cocking her head to the side to survey the bride on the round pedestal centered before the three paneled mirror. Vanessa's thick dirty blond braid slid over her shoulder, her fingers pinched as if plucking a roll of the fabric from the ether.

"I know you said you wanted more of a clean look," she continued, "but if you pair a lace overlay top with that darling strapless sweetheart trumpet dress, I think we can get the retro Hollywood glam vibe you were showing me on Pinterest."

Annika heard the bride's uncertain answer over the neutral tones of the acoustic love songs playlist Vanessa was streaming this shift. She smiled ruefully as she bent over her pride and joy, Greta, her sewing machine, to fix the cuff on the custom beaded bridal suit she was tailoring. The tiny glassine beads scattered across the silk chiffon made it difficult to work. She didn't want to go too fast and tear the delicate fabric, break a needle or a bead, or get the thread snagged on a bead, which she'd then have to cut and resew by hand. Which would be a giant pain in the ass when she had four other dresses she needed to alter this week as well.

"See, doesn't the lace just give it that extra oomph? Plus, you can remove it for the reception, and then it's like you get two outfits for the price of one," Vanessa exclaimed, and she actually clapped.

God bless her sales tactics, Annika thought as she stretched her neck before she leaned back over her machine.

She passively listened in to the rest of the appointment as she moved from one cuff to the other. The bride went with Vanessa's suggestion and proceeded to get emotional over the complete look Vanessa had crafted for her.

Annika rolled her eyes when Vanessa went to get the tissues because all the women at the appointment—the bride, her mother, and her two best friends—had begun to cry.

She heard the client's mother tell her she was *so proud* of her, and Annika scoffed. No matter how many times she heard it, it never got less ridiculous. Proud of what? Standing and looking nice in an expensive dress? Getting a man—Annika knew it was a hetero couple because the woman kept referring to her future hubby—to commit to her?

There was a reason Annika sat in the back developing neck issues rather than helping on the floor, besides the fact that she needed to keep her hands busy and her mind occupied at all times, or she'd explode.

Vanessa took the bride's measurements, chipperly narrating how she was going to look absolutely perfect on her special day and her fiancé was going to be positively stunned when he saw her coming down the aisle, and rang up her credit card for the one thousand dollar dress deposit. The bell on the door chimed as the woman, her mother, and her friends left the store, no doubt going to celebrate this momentous purchase.

"Another successful sale for me, your best employee," Vanessa chirped as she waltzed into the back room and plopped into the desk chair in front of the computer station next to Annika's sewing table.

"My only employee," Annika corrected, not looking up at her as she fiddled with the lapel of the suit jacket. "Good job upselling her on the lace separate."

Vanessa shrugged and said, "It did complete the look she was going for. If it just so happened to be an extra five hundred dollars, who am I to stand in the way of perfection? They can always say no."

Annika grinned at her over the machine. Vanessa might be all sunshine and smiles with the customers, but she had a practical streak that jibed with Annika's own cynicism. It was the reason they'd initially bonded when Annika started at the store.

Like Annika, Vanessa knew how feral people got when it came to weddings and had no moral issues about milking that insanity for every penny she could. Except, of course, if she knew that person really couldn't afford it.

Annika was fundamentally against driving someone into debt for one day of their lives.

"That's my last appointment for today," Vanessa said, stretching her arms over her head. She was dressed in black head to toe, a neutral palette for the bridal outfits to pop against, a rule set down by Anusha that Annika had kept.

"You sure you can't stay just a *little* bit longer," Annika asked, her voice almost a plea. Her legs bounced beneath the sewing table.

Vanessa shot her a look and folded her arms across her chest.

"As entertaining as it would be," she drawled, "I think you can manage this on your own. It's just an initial consultation. You show her pictures and fabric samples, she says what she likes and what she doesn't, you do a little sketching—"

"She tells me what I'm doing wrong, and then we get into a fight, and she storms out in a huff and leaves me with, like, sixteen unfinished sketches and no direction to go in, and then we both call our mom crying," Annika concluded sullenly.

Vanessa stood and grabbed her denim jacket and green canvas backpack from the hook by the door.

"See, sounds like you've got everything covered, Niki," she said.

Annika sighed and replied, "Yeah, yeah."

"And you can vent about it after, at trivia," Vanessa said as she fit her bike helmet over her thick hair. "Mindy and I will have a tequila soda with lime waiting for you. Just remember, you love your sister. Now, say it with me."

She gave Annika a coaxing gesture like she was a toddler with stage fright.

"I love my sister," Annika grumbled as her shoulders curled in farther.

"That's the spirit, my dude," Vanessa said. "Now, my hot wife is waiting for me to whisk her to the bar so we can get a little tipsy and make out in public before trivia begins."

She turned to leave the store and Annika called out after her, "You guys better actually have that drink waiting for me."

A minute later, she heard the bell on the front door tinkle and sighed, girding herself for the onslaught.

"Niki! I'm so excited. Aren't you, like, so thrilled for this?" came Maia's squeal of delight as she bounded through the door.

"Hey, Mai," Annika called, not yet able to lift herself from her chair, "just take a seat out on the couch. I'll be there in a second."

She braced herself and gathered her sketch pad and the book of fabric swatches she kept for custom orders.

"Welcome to Something New," she said, putting on a cheap imitation of Vanessa's chipper chirp as she approached her sister and deposited the fabric book on the low clear acrylic coffee table stationed between an emerald velvet love seat and a wingback armchair that had once belonged to their bubbe. "Can I offer you a complimentary glass of water or cup of tea?"

"What, not champagne?" Maia asked with a pout.

"Champagne is for when you come back with your bridesmaids and Mom for your final fitting," Annika said.

"Technically, *you* are my maid of honor," Maia replied.

"Ugh, don't remind me," Annika said. In the month since her sister had asked her, the idea still hadn't gotten any less horrible. "And *technically*, it's co–maid of honor. I don't see Gabi here."

"Can you *believe* she broke up with Matt?" Maia asked. She leaned forward, hand pressed against the oatmeal knit vest she wore over a crisp blue button up to emphasize her shock.

"Honestly, I know, it's totally wild," Annika said, leaning toward her sister. Gossip was one of the areas where their interests overlapped. "Just goes to show that lasting love is a lie."

Maia scrunched her face.

"Mom and Dad are still married," she pointed out.

Annika waved her hand dismissively and said, "They're the exception, not the rule."

"You don't even give anyone a chance to see if it could last, though. If you let someone get close to you—" Maia began.

"Are we here to talk about my romantic issues, or are we here to design you a wedding dress, huh?" Annika interrupted. She puffed her bangs out of her face and took a pencil from the messy bun on top of her head, snapping open her sketchbook.

Maia, distracted by the prospect of making a wedding dress from scratch, let the subject drop.

For now.

"You got the images I sent you?" Maia asked. Her tone was all business, but her eyes gleamed with excitement.

"Yes, I got the approximately one hundred images and pins you sent me over the last month," Annika deadpanned, flipping through the pages of her sketchbook until she came to the rough outlines she'd made. "Here's what I have for a silhouette."

She handed the book to Maia, revealing the two designs. The one on the right showed a full-skirted ball gown with a five foot train, a back that dipped below the shoulder blades in a graceful U shape, and a simple strapless neckline with a gauzy layer that draped down the shoulders. There was a small swatch of a pure white satin fabric textured with sunflowers taped to the sketch. A dress fit for a princess like Maia.

The left design showed a high-necked sheath from the front that left the shoulders bare. The back, however, dipped nearly to the waist, and a gigantic bow was attached right above the butt, wide enough to be visible from the front on both sides of Maia's slender hips. Modern, chic, and sleek, also like Maia.

"Hmm..." Maia surveyed the drawings before her eyes. She tapped her index finger against her lips and frowned as she inspected the designs.

"I combined some common elements together from the dresses you sent me," Annika said, tentatively explaining her design process.

"They're both really gorgeous, Niki," Maia said.

"But...?" Annika prompted, eyebrows raised, shoulders tensed.

"I mean, you're, like, so talented. You're totally right that these are elements I sent you," Maia enthused. She slid a hand down her smooth high pony as she sat back on the couch.

"But," Annika repeated.

"But," Maia said, annoyed at her insistence, "what if we added the sunflower pattern to the high neck design? And then maybe added a kind of dramatic train-overskirt combo? And the train and skirt are detachable for the reception so it's, like, a two in one?" Maia suggested.

"So basically, what if it was a completely new dress," Annika concluded with a sigh. She took the sketch pad back and flipped to a new page, roughly outlining Maia's additions to the design.

Thus began an hour of back and forth. Maia would describe a detail she thought might be interesting, Annika would sketch it. Maia would inspect it and then propose another.

They bickered and jabbed. Annika got frustrated and rolled her eyes, called Maia high maintenance. Maia adamantly swore she wasn't, she was just particular and exacting.

Then Annika brought up when Maia was eleven and threw a tantrum about the color of her Rosh Hashana dress because it was salmon and not magenta, like she'd specifically requested.

By the time Annika walked into the bouldering gym, having decided that climbing her frustrations out would be better than drinking them off, she was ready to tackle the hardest wall. She wanted to climb until her limbs ached with exhaustion and her head went quiet, the bickering with her sister sorted neatly into the proper section of her brain rather than rattling around, pinging off every thought that passed through her crowded head.

The thoughts that whispered Maia was being so difficult because she actually hated Annika's designs. That she wished she could get her dress made by someone else because she didn't think Annika was good enough.

That deep down, Annika's fear that she was actually terrible at everything and a failure was true.

"Hey, Annika, been a minute since you stopped in," said Michelle, the woman behind the register. She was a white woman about Annika's height and age with straight brown hair pulled back in a low pony under a backward flat-brim hat. Her arms, though, were like granite boulders, and she had strong thighs Annika wouldn't mind being strangled by.

"Hey, Mich," Annika replied, hefting the strap of her climbing bag up her shoulder, "yeah, been busy lately. But I had a consult with an annoying client. My sister."

Michelle raised her eyebrows, and Annika grimaced.

"Well, there's a V4 set up on the left back wall you might want to check out, if you're not too out of shape," Michelle said, teasing, and Annika grinned.

"Sounds perfect," she said.

She waved to Michelle, scanned the member fob on her keychain, and stashed her bag in her locker. She retrieved her chalk bag and her climbing shoes, which were thin like jazz shoes but with grips on the toes and heels to help her grab the holds on the wall. She pulled them on and clipped her chalk bag to her hip before leaving the locker room.

As she walked over to the side area with a pile of yoga mats, she swung her arms around a bit to loosen her shoulders and shook out her wrists before she executed a series of lunges to warm up her hamstrings and inner thighs.

Then she stepped out onto the floor of the gym, springy like a gymnastics mat, and eyed up the wall Michelle had suggested.

The gym was only sparsely populated at this time of night, just a few other climbers working their way up the walls, hands and feet gripping the colorful holds like the monkeys they'd all evolved from.

Annika was pleased to see that it was blessedly free of climbing bros, that special breed of dude who liked to hog the hardest passes and who made condescending comments to Annika when they saw her, her undercut and tattooed arm on display. She figured she was too visibly queer for them to try to impress, so they either made snide comments, were rude, or pretended she was invisible.

She stood before the wall and contemplated the pass with her fists resting on her hips. It was the same pose she struck to contemplate fabric when it was draped over her dress form, willing it to divulge the secret shape it wanted to take.

She chalked up her hands and began her ascent, losing herself to the stretch and burn of her muscles, the scrape of the rough surface of the holds against her hands when she sweated through the chalk.

Her racing mind only ever slowed when she was lost in sewing, or trying to work her way through a rough climb, or having sex. She settled in her body more after each attempt, making it slightly higher along the wall after each pass.

After the fifth time she reached a certain tricky part of curved wall, she pushed herself, willing her body to be just a little longer, to reach just a little farther. Her fingertips grazed the next hold, her torso bent backward to adjust to the angle, but she released her right foot too early, and her weight shifted too far backward. For one second, she was weightless, falling the six feet from the wall to the mat, knowing she was going to have the wind knocked out of her but not there yet. A thrill of anticipation mixed with dismay in her gut.

She landed butt first, let the padding there absorb some of the impact, and curled her head in for protection. The force of her fall left her winded, as she knew it would, and slightly giddy, as adrenaline coursed through her body.

She felt her ass begin to smart and caught her breath.

Failure, a sinister voice whispered from a crevice deep in her brain. *You always fail at everything. How can you ever let anyone close? Once they see you for what you are, they'll leave you.*

She took a deep breath, got up, and tried the climb again.

That was the thing people didn't get about Annika. What Maia, her mother, and that little voice didn't see.

Sure, she quit relationships, and college, and hobbies when they grew boring. But when it really mattered, when it made her mind go slow and calm and quiet and her heart beat faster, made her brain feel energized and alive for once, she kept going until she got it perfect.

She never gave up on the things that really captured her scattered attention, that required her whole self to be present.

The next climb, she made it halfway up the curve, body clinging to the wall with just finger and toe tips. Sensing defeat, she climbed down a few feet before she dropped with more grace to the mat, wrists and metatarsals aching.

It was always better to know your limits and exit with control than to try, slip, and end up smashed to the ground with the wind knocked from your lungs.

"Good effort on that pass," Michelle said, adjusting the brim of her hat and resting her hip on the corner of the check-in desk as

Annika walked past on her way out, "I was watching. You released early with your back foot when you went for the hold on the top of the hump. I could help you out next time, if you wanted a little one-on-one coaching."

Annika smiled, a little flustered Michelle had watched her. She wondered if this was a come-on, or just Michelle being friendly and good at her job.

Always so hard to tell with women.

"Thanks," Annika said and flipped the end of her sweaty braid off her shoulder, "some help on that pass would actually be wicked great."

Michelle smiled, and her eyes crinkled at the corners, already sun-worn from summers spent climbing on the craggy granite of Maine mountains.

"Oh, by the way, we've got another Queer Climb coming up this Friday if you're interested," she said, "starts at six and goes to nine. I know that last one you went to was…productive for you."

"Ha," Annika replied. A Queer Climb was an all ladies and femmes night at the gym that happened once a month. There was live music from local queer bands, food trucks, and beer from local breweries. Annika had met Lana the potter at the last Queer Climb she'd gone to back in June.

Their *relationship*, for lack of a better word, had been like all of Annika's previous flings: intense—like, nine dates in two weeks intense—and consuming. It was like Annika got caught up in a dream, the thrill of it as intoxicating as a good high. But just like any high, there was always a comedown. Always a moment where Annika would wake from the dream of the relationship to find the reality of the human before her and feel…exhausted by her.

She had no idea how people made it through that, how her sister had been with Jonnie for four whole years and still wanted him, wanted to spend even more time with him. How Gabi had spent eight years with Matt.

Although, she thought as she drove home from the gym that night, Gabi did get there eventually.

CHAPTER SIX

Since moving into her new apartment, Gabi's whole routine had changed. New coffee shop, new grocery store, new pharmacy. Her commute was shorter now, thank God. Those extra fifteen minutes meant she could collapse face-first on her full-size bed sooner after a twelve hour shift.

It also meant proximity to new activities, ones she could explore on her own. Ones she'd been curious about for a while but hadn't had the nerve or opportunity to try.

Like Queer Climb night at the rock-climbing gym three blocks from her new place. She'd seen the flier in the window as she'd walked past one day earlier in the week and had decided it was time.

She and Matt had been officially broken up for two months now, even if their relationship had really been over for much longer than that. And if she wanted to explore new activities, kissing-women-related activities, she had to meet women who might want to be kissed.

Plus, the gym was so far outside the territory of anyone she knew, geographically and demographically, that she could dip her toe into the sapphic waters without it having to be a whole thing.

Sure, she felt a little bit out of her depth as a thirty-year-old coming to terms with the fact that she might not be straight. Okay, she *definitely* wasn't straight. Years of sex dreams about her strong but nurturing attending that left her more turned on than any sex with Matt had more than confirmed that for her.

And yeah, she might have agonized over her outfit. Might have fussed with whether it was too cold in November for bike shorts, even if they did make her short and plump legs look longer. Might have fought the increasingly embarrassing and urgent impulse to google *lesbian workout attire* as she got progressively sweatier and her curls got frizzier from her hands constantly running through them.

But she was here.

And she was—hypothetically, only in the privacy of her head so far—queer, and there was nothing for it but to push open the doors of the gym and enter this new phase of her life.

As she walked through the lobby, Gabi passed groups of women of every shape and size, although the majority were white—this was Maine after all—hanging out in groups, checking in at the desk, chatting with the musicians as they set up a small drum stand and amps in the corner by a stack of yoga mats.

"First timer?" The receptionist, a white woman with long straight hair hanging loose around her face beneath a backward flat-brim hat, asked as Gabi checked in.

Gabi felt herself blush.

"Uh, how did you know?" she said. Her crimson cheeks screamed it was her first time for more than just rock climbing at this gym.

The receptionist smiled with the left corner of her mouth, and her eyes lingered on the blush in Gabi's cheeks.

"I haven't seen you around before. And I'd *definitely* remember you," she said.

If a man said that to her, Gabi would have groaned and rolled her eyes. But there was something about this obvious line from a woman that had her heart racing.

"Oh, um, I…" Gabi sputtered, and the right corner of the woman's lips quirked up, too.

"I'm Michelle," the receptionist said, and she handed Gabi a tablet from behind the register. "Welcome to Queer Climb night. If you've never done this before, I can show you the ropes." She leaned across the register desk, forearms crossed on the glass, strong wrist muscles flexed.

"Thanks," Gabi managed, face aflame, as she took the tablet with shaking hands, "but I've, uh, climbed before."

"Well, if you need anything else, you know where to find me," Michelle said. She stood and leaned back, hands stretched out on the smooth surface of the check-in desk, all but winking at Gabi. "There's beer on the patio, you'll get a voucher in your email after you register.

You're not allowed to come back in to climb after you go out there, so make sure you're really finished climbing before you go get a drink."

Michelle paused and then bit her lower lip and said, "Maybe I'll see you out there when my shift ends."

Gabi felt her stomach swoop and tried to keep her jaw from dropping. Okay, so Michelle was very much flirting with her.

She nodded, stammered, "Um, yeah, sure," before she turned and fled from the desk, heart hammering and palms slicked with sweat.

Taking a seat on one of the black faux-leather armchairs scattered around the lobby, Gabi pretended to fill out the forms on the tablet but was really willing her pulse to slow down before she went into cardiac arrest.

Okay, so a hot lady had flirted with her.

She could handle it, this was fine. She was not internally freaking out at all.

She was a doctor who had seven months left in her residency, gave women cancer diagnoses, and delivered babies every day. She was strong and confident and would not be brought down by long hair, strong arms, and a cocky smile.

She peeked up at Michelle, who caught her eye and grinned that one-sided grin again. Gabi quickly dropped her gaze back down to the tablet in her hands.

Okay, maybe she would be.

She turned her form in, thankfully to another woman working registration. Michelle now leaned across the counter to chat with a tall, willowy white woman with a coil of blond dreads piled on her head and a mandala tattooed on the back of her left shoulder.

Gabi scurried away with her rented climbing shoes before Michelle could catch her eye again.

It was pretty incredible, she thought, as she put on her shoes and surveyed her surroundings, to be in a place where it was women, femmes, and non-binary people only from wall to wall.

And everyone was so…hot.

So many lovely curves clothed in tight leggings and athletic shorts and clinging climbing pants. Buff arms and soft breasts of all sizes in tank tops and T-shirts and cropped sweatshirts. Long and short and dyed and straight and curly hair on heads, the casual glimpse of armpit and leg hair as people climbed the wall.

Her gaze kept flitting from group to group as she absorbed and feasted and tried not to look like a total creep. Gabi felt like she hadn't yet mastered how to check out women without also feeling like she was objectifying them, a delicate dance, she was learning.

She took a seat near an easier pass and chalked her hands as she waited for the woman ahead of her to finish. As she watched the woman on the wall, it struck her that she knew no one here and no one knew her. If she wanted to flirt with someone, talk to her and maybe touch her arm the way the blonde was doing to the tiny East Asian masc she was with over in the corner, she could. And no one would ever have to know unless she told them.

Total freedom flitted through her frame. She breathed in, and the knot of anxiety that had lived there for as long she could remember began to unspool in her chest. She felt lighter, like she'd unknowingly been carrying a backpack filled with rocks, and she could finally release it from her shoulders.

For the first time in eight years, she was just herself.

Solo Gabi.

Coming to this event had been a huge first step in her staking a claim to a future full of her independence and self-discovery. Of letting herself acknowledge not only what she wanted, but that she had wants at all that were separate from her medical career and the path everyone expected her to take.

She'd told Rachel she was coming to this event tonight—not that it was a *queer* climb night, God forbid, she wasn't ready for that conversation yet. But that she was striking out on a quest to figure out who she was alone.

"Just don't expect yourself to be, like, immediately the best at being single, Gab," Rachel had said, the pastel sounds of a children's musician singing an upbeat ditty about fish sleeping on a rock playing in the background. "Give yourself grace—you haven't been just you in eight years."

Gabi had bristled a little at the word *just*. There was nothing just about her. She was gloriously alone, ready to stretch her wings and see who she might have become if she hadn't devoted her twenties to a relationship she thought she should be in, that was easier to be in than examining her own identity and desires.

A relationship that had, she admitted, provided her stability and support when she was in med school and the early years of her residency, but that had chafed at her for longer than she'd known.

Rachel was right about one thing, though.

Gabi had come into tonight with grand ideas of picking up a woman and having her first queer sexual experience, or at least date. But now that she was here, that idea felt overwhelming. Plus, people seemed to have all come with at least one other person, if not in groups of threes and fours.

She scanned the floor, eyeing up anyone who didn't seem to be attached to another person. Gabi's gaze snagged on a woman on what looked to be the hardest pass. There didn't appear to be anyone cheering her on as she navigated a nearly ninety-degree bend in the wall. Her body flexed to accommodate the shape, one leg hiked up in line with her elbow as she shifted her weight from her back foot in preparation to move. As she tested her weight, her long French braid swung with the movement of her body, revealing an undercut that extended from the base of one ear to the base of the other and down to the nape of her neck. Her arms, currently straining with the effort of clinging to the wall, were soft but toned, and the right one was covered from shoulder to fingers in tattoos. Gabi was too far away to make out much detail beyond the black lines of ink on her pale skin.

After one, two more shifts of her weight, the woman seemed to admit defeat and inched her way back down until she could safely drop to the mat-like floor below. She stood for a minute, still facing the wall, and shook out what appeared to be a cramp in her left foot with her hands on a waist that dipped in from narrow shoulders and rounded out into an ass Gabi found herself transfixed by. It was round and tight and well-defined in the woman's purple leggings. Her thighs were thick to match it, while the rest of her appeared as trim and toned as her arms.

Gabi was still staring at the woman's ass when she turned around. Gabi's eyes darted up quickly, embarrassed at the idea of being caught checking out a strange woman's butt, only to find a pair of familiar brown eyes gazing back at her in confusion.

Gabi had been so wrong.

She did, in fact, know one queer woman.

Annika Silberberg.

As in, her best friend's little sister, Annika Silberberg.

Her co–maid of honor in her best friend's wedding, Annika Silberberg.

Owner of a rather extraordinary ass, Annika Silberberg.

The woman Gabi had just very openly been checking out who was now walking toward her, eyes still locked on her own, Annika Silberberg.

"Gabi?" Annika asked, wiping the sweat from beneath her bangs with her tattooed right forearm as she came to a stop in front of Gabi. "What are you doing here?"

Gabi had always wondered if she would have a fight or a flight response when struck with a situation she didn't know how to handle. In deliveries and appointments, she was cool as a cucumber, relying on her years of training and studying and knowledge to guide her through. Even in med school, she hadn't felt panicked about being cold-called in classes. She trusted her own intuition, and it usually didn't fail her.

But here, facing down her best friend's little sister at a queer event, a woman she realized she maybe found attractive, Gabi got her answer.

She fled.

Chapter Seven

Gabi? Gabi, wait," Annika called after her as Gabi, all thoughts of bouldering gone from her brain, rushed out of the gym and pushed open the first door she found.

Oh shit oh shit oh shit, Gabi thought over and over again.

No one knew, *no one*. Not Rachel, not Maia, not even her mother.

It wasn't that she was ashamed of being queer. It was just, she hadn't had a chance to explore it herself, what it all meant to her, beyond knowing that she was dying, *dying,* to know what it felt like to kiss a woman.

Belatedly, Gabi realized she hadn't gone out the front entrance, but rather the door to the patio where groups of people were gathered. They held cups of beer or hot cider and chatted in loose groups. Her sudden shivering also alerted her that it was, in fact, November in Maine, and despite the fact that she had been warm in the gym, her flimsy exercise top wasn't cutting it outside.

"Hey," she heard Annika say and felt a hand on her bare upper arm. The touch halted her mad dash.

"Gabi, hey, hold on," Annika said softly from behind her.

Gabi squeezed her eyes shut and willed her wild breath to slow, told herself that she wasn't in any danger, that she was safe. At least physically.

After a count of thirty, she turned around and faced Annika. Her brown eyes peered down at Gabi from beneath her bangs, long braid pulled over one shoulder. She was also dressed in just her climbing clothes, and Gabi's first thought was that she must be cold.

"You must be cold," her mouth decided to say for her.

Annika wrinkled her brow but ignored Gabi's obvious mental distress.

"Why did you run away like that?" Annika asked. "Are you okay?"

She was speaking so calmly, concern for Gabi clear in her eyes. Something inside Gabi's chest broke.

"I'm gay," she practically yelled at Annika, whose eyes went wide at her proclamation.

"Wow, okay," Annika said. She leaned back in surprise, hand still warm on Gabi's bare shoulder. Gabi closed her eyes and anchored herself to the feel of Annika's fingers on her skin.

"I just...you probably were confused why I was here, and you'd put two and two together eventually because you're pretty smart whatever Maia says, and I guess it would just be easier if I told you, and shit, I haven't actually said that out loud to someone else before," Gabi stammered. Words tumbled from her mouth like water from a burst dam, the pressure to contain them finally reaching a crisis point.

"Why don't you sit down over here," Annika said soothingly, and she guided Gabi to sit down at the nearest empty picnic bench. She wrapped one of the spare fleece blankets the gym had stashed out there around Gabi's shoulders. "I do want to revisit the part where my dear sister has been trash-talking me to her friends, but let's deal with one thing at a time, shall we?"

Annika sat straddling the bench seat perpendicular to Gabi while Gabi gulped down air. She rubbed Gabi's upper back over the blanket in soothing strokes while Gabi calmed down.

When she could breathe again, Gabi turned to look at Annika over her shoulder.

Annika gave her a small smile and motioned to the beer booth behind her. "Want to redeem your voucher?"

Gabi nodded enthusiastically. "Absolutely, I do."

After they'd both gotten their warm layers on and retrieved their sixteen ounces of local IPA from a queer women owned and operated microbrewery, they sat across from each other at a picnic table.

"If you want to know the truth, I was more confused to see you at a climbing gym than at a queer event," Annika said teasingly. She took a sip of her beer and went on, "I didn't think you were into physical activities."

Gabi laughed and, aiming for indignant, said, "I *am* a doctor. I need to be able to scale those shelves in the storage room without help. The nurses always pack the good gauze on the top. I think it's out of spite."

Annika smiled. "So, beyond improving your gauze retrieving ability," she said, "you came here to…"

"Pick up women, yeah," Gabi said, and her cheeks flared hot as she said the words.

"This explains a lot more about your breakup with Matt," Annika replied, nodding to herself, and Gabi grimaced.

"Yeah," she sighed, "poor Matt."

"Hey, no, none of that," Annika said as she reached across the table to grip Gabi's forearm. "He's a conventionally attractive white man with a good paying job who *wants* marriage and babies. He'll be totally fine."

Gabi snorted and felt Annika's strong fingers grip her forearm tighter through her fleece zip up.

"I'm serious, Gab. What you did was brave. You shouldn't feel bad about wanting to figure yourself out," Annika said, her usually buoyant eyes going still and serious as they met Gabi's.

Gabi swallowed and felt tears rise up her throat. Like Annika had when Gabi had told the Silberberg sisters about her breakup, she made it all seem so simple. Made it seem like choosing herself wasn't the selfish, unfeeling move Gabi had been afraid people would think it was.

"You have no idea how much I've needed to hear that," Gabi said and sighed. She took a long drink from her beer and then said, "Fuck, Annika, I have no idea what I'm doing when it comes to this shit."

She dropped her head in her hands.

"Yeah, I can't blame you. I've always known I was gay, and I'm awful with women," Annika replied.

Gabi snorted again and looked up at her.

"You don't seem to have a problem with getting them—it's keeping them around that seems to be where you get stuck, at least according to Maia," Gabi said before she could stop herself.

Annika's face pinched for a moment as if she'd been stung, but then she shook her head and rolled her eyes. "God, Maia really *does* talk serious shit about me behind my back." Annika grimaced, and she took a deep drink from her beer, licking foam from her lip when she was finished.

Gabi waved the comment away with her hand. "It's just out of love and worry."

"Uh-huh," Annika said, although something about the pinch of her brow made Gabi think she didn't believe her.

"Okay," Annika said after a moment, and she clapped her hands together. Gabi noticed her nails were cut short and filed round.

Did she need to cut her nails short now, too? Not that they were long, she was a doctor and long nails were impractical. They punctured gloves and got in the way when she was doing pelvic exams.

"Earth to Gab," Annika said. She waved her hand in front of her face. Gabi blinked and glared half-heartedly at her.

"First things first, you are going to stop spiraling right now," Annika said firmly. She sat up straight and laid her hands flat on the table, body language meaning business.

"Gee, thanks, I'm cured," Gabi deadpanned, and Annika grinned.

"I'm serious. I've known my fair share of baby gay girls in my life, and I bet I know exactly what's going on in that pretty little genius doctor mind of yours right now," Annika said, pointing to Gabi's forehead. She started ticking things off on her fingers. "You're questioning if you, slash your outfit, slash your whole vibe are gay enough. If you aren't, how can you make yourself gayer? Should you buy new clothes? Cut your nails? Cut your hair?"

Gabi opened her mouth, and Annika held up her hand to silence her.

"If any of those things feel affirming to you, go ahead," she continued, "but if you're doing them to conform to some preconceived notion of what a queer woman looks like because that's what society told you, you can fuck right off with that bullshit. A gay lady is whatever you are, because you are gay." She finished with a shrug.

"You just...believe me?" Gabi asked, a bit awestruck by Annika, *Annika,* her friend's kind of goofy, screwy little sister, making such an impassioned and eloquent and empathetic speech.

Annika gave her a look and raised her eyebrow. A small part of Gabi noted that it was kind of sexy when she did that. Then she mentally shook that part.

"Why wouldn't I?" Annika said. She rested her elbows on the table, one arm crossed in front of her on the scored wood, the other holding her beer aloft.

"Because I was in a relationship with a man for eight years? Because I've never been with a woman, never even kissed one?" Gabi said, a bit exasperatedly. "I mean, where's the proof?"

"Such a scientist. Do you want to kiss a woman?" Annika asked.

Gabi took a big gulp of her beer and swallowed. She let out a slightly shaky breath and said, "Yes."

Annika shrugged again. "Then there's your answer."

Gabi stared at her, dumbfounded. After a beat, she said, "That was actually my catalyst for breaking up with Matt."

"What was?" Annika said. She finished her beer with a toss of her head and wiped her mouth with the sleeve of her hoodie.

Gabi idly noted the line of her throat as she gulped the beer. When Annika turned back to her, she looked down into her own beer.

"I was on my computer one night when Matt was watching TV, and I thought about how the rest of our lives were going to look just like this. Then, out of nowhere, this thought popped into my head," Gabi said, finger scratching at the paint on the table.

"What was it?" Annika asked.

"I'll never get to kiss a girl," Gabi said. She turned back to look at Annika, who had her chin resting on her linked fingers.

She'd pulled a forest-green beanie with the name of her boutique on the brim in flowery script on over her braid. It was so incongruous with the rest of her aura—the puffy black vest, the dark gray hooded sweatshirt, the tattooed sleeve Gabi knew lay beneath her clothes.

"It made me so deeply sad, that thought, that I had to leave the room and go cry in the bathroom," Gabi said.

"Oh, Gab," Annika said gently, eyes alight with sympathy.

Gabi nodded.

"Anyway," she continued, "that's why I'm here, trying to work up the courage to flirt while having a panic attack every time a pretty girl looks my way."

"Oof, I know that life," Annika replied with a grimace. "Anyone piqued your interest?"

"Well," Gabi said tentatively and felt her face practically burst into flames from the rush of heat to her cheeks, "there's this woman at the register—"

"Michelle," Annika said and shook her head with a little laugh. "She would have clocked you."

"What do you mean?" Gabi said, feeling a little like Annika had popped her balloon.

"Let's just say some women get off on being someone's first time," Annika said, a sly teasing grin on her lips. "Michelle has a habit of ferreting out the baby gays and then breaking their hearts."

"Oh," Gabi said.

Annika must have noticed her slight disappointment because she nudged Gabi's foot under the table and said, "Hey, I didn't mean to discourage you. If you want, I can introduce you."

Gabi thought about Michelle's flirting and shook her head. She didn't have an interest in being just another first time for her.

Annika shrugged.

"If you change your mind, let me know. For what it's worth, I've heard she knows what she's doing, sexually," Annika said, raising her eyebrows suggestively.

Gabi gulped down the rest of her beer and felt the back of her neck sweat. Having this conversation with Annika was surreal. Saying these words out loud, when they had been trapped inside her for her whole life, was overwhelming. Too many emotions flooded her body for her to parse out.

But the overall sensation was...relief.

"It feels amazing to say all of this out loud to another human being," Gabi confided to Annika.

"I'm honored it could be me," Annika said. She pressed her hand to her chest, half joking, half sincere.

"You *are* basically the only queer woman I know, anyway," Gabi said.

Annika had started shredding a napkin. She was always fidgeting, Gabi noticed.

"I can't believe that's true," Annika said. "Look around you"— she spread her arms wide and gestured expansively to the surrounding area—"it's Portland, we're everywhere. I am impressed you started with an in-person event and not an app, by the way."

Gabi looked at her blankly.

"You do know queer women are on the apps, right?" Annika asked with a cock of her head.

Gabi just blinked at her.

"Oh my God, give me your fucking phone," Annika demanded, holding her hand out for Gabi's phone.

Gabi felt so stupid for not having thought about downloading an app, but honestly, she'd never used them. She'd met Matt in college and the rest had been history.

"Okay, you've officially got yourself a gay guru for this journey of self-discovery," Annika said as she flicked through the app store on Gabi's phone. "Are you interested in dates? Hookups? Threesomes? No, better walk before you run, I think."

"Uh, I think dates," Gabi said.

"Yeah, you don't really strike me as the hookup type," Annika agreed with a nod.

"Wow, what does that mean?" Gabi asked, feeling oddly hurt.

"Just that, you know, you're kind of *wicked* serious," Annika said. She let the phone flop from in front of her face to meet Gabi's gaze.

"Don't you *wicked* me," Gabi said. "I could hook up if I wanted to."

"I'm sure you could," Annika said patronizingly. She patted Gabi gently on the hand and went back to tapping at her phone. "But really, I bet you'll be wifed up in, like, four months. A hot gynecologist? Someone'll snatch you up quick."

Gabi swallowed and felt her heart sink.

She hadn't thought beyond getting a woman to kiss her on the lips, not really. But she did know she didn't want to dive back into another serious relationship that quickly. Didn't want to surrender her desires to another person's again.

"I'm not looking for anything serious right now. I want to keep it casual," she said, with more conviction than she felt.

"Cool," Annika said, bobbing her head in acknowledgment. "Okay, there," Annika said, handing the phone back to Gabi, who saw three new apps nestled together on her home screen. "I've downloaded the most popular apps for dating and casual fun." She wiggled her eyebrows. "You can customize the profile when you feel like it."

"Women aren't going to shun me because I don't have any experience?" Gabi said, phone clenched tightly in her hands. "They aren't going to, like, be turned off and think I'm just experimenting?"

"Some might," Annika conceded with a shrug. "There are some

people out there who just don't want to be someone's first. And there are some ladies, like Michelle, who will *really*"—she raised her eyebrows in emphasis—"want to be your first. You can use your discretion to try to figure it out. Plus, you don't need to, like, watermark all of your pictures with *I'm a baby gay.*"

Gabi laughed.

"Thanks, so much, Annika," she said, and her voice practically sagged with her body. "Really, this is so, so, so, so helpful, you have no idea."

Gabi's whole body ached from her earlier panic, and exhaustion flooded in to replace its receding tide more quickly with every passing moment. What she needed now was her couch, her fuzziest robe, some red wine, and her favorite animated comfort watch.

"Hey, if any good can come from my many misadventures in lesbian dating, I'm happy," Annika said. She shot Gabi a broad smile and a wink. "Anything for my co–maid of honor."

Gabi's heart gave a not unpleasant lurch at the teasing look, but she rolled her eyes. "Speaking of," she said, "do you mind if we keep this between ourselves? Just for now?"

"Of course," Annika said without hesitation, "besides, Maia is still freaked out you broke up with Matt. I don't think she'd react in the best way to this news right now even if you did want to tell her."

"I love that woman like a sister, but she does *not* like change," Gabi said, and she levered herself up from the picnic bench and gathered her things.

"She *is* my sister, if you can believe it," Annika responded, a small tender smile playing on her lips.

Gabi had known Annika for a long time, since she was twelve and Annika was ten. But she'd never *really* known her, just the version of her Maia saw and complained about in typical sisterly fashion. The glimpses she'd seen when she'd come to visit while they were growing up.

She'd kind of missed when Annika had gone from gawky kid sister to full-grown and fully realized person.

But tonight, she'd seen a woman comfortable and confident in her own skin, so self-assured she could calmly handle a panic attack and a coming out in stride.

"By the way, you handled that panic attack like a pro," Gabi said to Annika as they dumped their plant-based plastic cups in the giant compost bin by the exit to the patio.

"You'd be surprised how many people panic during fittings," Annika said as they strolled back through the gym to their cars. "Plus, I dated a social worker a few years back, and she taught me the basics for getting someone through one."

"See, those dating misadventures do have their uses," Gabi said with a smile, and Annika shot her a one-sided grin.

Michelle was still at reception, and she tossed a wave to Annika when she passed. Annika waved back, and when Michelle saw Gabi at her side, she shook her head and smiled ruefully.

"What's that about?" Gabi asked, gesturing with her head back to Michelle when they pushed through the gym doors out onto the street.

Annika scratched at the shaved part of her head beneath her beanie almost self-consciously.

"Let's just say this isn't the first time I've left Queer Climb night with someone by my side," Annika said, a blush high on her cheeks.

"Wow, you really are a player, aren't you?" Gabi said. She regarded Annika thoughtfully. Tried to see her separate from the history she knew.

She wondered what it would be like to meet Annika as a stranger, to see her from across the room and lock eyes. Would Annika smile? Make the first move? Wait for Gabi to come to her, drawn to her beauty like an asteroid into a planet's gravitational field?

"No, no, it's nothing like that," Annika said dismissively. "I just...I don't know, like dating, I guess."

Gabi snorted and said, "No one likes dating."

"Not true," Annika said, "I love meeting people. First impressions, the anticipation of if there will be a spark or not. The millions of what-ifs that dance around in your head when you're asking them about their siblings, and first kisses, and the little everyday dreams they have for themselves."

Gabi's felt her pulse kick up at just the idea of sitting across from Annika...or any women...at a dimly lit bar. The way their knees might brush under the table. How every word, every accidental touch would be laden with the promise of the unknown.

"You make it sound so exciting," Gabi said, a little breathlessly.

"It *is* exciting," Annika said. Her eyes shone under the streetlight, her face lit up from within as she spoke. "The rest of it, when they start wanting things from you beyond a conversation and sex, wanting to know you on a deeper level, not so much."

"I've never really dated," Gabi said, tucking her hands in her pockets and shrugging. The air was crisp now. Her exposed skin almost smarted with it. "Just drunk hookups in college and then Matt. Maybe you should coach me."

She meant it as a joke, mostly, but Annika smiled.

"If you need a consultant, I'd be happy to advise," Annika said. "I already told you I'd be your gay guru."

"I'm seriously going to take you up on that," Gabi said. "You're the only person besides Matt who knows I'm not straight. And I only told him because he knows me so well that the whole *I just need a change* explanation wasn't cutting it. I'm not ready to come out to"— she waved her arms around in a gesture that encompassed the whole of Portland—"people yet. I want to try to figure things out for myself first before I start getting hammered with questions and handed the number of everyone's single queer cousin."

"Can I ask you why you came out to *me*?" Annika asked. "Not that I mind, I'm just wondering what I did to deserve such an honor."

Gabi looked up into the star strewn sky above her and took a deep, chilled breath.

"Besides the fact that you caught me red-handed at a queer event? I guess because we don't really have a relationship," she said.

"I'm hurt," Annika said, and she pressed her hand to her chest in mock offense.

"I just mean, you're my friend's little sister. We know each other, but we don't, like, *know* each other, not really," Gabi finished, feeling like she was making no sense, but Annika nodded.

"I get that. It's easier to be someone new with someone who has fewer expectations of who you were," Annika said. She tucked her hands in her vest pockets and hunched her shoulders against the night air.

"Yeah," Gabi said. Once again, Annika seemed able to sum up her thoughts succinctly. "Exactly."

Annika stopped next to a beat-up black Subaru Outback and turned to face Gabi.

She held out her arms and Gabi stepped forward, letting Annika give her a brief squeeze.

"This whole dating thing will be fun, I promise," Annika said as she released Gabi and turned to open her car, "and if you find yourself panicking, just text me."

"Yeah, okay," Gabi said.

Someone else knows, she thought as she walked to her own car. She tilted her head to the sky and let a tear roll down her face as a huge grin split her cheeks.

Chapter Eight

Annika hadn't really expected Gabi to take her up on the offer of dating coach. She'd suggested it mostly as a joke, trying to get Gabi to smile and lighten the mood after her panic attack and confession.

She still couldn't believe Gabi had been there at Queer Climb night. At first, she had been so absorbed with trying to figure out that bend on the V4 climb she hadn't really paid attention to what was going on around her.

Then she'd turned around to find a hot girl checking out her ass, then looking away very quickly to pretend that she hadn't been checking out Annika's ass.

Annika hadn't taken in more than the barest of details of the woman—short, curvy in all the right places, curly hair secured in a lopsided bun at the top of her head—before her gaze had snagged on the woman's and she'd realized, with a huge jolt like lightning through her stomach, that the woman who had been checking her out, who Annika herself had thought was hot, was none other than Gabi Mendon, her sister's oldest and best friend.

And then Gabi had run from her, really and truly run, and Annika had chased after her, driven by pure instinct, loyalty to Maia, and more than a little curiosity.

It was hard, still, to wrap her mind around it. To try to let the image of Gabi she kept in her head dissolve and reform as something new.

Annika had known she was a lesbian since she hit the age of twelve and suddenly felt like there were bubbles in her stomach whenever she was around Shoshana, her fourteen-year-old bat mitzvah tutor. She couldn't imagine having to come out as a grown adult.

So, she'd kept Gabi's secret, and she would as long as Gabi wanted her to. No way was she ever going to out someone, not intentionally, anyway.

Besides, Gabi's sexuality didn't really affect her. Gabi was right—they were friendly but weren't exactly friends. Friday was the first time Annika could remember them hanging out one-on-one.

Still, one night that next week, Annika found herself swiping on one of the same dating apps she'd downloaded for Gabi as if she was searching for something. Someone.

Unfortunately, she didn't find Gabi, which made a restlessness settle under her skin.

That next Saturday night, she was working on the latest sketch for her sister's wedding gown. She fiddled with repeatedly adding and subtracting a ten-foot train with the stylus of her drawing tablet and saw a text notification come up on her screen.

Gabi: *Okay, so you know how you said I could call in your dating coach services?*

Gabi: *I'm in dire straits.*

Annika read the messages and sighed, swiping over to the texting app and leaving the sketch unfinished.

Annika: *What's the problem, doc?*

Gabi: *Original*

Gabi: *Sorry, I get snarky when I'm stressed.*

Annika: *Have I ever seen you unstressed?*

Gabi: *Ha ha, way to kick a girl when she's down.*

Annika smirked and typed back.

Annika: *What's got you down?*

Gabi: *I took your advice and made a profile on an app. I matched with this girl, and we chatted a bit and we're going on a date tonight.*

Annika: *THAT'S HUGE, mazel tov!!!*

Gabi: *Yes!*

Gabi: *BUT it's also possibly more terrifying than anything I've ever done in my entire life?*

Annika: *You're literally a doctor.*

Annika: *You bring life into this world with your own two hands. This is just drinks with someone—at most it will be two hours of your life.*

Gabi: *I seem to remember Maia once mentioning that your average first date is seven hours long.*

Annika: *Yes, but I'm the exception, not the rule.*

Gabi: *And during deliveries there are nurses and doulas and attendings. This date it's just me and this girl. What if we have nothing to say to each other? What if I tell her a story from work and it's accidentally grosser than I think it is, and she freaks out and leaves?*

Annika heard the question beneath the questions and switched to her phone. She clicked her video call app and summoned a disheveled Gabi onto her screen.

"Oh, thank *God* it's you," Gabi said when she answered. Her face was free of makeup and freshly scrubbed, her hair tossed up into a messy bun on top of her head. "I nearly panicked that it would be Maia or Rachel insisting on coming over to help me get ready, and I could *not* handle that right now."

"Seems like you're doing really well with this," Annika replied evenly.

On screen, Gabi flipped her off.

"The last first date I went on was two presidential terms ago. It was to the dining hall on campus and ended with us making out in a frat basement. Matt was so drunk he spilled beer on my back, and I was so drunk I didn't notice," Gabi said.

She put the phone down on her crowded bathroom counter so she could apply moisturizer to her round cheeks.

Annika very studiously avoided looking at the way the towel Gabi had wrapped around her soft frame pushed her breasts together as Gabi leaned over to rummage in her makeup bag.

"It was just so much simpler then, you know?" Gabi said, rubbing a raspberry tinted blush on her cheeks and dotting it along her lips, then leaning back to survey the effect and making a face.

"Ah yes, those days of yore when romance meant getting drunk and grinding on a sticky basement floor and then going back to a dorm room to hook up sloppily while your roommate waited impatiently in the lounge. What a time to be alive." Annika sighed dramatically and leaned back into the pillows on her couch. She forced herself to be extra relaxed in the face of Gabi's manic energy. "I knew you and Matt dated forever, but I never actually got the story of how you got together. I just came home one day, and Maia was talking about you guys like it was a done deal."

Gabi sighed and leaned one plump hip against the side of the counter.

She said, "I met Matt the spring of my senior year in a history elective I was taking. He was cute and nice. It was just so…"

"Easy?" Annika supplied as Gabi looked unseeingly into the mirror, no doubt transported back to a lecture room eight years in the past.

"Yeah." Gabi shrugged. "He was so easy. I never had to think too hard about whether or not he loved me or wanted me, he just told me. And he was always so happy to take control of the parts of our life I couldn't devote time to because of med school and interning. He picked out our apartments and bought the groceries and scheduled our social calendar, and I studied. And occasionally, we did things together."

Annika nodded.

"Is it weird I'm just spilling my guts to you like this?" Gabi said, scrunching up her nose in concern. "I mean, I know we've known each other forever, but we aren't really this close."

It was Annika's turn to shrug now.

"Honestly, it feels kind of natural. I'm used to people spilling their secrets to me. There's something about a fitting—it's like getting your hair cut, people just feel the need to talk. Little do they know, I'm only listening to them because it helps block out the intrusive thoughts that tell me to stick my pins into their thighs. I've been the first person someone told they're pregnant, like, six times in the last two years. Oh, also three different people have told me they're cheating on their fiancés, and one girl came out to me at a climbing event recently."

Gabi's face softened, her cheeks round and rosy from her blush as she smiled. Annika felt a familiar flutter in her stomach and shifted on the couch.

"That's wild. You're truly doing Hashem's work," Gabi replied, and Annika laughed.

"Quick question for you, though," Annika said. "When you were dating Matt, did you ever ask yourself whether or not you wanted him, or if you just wanted him to want you?"

Gabi froze midmotion, mascara wand lifted halfway to her eye, and glared down at the screen of her phone.

"Annika Silberberg, you can't just drop huge, perspective-altering questions on me forty-five minutes before a date I'm already on the verge of canceling," Gabi said. She pointed the mascara wand threateningly at Annika through the screen.

Annika sat up and crossed her legs, leaned her back against the couch, and tucked a strand of her long wavy hair behind her ear, tablet discarded on the cushion beside her and attention fully devoted to Gabi.

"Gabriella Mendon, MD, you are not canceling this date," Annika said, and her voice came out more serious than she had been meaning it to. "Okay, I'm going to spit some hard truths at you."

"Spit away," Gabi said, waving her hand to indicate the floor was now Annika's.

"It's like this," Annika said. She sat up straight and spoke slowly. "Big, life-changing first steps are terrifying—"

"This is supposed to help me, how?" Gabi interrupted.

"Just let me finish. Damn, girl." She rolled her eyes at Gabi and cleared her throat to continue. "As I was saying, they're heart-pounding, pee-your-pants scary. My first day opening the store without Anusha I thought I was going to have a stroke, but I did it. And you know what?"

Annika widened her eyes at Gabi, who huffed and reluctantly replied, "What?"

"Every day afterward was easier. This is probably not going to be the best date of your life. First dates are always awkward, even the best ones. But that's the beauty of it. The more you do it, the more you can roll with the awkward"—Annika moved her left arm in a rolling motion—"and the easier it gets."

"Seriously, does Maia know you're this wise?" Gabi said, her breaths more even, her hands steadier as she turned to finish applying her mascara.

"Ha, fuck no," Annika said. She flopped on her back on the couch and gazed at the white plaster ceiling of her studio apartment, her right arm flung over her head. "I save my wisdom for my clients and baby gays. Besides, my sister doesn't need it, she's all *bridal* this and *wedding* that. We've had three different consultations on her dress design now, and she keeps tweaking the tiniest things, it's driving me absolutely batshit. Sorry, I probably shouldn't bad-mouth my sister to you since she's, like, your bestie."

Annika glanced up at the screen and saw Gabi's eyes fixed on her. She traced Gabi's gaze with her own and saw she was looking at her biceps, at the vines tattooed on the underside curling from a peony in full bloom, the ends of it disappearing into the dark hair in her armpits. She felt her cheeks heat and her hand jerked the camera slightly, breaking Gabi from her inspection.

Okay, so that was the second time she had caught Gabi checking her out in the last week. Didn't mean anything, though, Annika reasoned with herself. She was just acknowledging her own attraction to women. Her eyes were bound to linger when she saw something she liked.

She shushed the small voice in her head that preened and said the something she liked was Annika. Pushed down the subtle thrill that idea sent through her.

"You can trash talk bridezilla Maia to me any day," Gabi said, now moving through what Annika assumed was her new apartment. She glimpsed white walls, still bare, behind Gabbi's naked shoulder. "I love her, but the last thing I need on my breaks at work are texts asking my opinion on types of folding chairs."

"How long have you been living in that place?" Annika asked, eyeing the blank white walls behind Gabi.

"About three weeks, why?" Gabi said.

She balanced her phone on her dresser in view of her closet as she went to contemplate outfit choices.

The bedroom held only a full-size mattress on the floor, the dresser, a heap of boxes in one corner, and a nightstand. The walls were blank in here, too, not a poster or picture or inspirational quote on the wall. Not a single effort to make it a home.

"It looks kind of spare," Annika, whose own studio apartment was crammed to the gills with work she'd taken home from the shop, her personal sewing machine, and trinkets she loved of all types, noted.

"Yeah, well, the life of a resident doesn't give much time for decorating," Gabi said over the clink of hangers sliding across the rod in the closet, "and what little time I have has been devoted to being gay."

Annika laughed and relaxed against the back of her couch, picking up a stray hair elastic and twisting it around the index finger of her left hand.

"You'd be surprised how much of your free time it does take up.

All the meetings and potlucks. So. Much. Processing," she said. "What are you and this woman up to tonight anyway?"

"Just getting drinks over by the harbor," Gabi said. Her voice emerged from the depths of her closet.

"A classic." Annika nodded. "Very chill, very low effort. What are you going to tell her if she wants to go back to your place? *I swear I'm not a serial killer, I just like sleeping on the ground*?"

"Back to…my place," Gabi whispered, and a look of anxious horror crept over her face as she popped her head out of the closet. "Niki, what if she wants *to go home with me*?"

"That is a possibility, yeah." Annika nodded calmly. "But remember, just because she asks doesn't mean you have to say yes. You should think about what *you* want, too. Not just what she wants."

She saw Gabi's shoulders slump.

"What I want, yeah," Gabi echoed.

She seemed to be absorbing that for a moment, but then something complicated went on behind her eyes, and they were back to panic.

"Annika, what the fuck do I wear?" Gabi said exasperatedly.

"I don't know, whatever you'd normally wear to get drinks at a kind of hip bar," Annika replied in the same tone.

"But, like…" Gabi trailed off, widening her eyes so she looked like a lost little lamb separated from its mother, pitiful and adorable at once. Her voice was hushed as she said, "It's *gay* drinks."

Annika couldn't help it, she spit out the water she'd been sipping, coughed and spluttered as a laugh rocked through her. Vera Wang gave her a reproachful look and flicked her tail in irritation from the opposite arm of the couch.

"I can't believe my literal gay panic just made you do a spit take!" Gabi whined.

"Are the drinks all going to be rainbow and have signs that say things like *love is love* on them? Will they make quippy little remarks that read you for filth? Will—"

"Yeah, yeah, okay, I get it," Gabi said, putting her hands on her hips as Annika's peals of laughter died down. "I'm serious, though."

When Annika was calm again, she felt bad about teasing Gabi when she was so clearly in distress.

"Just wear what makes you feel comfortable and sexy," Annika said and watched Gabi nod, face as serious as if she'd just told her the steps to a complicated procedure.

"Comfortable and sexy," Gabi repeated to herself. "Okay, I think I can do that."

"Do you want to bounce outfit ideas off me?" Annika asked, flipping her long hair in an imitation of Maia.

"I'm a big girl. I think I can handle that part on my own," Gabi said.

"Says the woman who texted me *I'm in dire straits* not ten minutes ago," Annika said.

Gabi rolled her eyes.

"I have Maia and Rachel to consult for outfits. They do know I'm going on a date, just not with who," Gabi said, her attention turned back to her closet as she pulled out a few tops on hangers and tossed them on her bed.

Ah, Annika thought, *her real friends.*

She waited for Gabi to say good-bye and end the call, but neither of them made a move to do so.

After a moment, Gabi turned back to the camera, genuine fear in her eyes as she asked, "What if I'm bad at this?"

Annika felt something in her chest crack and melt, a warm tenderness spreading like butter over hot toast.

"You're smart, you're hot, and you're funny," Annika listed matter-of-factly, trying to keep the sudden warmth that crept through her chest out of her voice. "You won't be bad at dating."

Gabi's cheeks turned a little pink when Annika called her hot, but Annika firmly did *not* notice that.

"Thanks, Niki," Gabi said with a tender smile.

Annika also chose not to notice the way her heart thumped when Gabi said her nickname like that, all soft and gooey, like freshly baked chocolate chip cookies.

"Okay," Gabi said. She drew in a deep breath and clapped her hands together. "Time to put clothes on my body and talk to a lady about her interests."

"Hear! Hear!" Annika said, and Gabi grinned.

"Bye, Annika," Gabi said.

"Bye, Gabi," Annika returned. She hit the call button and flopped onto her back.

She couldn't believe she had just coached Gabi Mendon, her sister's best friend, through getting ready for her first date with a woman.

A date her sister didn't know about. Well, didn't know the full truth about, at least.

She lay on her couch and stared up at her ceiling. One arm dangled off the couch and trailed on the carpet.

It felt strange, knowing she knew something about one of Maia's best friends that Maia didn't. The part of her that would always be twelve and wanting, desperately, to be included with Maia and her friends buzzed to life at the idea of it. The fact that it was Gabi, studious, serious, sexy Gabi, made it that much more surreal.

Her phone vibrated ten minutes later with a picture from Gabi.

She was standing in front of the mirror showing off her outfit. High waisted blue jeans that clung to her round hips and lush thighs and flared around her calves paired with an orange and white smocked top with loose sleeves that gathered at the wrists and left her collarbones and sternum bare. It was short enough to offer a glimpse of hospital-pale stomach between the hem of the shirt and top of the jeans. A trio of simple gold chains with pendants too small for Annika to make out were slung around her neck and matched the thicker gold hoops in each earlobe. Black leather heeled ankle boots were on her feet, and her dark curls fell in tight coils below her shoulders.

Annika sent back three fire emoji and then dropped her phone on the carpet before she could spend too long gazing at the image. She slung her right arm across her eyes and let out a little groan.

She always was a sucker for a soft, beautiful femme all dressed up in her glory.

The urge to take out her phone and scroll for a date of her own surged through her as she thought about Gabi entering the dimly lit bar by the harbor, the nerves that would flutter in her stomach as she searched the crowd for the woman she was meeting. The held breath, knife's edge moment of possibility when their eyes first met.

Then she thought of Lana. Of the tears that had been in her eyes when Annika had broken it off after just two months, when it became clear Lana wanted to enter the sleepovers and lazy mornings and making future plans stage.

Annika didn't know why other women's interest in building a

future with her turned her off. Even the hint of interest in getting to know her better made her suddenly see their flaws. It was like the moment it went from possibility to reality, the fun drained from it, and she got this impulse to get as far away from the other woman as possible.

If she was ever going to be with someone long term, it would have been someone like Lana, she mused as she inspected a water stain on her ceiling, and Vera Wang butted her dangling hand for pets.

Lana was gorgeous and creative. Tall with soft curves she covered in gauzy fabrics splattered with clay. She sold her pottery in one of the touristy stores in town but also did more experimental commissions and pieces for herself on the side. They'd bonded over their artistic sides and love of nature, taking Lana's dog Skipper, a flat coated mutt who loved to wallow in the muddy summer streams, on long winding walks through the woods around Portland. And she had been good in bed, too.

The idea of it had felt so right, so good. But then Annika had woken up next to Lana after a postsex nap, and the sight of her face smiling at her, expecting things from her, made her feel suddenly exhausted and trapped. The reality of having to deal with another person invading her life, making her adjust to their desires and schedules and plans, needing her, wanting to know her, the truth of her, had her heart racing in all the wrong ways.

It had been more or less the same story for all of her romantic history since her first girlfriend when she was fourteen.

Maybe I should figure my shit out before I go on any more dates, Annika thought.

She wondered if Gabi had made it to the bar yet.

CHAPTER NINE

That first date hadn't been bad.

Not terrible in the way that Gabi had feared it would be. She didn't spill anything on herself, or forget how to talk, or tell stories about abscesses she had to drain or the effects of untreated chlamydia.

She didn't physically recoil when her knees brushed the woman's under the table, suddenly realize that she had been totally wrong about her sexuality, and had blown up her life with Matt for no reason.

It had actually been nice when their knees brushed. Not fireworks, but still sent a pleasant zing of warmth up her thigh.

Gabi had babbled a bit, she was a nervous talker after all, and there had been some lulls in the conversation. But over the course of two hours, two Negronis, and a shared plate of fried goat cheese stuffed olives, she had had a decent conversation with an attractive woman and the world hadn't ended.

At the end, they split the bill and hugged on the sidewalk before going their separate ways. Gabi, who had been secretly obsessing about the parting and the paying for the last twenty minutes of the date, was relieved she didn't have to navigate bringing someone home to her apparently serial killer-esque apartment.

She'd gone home alone and promptly changed into her pajamas and collapsed onto her bed, exhausted from the adrenaline withdrawal and drowsy from the two drinks and little food. Sleep was about to take her when her phone buzzed.

Annika: *How'd it go?*
Annika: *Is she the love of your life?*

Gabi smiled at the sight of the texts on her screen. Who knew having someone to confide in, to talk her down from the ledge, would be such a massive relief?

She'd already updated Maia and Rachel, in separate texts, about her date with the *person* from the app. How it had been so weird to be on a date again after nearly a decade of coupledom, but a good weird.

Annika was right—the anticipatory thrill that went through her when she'd spotted the woman in the dim ambient lighting of the trendy bar had been like a bump of cocaine, buzzing her brain to life after years on autopilot.

It hit her that she was texting Annika, who she sometimes still expected to have braces and terrible acne like she had when she was fifteen.

But now, she was her lifeline to queer culture. Gabi hadn't been lying when she said she didn't know any other queer women, at least not well enough to consult with them about dating, to give them a glimpse of her deepest vulnerabilities.

But it felt almost normal, talking to Annika this way.

Maybe it was familiarity, the long years they'd been in each other's orbits, not quite friends, but not quite strangers either. Maybe it was Annika's easy manner, the fact that she didn't want anything from Gabi but to help her understand herself better.

Gabi: *It was actually *gasp emoji* fine.*

Gabi: *Not amazing, I probably won't see her again, but also not a huge horrible disaster.*

Annika: *Wow!!! Ten out of Ten stars! Congrats on your thoroughly average date with a woman!!!*

Gabi chuckled to herself at Annika's overly enthusiastic reply.

Gabi: *Were you waiting for me to text you about how it went?*

Annika's reply came before she could put the phone down.

Annika: *Absolutely, yes I was. That's why I've been scrolling on my phone for the last two hours and no other reason.*

Gabi rolled her eyes. After a pause, her phone buzzed again.

Annika: *How do you feel about it? Still spiraling?*

She paused with her thumb hovering over the keyboard.

How did she feel?

Gabi: *Like I can make dating my bitch.*

Annika hearted her message, and Gabi smiled.

PART THREE

Bachelorette Party Brainstorming

November–December

Chapter Ten

Gabi was eating those words three weeks later after as many bad dates and still no kissing.

There had been the woman whose whole personality was the WNBA, particularly the Connecticut Sun. She spent a good hour talking Gabi through every play from their recent game against the New York Liberty even though Gabi had said she didn't really follow sports. When Gabi had asked her if she had any other interests, the woman had stared at her blankly.

Then there was the pediatric nurse practitioner who suggested they meet for tea and dessert instead of drinks when Gabi was on a night rotation. At first, they had connected over their most recent patient stories. But then Gabi had quipped that while kids come out of vaginas, she didn't have much interest in them once they'd left the delivery room. Her date, who was twenty-seven, said she was really looking for someone she could start a family with soon, that she didn't have time to waste, and that while it had been nice to meet her, she should probably be going.

"You actually have a good decade before you have to worry about your fertility declining," Gabi called to her retreating back as she walked out of the café.

Gabi finished her cake, and then her date's, while texting Annika all about the storm-out.

It had become a regular thing, texting Annika before and after dates, getting Annika's input if a certain answer to a prompt was a red flag, or what an acronym meant.

"I can't believe you don't know that enby is non-binary and ENM means ethically nonmonogamous," Annika said now as she peered down at the profile on the screen of Gabi's phone. "What are you, in a nursing home?"

They were sitting next to each other on Maia's couch while Maia fussed with something in the kitchen. Gabi only risked pulling out her phone because Maia had told them she was assembling snacks, and knowing her, that meant something elaborate and time consuming that would take all her attention.

"Niki," Gabi replied, "I spend eighty percent of my time talking to your heterosexually engaged sister or my heterosexually married mom friend. Why would I know those things?"

"I don't know, the zeitgeist?" Annika said, and she waved her arms around vaguely.

Gabi gave her an exasperated look.

"What do you think, though? Worth a swipe right?" Gabi said.

She contemplated the person on her screen. They had short reddish-blond hair that was styled in a swoop over their forehead, and a nice smile. The majority of their pictures were solo shots, something Maia, Rachel, and Annika had assured her was crucial to weeding out the weirdos, although most were outdoor shots in hardcore hiking gear or posed with dogs.

"Says they're a photographer. I don't usually go for the artsy types," Gabi mused.

"What do *you* think?" Annika replied. She leaned back on Maia's couch, tucked her woolen-socked feet under her legs, and crossed her arms over the front of her well-worn red and green checked flannel.

She looked soft and inviting, and Gabi had to fight the sudden and strange urge to curl into her and rub her cheek against the flannel over Annika's chest. It would probably smell like citrus and musk and the lingering scent of the lavender and eucalyptus room spray they used at the boutique.

Instead, she looked back down at the person on her screen.

What *did* she think?

"Left swipe," Gabi narrated as her fingers completed the motion.

"That's my girl," Annika said, a smile crinkling the corners of her eyes.

Gabi felt a small thrill hum through her at the praise.

"Are we swiping?" Maia exclaimed as she swept into the room. Her high pony swayed as she placed the olive wood board in her hands on the coffee table in front of Gabi and Annika, "You let Niki give you advice, but you won't let me?"

"You're basically an old married woman," Annika said, leaning over to pick up a piece of cheese from the elaborate spread on the board Maia had assembled.

"You're a lesbian," Maia retorted.

"Exactly, I have excellent taste," Annika said. Catching Gabi's eye, she gave her a little smirk. Gabi felt her cheeks heat and bent toward the snack board to hide them.

"Okay, and can we talk about why you're consulting my baby sister, a huge raging lesbian who has not kissed a man since she was eleven and kissed Jonah Mizrahi as a dare one Shabbat, on your dating life?" Maia asked incredulously.

"Wow, I totally forgot about Jonah," Annika said. She scrunched up her face in distaste. "His mouth was so wet."

"Gross," Maia said and grimaced, and Annika nodded in agreement.

"I mean, she does have more experience with dating in general than most of my friends do," Gabi hedged. "I'm sorry, but you're all a bunch of serial monogamists."

Maia nodded thoughtfully. "I guess that's true. She is a slut for dates."

"Excuse me, I'm sitting right here," Annika interjected. She raised her right arm and waved her hand a bit, loose sleeve slipping to her elbow, granting Gabi a glimpse of her tattoos with the motion.

"I'm so sorry," Maia said, not sounding sorry in the least. "*You*"— she turned her head to look directly at Annika—"are a slut for dates."

"Thank you for acknowledging me," Annika said primly, and Maia threw a grape at her.

"I'm trying my best, but it's hard out here," Gabi groaned, ignoring the sisters' bickering. "There are so many perfectly nice people I am just *not* into."

"So kiss someone you *are* into," Maia said simply, and she popped a grape into her mouth.

"Like who?" Gabi asked. She flopped back against the couch cushions and felt her thighs brush against Annika's toes.

"I'm just saying, isn't there, like, someone at work or somewhere else in your life you vibe with, who makes you feel comfortable and who won't be weird about it if you ask them to make out a little?" Maia suggested. "I just think the longer you put it off, the more you'll build it up in your mind, and the bigger and bigger a thing it will become."

Beside her, Annika shifted. "For once, I agree with Maia," Annika said.

"Okay, you know it's a good idea if both Silberberg girls endorse it," Maia concluded. "Also, not to change the subject, but let's focus on me now."

Maia settled on the floor and brushed her hands together.

"I hereby declare this meeting of the Maia's Bachelorette Party Planning Committee to session," Annika declared, raising her glass of wine.

"Hear, hear," Gabi chimed in, raising her own glass.

Maia gave a small cheer and wiggled her hips as she raised her glass, and the three of them clinked.

"Okay," Maia said, spreading some soft goat cheese on a seeded cracker and popping it into her mouth, "I have ideas."

They spent the next thirty minutes listening to Maia detail an increasingly more expensive and intricate trip including ten of her best gals flying across the country to the Napa Valley for five whole days of drinks, spa treatments, and farm-to-table debauchery.

"And whose millionaire partner is paying for all of this?" Annika replied after Maia had handed her her phone to show her the resort she'd seen in a video on social media.

"Yeah, Mai. I love you, but I'm not selling my eggs to fund your bachelorette," Gabi joined in.

"Ugh, fine, but a girl can dream." Maia sighed, holding her phone to her chest and gazing off into the distance wistfully.

After some more back and forth, they finally settled on a three-day weekend in Nashville, Maia's fourth idea after Paris and Cabo.

"Okay, we'll reconvene in two months to book accommodations and plan an itinerary," Maia said, and she pressed a button on the screen of her tablet.

"Sounds good," Gabi agreed and poured herself another glass of wine.

Annika opened her mouth, but Maia smoothly cut in, "I will send you a calendar invite now, then text you reminders every day leading up to the event."

Annika grinned. "She knows me so well," she crooned at her sister, who yanked her ankle in response.

"Now," Maia said, swiveling her whole body to face Gabi, "back to you and your dating journey."

Gabi's heart dropped into her stomach.

"How was the date you went on earlier this week, the one in business school?" Maia prodded.

"Um, it was fine," Gabi said, twisting one loose curl around her finger and not quite meeting Maia's eyes. She wasn't exactly lying to Maia. She had gone on a date with a woman in business school. She'd just left out the *woman* part.

"Just fine?" Maia pushed.

"Yeah, I mean, it was nice," she stammered and felt Annika shift beside her on the couch as she settled back against the arm and wrapped a fleece blanket around her shoulders, wineglass in hand, undivided attention on Gabi.

She glanced between the two Silberberg sisters and felt sweat prickle the back of her neck.

She should just do it, tell Maia now, Gabi thought. Get it over with so she could stop feeling like she'd swallowed a horde of eels who were having a hard time settling into their new home.

"Just nice?" Maia echoed. "Gab, we need to find you a guy who is hot who you vibe with and want to make out with his face so the last face you've kissed isn't Matt's."

"I agree," Annika said. "I've been telling her that she's overthinking this."

"Actually," Gabi said before she could stop herself, "I'm a lesbian."

Maia actually spit the sip of wine she'd just taken back into her glass and began coughing and spluttering.

"Holy shit, Mai, it's not like she said she's dying," Annika said as Gabi took the wineglass from Maia, and Annika poured her a glass of water and handed it to her.

"I'm sorry," Maia said, blinking rapidly up at Gabi. "It just sounded like you, my best friend of nearly twenty years, came out to me like it was no big deal."

Gabi shifted in her seat as a sudden weight landed in her stomach.

Then Maia launched herself at Gabi and tackled her into the soft embrace of the couch.

"Mai, your boney elbow is poking me in the boob," Gabi complained, but her insides were soaring as Maia continued to squeeze her tightly.

Gabi caught Annika's eye over her sister's shoulder and saw Annika's wide grin directed at her, eyes sparkling beneath her bangs.

"I told you so," Annika mouthed and shook her head at her sister's antics.

"Okay," Maia said, letting go of Gabi and scooting back only far enough that she could look Gabi in the face. She pressed her slender hands into Gabi's cheeks, the metal of her engagement ring cool against Gabi's flaming skin. "Tell me everything, babe."

So Gabi did.

She told her how she had been feeling, for years, like something wasn't quite right but had gone along with Matt's plans for their future regardless because she was so focused on medical school, on her internship, on residency. How she'd felt drawn toward women, had dreamed about kissing them and holding them and touching them, her whole life but thought it was just how everyone felt, until that moment last summer when it suddenly became clear to her.

"Well, I'm over the moon that you're stepping into your truth," Maia said, and a few tears slipped out as she hugged Gabi again. "I love you, and I want happiness for you no matter what. If that's with a woman or alone on a ranch with a thousand dogs, I will support you. I might have some logistic questions about where all the dogs will sleep, but that's just who I am."

Gabi was crying, unable to hold anything back now. She laughed as she gripped Maia's wrists.

"I'm sorry I didn't tell you sooner," Gabi said, wiping her nose pitifully on the sleeve of her sweater. "I just needed some time to adjust to the idea of everything myself and work through some things on my own."

"Oh my God, girl, don't even with that. You have nothing to apologize for," Maia said, and she waved Gabi's apology away with a flick of her hand.

Maia's eyes darted back and forth as if she was calculating the amount of medication to give a patient based on their weight.

After a moment, Maia said, "But all those dates…"

"Were with women, yeah," Gabi said, and nodded.

Maia looked thoughtful for a moment, turned to Annika, and said, "You knew, didn't you."

Annika just said, "Yeah."

"Explains why she was consulting with you rather than me," Maia said and then turned back to face Gabi. "Now back to this whole kissing debacle. I really do think you need to just find someone and smooch the hell out of them. Annika, are there any events at that clam bar you go to you can take her to?"

Gabi felt like her organs had been replaced with helium balloons and she might just float away at any moment.

Just like that, Maia had accepted her. No pushback, no questioning, just support.

God, she'd lucked out when those counselors were making bunk assignments all those years ago.

"I still keep kosher," Gabi said, mind still mostly blissfully blank with relief.

"It's a lesbian bar called The Clam Shack," Annika said as Maia giggled.

"You get it," Maia said, elbowing Gabi in the ribs, "clams, like…" She pointed at her crotch.

"Yes, Mai, clams like pussies," Annika said, her tone fed up with her sister's heterosexual dramatics.

Gabi felt her stomach clench at the sound of the word *pussies* falling from Annika's lips and tried her best not to show it.

"That's clever," Gabi said.

"It's just a little dive bar in downtown Portland," Annika said and shrugged.

"It's perfect, you should totally take her, Niki. Introduce her to some queer women who aren't you she can kiss," Maia said.

Yeah, she totally couldn't kiss Annika, Gabi mused a few minutes later as Maia and Annika were once again bickering, this time about how much money Annika owed to the wedding bin for her behavior that evening.

Even if Annika did make Gabi feel safe to be herself.

Even if she looked so cute in that flannel, her dark hair pulled up in her habitual bun, undercut freshly shaven.

Even if Gabi wanted to trail her fingers over the ink of her tattoos, trace the designs with her tongue to know how the salt of her skin tasted.

Annika came back into the room then, coat in hand, almost like she'd sensed Gabi's thoughts as they took a horny turn.

"Everything okay, Gab?" Annika said quietly.

She squatted so her eyes were level with Gabi's and rested her hand on Gabi's thigh, squeezing a little. The heat from it suddenly seared through Gabi's jeans.

Gabi glanced down at that hand, nails short and rounded off, nicked from needles, a plain beaten silver band on her forefinger. She wondered how Annika would react if Gabi covered it with her own hand, slid her hand up to grab Annika's wrist, and pulled her closer to let their lips brush.

"I know tonight might have been intense for you, and I wanted to check in," Annika said, voice low.

Well, now, what was Gabi supposed to do with this sweet and considerate side to this woman? The urge to wrap her arms around Annika's neck and kiss her surged like a blown fuse through her body.

"Uh, y-yeah," Gabi stammered, unable to look away from Annika's warm gaze. "I mean, I didn't plan it, but I think it was better that way. Less chance to overthink myself into knots."

"Like you're doing with this kissing thing," Annika said.

"Maybe," Gabi said. "I was just thinking about what you and Maia were saying"—she drew her gaze up from Annika's hand to meet her eyes. Annika's face was closer than she expected it to be. She realized she was leaning toward Annika but didn't do anything to stop herself— "about a low-stakes way of kissing someone I'm attracted to so I'm not so in my head on dates."

She thought she saw Annika's eyes dip down to Gabi's lips for just a second before Annika said, "It would have to be a wicked good kiss to get *you* to stop thinking."

There was a quality to her voice, her usual teasing mixed with something more, something smoky and dark like a well-aged scotch.

Gabi felt her heart rate kick up as she moved even farther into Annika, and Annika's hand slid ever so slightly higher up her thigh.

After a moment, Annika sat back and pulled her hand from Gabi's thigh as she stood.

Gabi's heart was pounding. A sense of almost disappointment flooded her as she took a moment to get herself in order.

What the hell had that been?

She didn't really want to kiss *Annika*, did she?

And did Annika want to kiss *her*?

"Hey," Annika said a little later when they were on the street and walking to their cars after Maia had dismissed them, "you should check out trivia night at The Clam Shack. I go most Thursdays with my friend Vanessa and her wife Mindy."

The casual use of the phrase *her wife* sent an electric zing through Gabi.

"It's a very chill environment, just a bunch of queers nerding out about pop culture and movies and music," Annika went on, using her hands to emphasize her words.

Despite her blasé description, Gabi could tell this was an event that Annika loved.

She found the idea of seeing Annika in a setting like that, loose and free and surrounded by her people, appealing. She'd only ever known her in the context of Maia and her family, but she was coming to know Annika as someone wholly different from who she'd thought she was. And the more she uncovered, the more she wanted to know.

"I'm terrible with pop culture," Gabi replied, and she tucked her hands into the pockets of her black wool coat.

"There's usually a few Disney questions thrown in there," Annika said. She waggled her eyebrows and elbowed her until Gabi elbowed her back playfully, a smile on her lips.

"Plus, it's, like, a feeding ground for single queer women, so I could totally wing-woman you into the low-stakes kiss of your dreams," Annika said.

"That actually sounds kind of perfect," Gabi said.

She quickly stomped out the small fizz Annika's teasing had shaken up in her blood.

"Mm-hmm. We'll get you a couple of drinks, loosen you up a bit. I promise, there will be no shortage of women and theys there who will be interested in kissing you," Annika said, and that grin tipped up her lips, shaking Gabi up again.

Annika looked away and surveyed the cars lined up along the curb.

"Any chance you remember where I parked my car?" she said, head swiveling up and down the block.

Gabi shrugged. "You were already here when I arrived," Gabi said as she unlocked her own car door.

Annika groaned.

"Well, if you don't hear from me before bed, I'm probably still out here wandering like the Jews of old," Annika said, and Gabi laughed.

"I'll see you Thursday, I guess," Gabi said as she opened the door to her silver Prius.

"You will *definitely* see me Thursday," Annika shot back. She pointed the hand holding her keys at Gabi almost threateningly.

Gabi shook her head as she got into her car and watched Annika walk away, shoulders hunched in her flannel-lined denim coat against the chill of the evening.

CHAPTER ELEVEN

A h!" Annika jumped when she glanced up from her sewing machine that Thursday afternoon to see a person in black standing in front of her.

"Woah, dude, you need to take a break from that," Vanessa said.

She dropped down into the seat opposite Annika, crossed her legs, and balanced her wrists on her knee. Today, she wore loose-fitting jeans with a turtleneck tucked into them and belted, her waist-length blond locks loose and held back from her face with a thick black headband.

"You've been at it for, like, four hours uninterrupted," Vanessa said. "I've had two appointments and a walk-in since one, and every time I come back here, you've been in the zone. Have you even peed?"

Annika sat up stiffly. Her back muscles protested after having been hunched over the machine for four-plus hours. She reached her arms toward the ceiling and felt something in her lower back pop.

"I got into a flow," Annika answered. "I fell out of space and time for a bit there."

"Uh-huh, you better eat something before trivia. I don't want a repeat of that time you skipped lunch and dinner, had four whiskey gingers, and nearly threw up on Mindy on the ride home."

Annika grimaced at the memory. "I like to think I'm a bit older and wiser these days," Annika said.

She stretched side to side to work out a kink in her back.

"Keep telling yourself that, babycakes," Vanessa said, rolling her eyes at her, "especially since you're bringing a date and all."

"It's just Gabi," Annika replied. She slumped back in the chair, grabbed her still full—oops—water bottle, and took a long pull from the straw on top.

"Just Gabi?" Vanessa said, and she raised her eyebrows. "The Gabi you've been texting nonstop for the last month? The Gabi who has you smiling to yourself like a little lovestruck puppy dog?"

"I do not," Annika said, a bit defensively, and she willed herself not to blush. "I've been helping her out with dating stuff. She's new to this whole complex world of ladies loving ladies. I remember how agonizing it was to figure out, so I'm just trying to keep her from making some of the same mistakes I did."

"And that requires texts that make you basically have hearts falling out of your eyes like a cartoon?" Vanessa said, tossing her hair off her shoulder and sitting back in the chair.

Annika took another long pull from her metal water bottle for cover. She could admit they'd been texting a lot in the past few weeks. Frequently about nondating things.

It had started one night when Gabi had sent her a picture of the scene of the mice from the animated *Cinderella* movie sewing a dress, texting: *Is this what you do all day? *monocle emoji**

It was obvious from the picture that she was watching the movie on her couch, a glass of wine just visible in the lower left corner of the image. Annika had texted back a joke about the cost of keeping domesticated sewing mice being way beyond her budget and then teased Gabi for her choice of comfort movie.

It had grown from there. Gabi asked her about her own comfort watches and reads, Annika surprised to learn that Gabi might be just a touch of a Disney adult. Gabi told her how she'd begged Matt to go on a vacation there for years, but he'd reply that he'd rather save their money for a house.

Gabi: *I mean, how boring is that?*

Annika: *Aren't you, like, severely in debt from med school?*

Gabi: *Exactly, so putting a couple grand on the credit cards is basically a drop in the bucket at this point.*

Annika: *Yeah, past Matt! How dare you try to be financially responsible when you could be visiting the OG mouse's own house! You should just take yourself.*

Gabi: *Nah, it's not as fun unless you have someone to go on the* *rides with. Otherwise, you get stuck with someone's spare kid.*

Annika: *Spare kid?*

Gabi: *You know, you're a family of five, there's always a spare.*

Annika: *You should make that your tagline on the apps. Looking for someone to go to Disney World with.*

Gabi: *Hmm, maybe.*

Annika could admit it to herself. She loved texting with Gabi. Their conversations flowed, quip for quip. Annika never had to worry if Gabi would get that she was joking, and Gabi dished out as good as she got.

She'd find in those restless moments at night when it was just her in her empty apartment with her racing brain when she'd usually reach to swipe on a dating app to distract her, there'd be a text from Gabi to occupy her instead.

If Gabi was at work, it was a picture of something ominous and gooey looking on her scrubs with the caption *guess the bodily fluid*, or a story about a particularly weird or obnoxious patient. Like the woman who wanted to know if garlic salt would cure her yeast infection, or the teen girl who'd stuck a quartz crystal up her vagina because she'd heard it could cure menstrual cramps.

And Annika would text Gabi about her own day. The garments she was working on, the demanding brides who came in with completely contradictory desires and no idea what was actually within their price range. The rare, sweet love stories that tugged at her own cynical heart.

Annika: *I mean, you just can't do velvet for a May wedding in New England.*

Gabi: *No?*

Annika: *Not if you don't want to look like your scrubs from two days ago.*

Gabi: **Crying laughing emoji**

And the wildest thing was that Gabi listened. She let Annika ramble on about the benefits of cotton organza versus tulle, about how she wanted to start her own silkworm farm if only so she didn't have to deal with the man who worked in sales at her silk supplier who always judged her.

She didn't want to date Gabi, she was sure she didn't. It was just so nice to have someone to talk to like that, to feel close to without the expectations of romance and commitment.

"Besides, I did my time in the baby gay trenches," Annika said now as she tilted back in her chair and locked her hands behind her head, legs stretched out before her under her sewing table. "Remember Charlotte?"

Vanessa grimaced at the reminder of Annika's ex who had shown up at the store every day for a week after Annika had broken up with her to beg Annika to reconsider.

"Btdubs, I recently saw online that she got married to the woman she met immediately after me, so that's something," Annika said with a shrug.

"Good for her," Vanessa said. "There truly is a fish for every hook in the sea."

"I don't think that's a thing, Ness," Annika replied. "Besides, Gabi's still figuring it all out. I remember trying to go through all that shit. And she's thirty and just exploring now—that's got to be, like, ten times harder. If I can give her some guidance the way I would have loved someone to do for me, then why not?"

"And that's all you're doing," Vanessa said, and the statement sounded more like a question. "Just giving guidance."

"Yes, Ness," Annika answered exasperatedly, "plus, I'm looking for something serious, and she's deep in casual dating mode."

"Looking for something serious, huh?" Vanessa repeated, an arch in one dirty blond brow.

"Why do you sound so skeptical about that? I want something that lasts. It just never really seems to, at least for me. I mean, why else would I spend so much of my life dating if I'm not looking for something real and long term?"

Annika meant it to sound like an explanation, but instead it came out as more of a genuine question, like she was asking Vanessa to explain her own behavior to her.

Vanessa just shook her head and shrugged her shoulders.

At that moment, Annika's body remembered she hadn't gone to the bathroom in over four hours.

"Whoops, got to pee," she said, standing and making a beeline for the tiny staff bathroom at the back of the workshop.

"You deserve to pee your pants," Vanessa called after her. "Serves you right for being so oblivious."

She met Gabi on the sidewalk by The Clam Shack later that night. On the outside, it looked just like any other pub in town. A touch grimy and worn from the sea salt air, not hip and artisanal like many of the stores and restaurants in town. A place where you were just as likely to find crusty old fishermen as younger queer folks.

"Hey," Gabi said, and she shifted nervously on her heeled boots on the cobblestones of the street outside the bar. Annika, a cool eight minutes late, hurried to meet her, long hair blowing loose around her face in the chilly late November wind.

"Sorry, sorry, got swallowed by a ball gown, almost literally," Annika said in a rush. She pushed her hair out of her face as she came to a stop before Gabi.

"That's okay." Gabi smiled. "I've just been working myself into an increasingly panicked state as I waited for you."

"Sounds like a productive use of your time," Annika replied, and she returned her smile.

Gabi's eyes flitted over her, took in her loosely waving hair, her black jeans and forest-green hoodie beneath her favorite flannel-lined oversized denim jacket. The weatherized Chelsea boots on her feet with the leaves she'd embroidered on the elastic around the ankle.

"Your hair looks nice like that," Gabi said, and her cheeks tinged the loveliest shade of pink.

"Oh, um, thanks," Annika said, lifting a tentative hand to her hair and tucking it behind her ear.

"You never wear it down. It's so long," Gabi said. She plucked some strands the wind had captured and tucked them behind Annika's ear. Her fingertips grazed the top of Annika's ear, shockingly warm against the chill of her skin.

"What?" Annika stammered, "I mean, you look nice tonight, too."

"You can't even see what I'm wearing yet." Gabi smiled, and she gestured to her calf-length black wool coat. "It could be a long-sleeve leopard bodysuit."

"Okay, *please* tell me it's that," Annika shot back with a grin.

Gabi just laughed and shook her head. "Are you taking me to lesbian trivia or not?"

"This place used to be an Irish pub until about five years ago," Annika said as she pushed open the door to The Clam Shack, "then Glory and Maria, the owners—and ex-wives, naturally—bought it and turned it into Portland's only lesbian bar."

"Wow," Gabi breathed in awe when they entered.

Annika looked over her shoulder and saw Gabi glancing around the little bar like it was some grand palace.

It looked just as generically bar-like as the outside. If not for the art on the walls, it could have been any pub in New England. Rather than covering every inch of the place in rainbows, the owners had gone for a more subtle approach. The walls were covered in images of women. Nineteen fifties style pinup women alone, draped over more clothed partners, or kissing other lingerie-clad women. Posters for lesbian pulp novels and contemporary movies. Stills from porn of women in the throes of passion. Nude figure drawings and oil portraits of women of all shapes.

Photographs of various sizes featuring couples through the ages also hung between the posters and art. Women in ball gowns and suits, dressed as drag kings with fake mustaches and top hats, in jeans and sweaters holding hands and kissing. In color and sepia and black-and-white, separated by time and space, but united by the same thing that brought Annika and Gabi here tonight.

Living women kissed and held hands beneath their paper gazes. They lined the wooden bar and waited to order, or sat at tables and booths where they sipped their drinks, laughed, and chatted a little louder than they would in mixed company. A lone microphone stand stood behind the pool table and between the bathroom doors. Annika spotted Mindy and Vanessa cozied up in one of the little booths on the right side of the room, pointed them out to Gabi, and headed over to them.

Gabi followed close behind.

"Hey," Annika said in greeting, "Vanessa, Mindy, this is my sister's friend Gabi."

"Also your friend," Gabi said when she drew up next to her. She gave a small wave to the couple.

"Oh, you think we're there in our relationship now?" Annika said and raised an eyebrow at her.

"I'd say so," Gabi said, and that smile grew a bit sly on her lips.

"Hi, Gabi," Mindy said from her perch across from Vanessa, who held her hand across the table. Mindy was thirty-three, and Korean American. She kept her midnight hair cut short in a blunt bob just below her chin and wore clothes as billowing as her haircut was severe and her frame was tiny.

Tonight, she wore a chocolate-brown knit turtleneck embroidered with the classic Macy's Thanksgiving turkey on the chest and black cargo pants. Vanessa sat across from her, still clad in head to toe black, her blond hair wound into a thick doughnut of a bun on top of her head. They were obvious opposites, but that's what made their love burn so brightly.

Gabi gave a little start, blushed, and said, "Hi, it's nice to meet you both. Mindy, I love the turkey. Annika neglected to tell me tonight was Thanksgiving themed, I guess."

She shot a playful glare at Annika over her shoulder as she pulled off her wool coat.

"Yeah, yeah, Annika forgot something, big whoop," Annika said as she shrugged off her own jacket and hung it on the hook by the booth before she turned back for Gabi's jacket. And froze.

Gabi looked…sexy as hell.

She wore tight dark-wash jeans that emphasized the dip of her waist and the flare of her hips, hugged her lush ass and thick thighs like they were their best friend they hadn't seen in years. A dark red wrap sweater tied at her waist and revealed a deep slice of her ample chest. Three layered dainty gold chains hung around her neck. A small *G*, a hamsa, and a Star of David dangled from them and nestled in the hollow of her collarbones, matching the habitual small gold hoops she wore in her ears.

She nervously played with a pendant as Annika swallowed and took her coat from her, turning around to spare herself from visibly drooling over her sister's best friend.

Gabi slid into the booth next to Mindy, who immediately turned to face her and began to pepper her with questions about herself. It made Annika smile.

She looked over at Vanessa to see that she was already shooting her a knowing look.

"I'm going to grab a drink. Gab, you want anything?" Annika asked as she jabbed her thumb across the room in the direction of the bar.

"Oh, uh, sure," Gabi said, turning from Mindy's interrogation to face Annika. "Just grab me a beer."

Annika nodded and left them, trying to look like she wasn't making a quick escape.

It wasn't the first time Annika had thought Gabi looked good, she mused as she pushed through the growing crowd to reach the bar. She'd always thought Gabi was attractive.

But it *was* the first time she'd looked at her and known the thought, the anxiety, the cautious care with which Gabi had probably gotten dressed before coming tonight. For some reason, that knowledge made her want to peel Gabi's clothes off her with her teeth.

She swallowed as she waited for the half-priced trivia special beers she'd ordered to arrive and tried to clear the image of sliding Gabi's pants off her and running her tongue over the curve of her ass from her head.

"So," Vanessa said once Annika had returned to their booth and handed Gabi her drink, "Gabi, I heard you're a baby gay."

Annika smacked Vanessa on the arm with the back of her left hand.

"Dude," Annika said.

Gabi blushed and took a swig of her drink before replying, "Um, yeah, I am. Annika's actually been very helpful in easing me into this whole"—she gestured to the room of women, some obviously in relationships with each other or close friends, others clearly looking for someone to take home for the night, some a mixture of all three— "scene. She's been guiding me a bit through the adjustment process."

"I bet she has," Vanessa said in an undertone and snorted into her drink.

Annika cut in and prayed Gabi hadn't heard that. "Along with being a very useful trivia team addition for obscure science facts, Gabi's here to try to find a lovely lady to make out with tonight."

Gabi's face went an even darker shade of red, and she kicked Annika's shin under the table.

"Hey! I figured four heads are better than two," Annika said, "plus, Ness and Mindy know, like, basically everyone in here and what their deal is."

"It's true." Mindy shrugged. "Vanessa is the gay daughter of a late-in-life lesbian and her older butch wife, so between the three of them, they've got multiple generations of the Portland queer scene covered."

"And Min teaches yoga at a studio in downtown and walks dogs on the side, so she's got more or less everyone else I don't know," Vanessa added. She gave her wife a loving glance and took her hand across the scarred wooden tabletop again.

"It's why I hang out with them," Annika said, and she popped a peanut from the small bowl of complimentary nuts on the table into her mouth, "their queer connects."

"Yes, our dearest Annika here is so grateful that we deign to allow her in our exalted presence," Mindy replied. She put on a fake fancy accent, and waved her slender hand royally.

Annika tipped an imaginary hat in return.

"Nerds," Vanessa said to Gabi, who grinned back at her.

"Do you have a type?" Mindy asked, directing her laser focus back to Gabi.

"I mean…I'm not really sure?" Gabi spluttered, and she wound a curl around her finger nervously. "Women, I guess?"

She's adorable when she's flustered, Annika thought. The way the tops of her plump cheeks went pink and her hands couldn't stop fidgeting. Gabi touched her pendants, twirled her hair, shifted her hips in the seat so her knee pressed against Annika's under the table.

Annika wanted to grab Gabi's busy hand and twine her fingers with hers, give her something to squeeze to help ground her, keep her anchored. Let Annika absorb a piece of her anxiety.

But she didn't.

Instead, she said, "Cheers to that," and raised her beer to Gabi. A small thrill of accomplishment whizzed through her when she saw Gabi's eyes crinkle as she smiled and her hands stilled.

"Any physical features you're into, so we can narrow down our options a little?" Mindy pressed. She tapped her dark red lips with her index finger, which was nearly taken over by a giant crystal ring, as she surveyed the options on display before them at trivia tonight.

"Tattoos," Gabi said at once and swallowed, eyes fixed to the label of the beer before her as she scratched it with her nail, "I like tattoos. And, um, someone who dresses a little more femme but, like, with an edge to them?"

"Is that a question or an answer?" Mindy replied.

"An answer," Gabi said firmly, looking up to meet Mindy's gaze.

Annika would not allow herself to feel anything about the fact that Gabi said she liked women with tattoos. She already suspected Gabi was into hers, but it didn't mean anything about her interest in Annika specifically.

"Hmm," Mindy said thoughtfully as she surveyed the people talking and drinking around them, "a femme with an edge who also has tattoos."

"Sounds like Annika," Vanessa pointed out, and Annika didn't need to turn her head to know Vanessa had a smug grin on her face.

Annika looked down at herself self-consciously.

People were often surprised when Annika told them she was a tailor and a designer because, most of the time, she couldn't care less about her own clothes.

What she loved was imagining and creating beautiful things for other people's bodies, not her own. Most days she wore jeans and hoodies or leggings and flannels. Often she simply opted for coveralls, preferred a one-and-done approach. She would never wear most of the clothes she made and tailored, but she loved the feel of the fabric as she fed it through the sewing machine, the way a dress could take shape behind her eyes just from draping a swath of silk across a dress form, or a body.

Gabi was spared responding by the trivia MC—a masc in their midtwenties with a furry brown mullet dyed green at the tips and dressed in a grandpa sweater and baggy jeans—stepped up to the mic. They had a hat shaped like a turkey drumstick perched on their head.

"Welcome ladies, theydies, and gentlebutchs to The Clam Shack trivia night, Thanksgiving edition," they called into the mic, "and while this holiday may be based on a bunch of lies written to favor straight white men, we gays can still have a good time."

The room erupted in cheers, hoots, and clapping.

Annika glanced at Gabi to see a look of excitement on her round face and smiled.

CHAPTER TWELVE

Gabi couldn't stop herself from looking around in amazement. The sheer variety of the female forms on display before her in this one little bar was boggling.

And the fact that they were all some flavor of queer?

Literally mind-blowing.

She kept finding something else that snagged her attention. Two women with long hair who leaned in and laughed together, one with a hand tucked into the other's back pocket as she showed her something on the screen of her phone.

A pair she was sure had just met made out in a corner by the pool table as their friends laughed at them from their respective tables.

A tiny masc with a shaggy haircut held hands with a statuesque woman with a shaved head as they walked to the bar. The taller woman bent down to kiss her partner's cheek while they waited for their order.

"You look like a kid in a candy store right now," Annika said, as she slid into the booth and passed her another beer. Gabi was on her fourth and felt it, her fingertips gone fizzy, but she didn't care.

"It's just…" Gabi started and gawked again. "Look at them all."

Annika laughed as she took a swig of her beer, eyes bright with mirth.

"Hey, this is all new to me," Gabi said defensively.

"I know, I know." Annika smiled. "It's cute."

Gabi took a swig of her beer to cover the little flutter Annika calling her cute caused in her stomach.

Trivia had been a blur, Gabi too distracted to really be much help.

Vanessa and Mindy and Annika didn't seem to mind, though. They squabbled over answers like old teammates, and broke down in laughter more often than not. Mindy shouted answers increasingly loudly, and wrongly, as the game wore on. Annika ended up with her head against the sticky table, groaning in mock frustration while Vanessa just gazed soppily at her wife.

Vanessa and Mindy now sat by the bar and chatted with friends of theirs, leaving Annika and Gabi alone in the booth. This meant Gabi got to survey Annika without an audience.

Annika was so free here, limbs looser and smiles freer. A tension she had around her sister melted away.

It made Gabi's breath catch in her chest each time she laughed, each time their eyes met as she sipped her beer, a little grin permanently etched into her lips.

She had shed her green hoodie and now sat in just a black cotton tee in the corner of the booth, tattooed arm draped over the back of the seat and on full display, body open and easy as she watched Gabi take in their surroundings, brushed her bangs from her eyes with silver-ringed fingers.

Was Annika…sexy?

No, Gabi scolded herself, she couldn't be.

Sure, she was hot. Gabi couldn't deny that.

But she was Maia's little sister. The one who had melted all the hair off Maia's American Girl doll when she was nine and had tried to straighten it. The one who'd once waxed her eyebrows off when she was fifteen and attempted to do it herself but was too impatient to do it right.

But she couldn't think of her as Maia's dorky little sister, not with the way she was right now. Confident and cool, her long hair falling off the arch of her neck, her tattoos twined around the soft curve of her biceps and triceps in the low bar light. She wondered what that spot just below Annika's jaw would smell like, feel like if she grazed it with her lips. What sounds Annika would make if she bit her there.

Gabi felt herself biting her own lip and opened her mouth to make herself stop.

"How did you meet Vanessa?" she asked when she realized Annika would expect something to come out of it.

"I forget that you don't already know everything about my life,"

Annika said with a smile. She rested both forearms on the table and leaned across it to be heard over the clamor of the bar.

"The summer after I finished design school," Annika began, "I took a six-week seminar on constructing the ball gown. I'd made a few before in school and enjoyed the challenge of them, how you have to build some of them like you would a structure. Anyway, the instructor, Anusha Malik, took a liking to me. After the course, she offered me a paid apprenticeship at her boutique, which I was thrilled to accept. It was mostly tailoring and hemming for the first few years, but then Anusha started letting me consult on special orders and custom dresses, and then I started to design and sew my own customs. Vanessa worked the register and did bridal consultations, still does. Anusha loves the spectacle of weddings, the pomp and circumstance, believes in the whole fairy tale of a wedding being the best day of your life. Vanessa and me? Not so much. We bonded over our shared cynicism."

"I feel like I should be charging you on Maia's behalf," Gabi joked.

"Hmm, and I thought you were supposed to be here as *my* friend," Annika replied, and that dark, smoky whiskey quality crept into her voice again. She raised her eyebrow at Gabi in teasing challenge.

Gabi found herself biting her lower lip again.

She saw Annika's eyes drop to her mouth, and her stomach swooped.

Then Annika seemed to realize what she was doing, and her eyes flitted away.

"You were, like, weirdly good at the nineties pop culture questions for someone who was barely conscious then," Gabi said into the suddenly awkward silence.

"I *have* been told I'm wise beyond my years, you know," Annika joked.

They grinned at each other, and their eyes held for a second too long. Gabi felt her face heat up and a tingle begin to build between her legs. She couldn't be turned-on just from eye contact, could she?

"Hey, Annika!" a voice called.

Annika blinked at the sound of her name, and it broke the intoxicating moment.

Gabi and Annika both looked up to see a tall woman with shoulder-length light brown hair arrive at their table. She was dressed in corduroy overalls patterned with turkeys on them with a white cotton turtleneck beneath.

"Oh, um, hey, Harley," Annika said. Gabi noted that the greeting was a bit stiff and felt her curiosity stir and prick up its ears. "I didn't realize you were back in town."

"Yeah, just for the week," Harley replied. "I'm staying with my parents for Thanksgiving and thought I'd check out the old stomping grounds."

Something about the tight set of Annika's shoulders, the overly friendly smile on Harley's lips, told Gabi that this was one of Annika's many exes.

"This is Gabi," Annika said, gesturing to her. Gabi gave Harley a little wave and then cringed inwardly at herself.

"Nice to meet you!" Harley said in a voice so bright it was nearly blinding.

"What's it been, two years? It's good to see you looking so well, Anni," Harley said. She turned her back on Gabi and gave Annika's forearm a squeeze with a hand that lingered.

Gabi saw Annika grimace at the nickname. A lick of irrational anger coursed through her at the possessive way Harley touched Annika, at the use of a nickname she so obviously loathed.

"Yeah, you, too," Annika said dryly. She pulled her arm out of Harley's reach.

"I better go find my *girlfriend*," Harley replied, with emphasis on the word. "She's lost somewhere in the crowd." She gestured over her shoulder with her thumb. "Don't want her to find someone else to go home with. Has everyone in Portland always been this hot?"

She laughed, overly jovial, and her eyes glanced down at Gabi again and then flicked back to Annika.

"Some of us have," Annika said and smirked. She leaned back and crossed her arms over her chest, sleeve riding up to show off more of the delicate tattoos inked there. Then her gaze flicked to Gabi, and Gabi felt nearly pinned in place by it.

Something new sparked there in the depths of Annika's eyes, something that called to Gabi, made her aware of everywhere her clothes touched her skin.

It's a show for Harley, Gabi tried to reason with her body. *She's just trying to get Harley to think we're on a date so she'll leave us alone.*

Harley tracked Annika's gaze, and her smile dimmed a few watts.

"Well, it was, like, *so* good to see you, Anni. Let's get coffee or something sometime," Harley said.

She gave Annika one last parting smile, which Annika missed because her gaze was still fixed on Gabi.

"Who was that?" Gabi asked. "She had, like, a super weird vibe."

"An ex of mine," Annika said and shrugged. "We dated for a few months a couple of years ago, but I broke up with her."

"Yeah, I could tell. She really wanted you to know she had a *girlfriend* now," Gabi said.

Annika crinkled her nose.

"Why'd you smash her heart to bits?" Gabi asked lightly, toying with her beer bottle and trying to hide her interest.

Annika shrugged again, and her eyes finally left Gabi to focus on the bottle she idly twirled in her hands.

Gabi felt both relief and disappointment with the loss of her gaze.

"I felt like she was always kind of judging me," Annika said. "Plus, she likes telling people she has a girlfriend more than she actually likes having one. Case in point, her checking you out the whole time we were talking."

Annika's eyes flicked back to Gabi as she grinned.

Gabi froze with her beer halfway to her mouth. "She was checking *me* out? I thought she was hitting on you."

Annika snorted.

"She'd probably have settled for either one of us. Or both. But she kept, like, darting her eyes over to ogle your boobs," Annika said. She gestured with a wave of her hand to Gabi's chest.

Gabi glanced down at the admittedly significant cleavage she'd put on display tonight and preened a little, pulling her shoulders back to give the room a better view.

Annika shook her head at her, but there was a smile on her lips.

"I thought she was just sizing up the competition. She definitely thought I was with you," Gabi replied.

"I should be so lucky," Annika said, and then took a long pull on her beer.

Gabi felt a shiver run through her. What did that mean? Needing a moment to collect herself, she let her gaze rove over the crowd again.

"Any more of your exes here?" she asked. Gabi turned back to Annika and caught her eyes darting away from the vicinity of Gabi's chest.

Gabi felt a flush rise on her sternum and took a swallow of her beer to gather herself.

Annika shivered. "God, I hope not. One run-in is as much as I can take."

"Mmm, you sure do date a lot for someone with such a strong disdain for serious romance," Gabi mused. She took another sip of her beer and licked a drop of it off her lips when she lowered the bottle.

Annika turned her gaze back to the crowd and answered, "I don't *disdain* serious romance. I love love as much as the next gal. I just haven't found that it lasts for me for some reason. But speaking of, anyone catch your eye tonight?" Annika asked, not so subtly changing the subject with a suggestive waggle of her eyebrows at Gabi.

"Oh," Gabi said. In all honesty, she'd been too overwhelmed to really look.

"If you're still game for that," Annika said, backpedaling. "We can just keep hanging out if you'd rather not put that kind of pressure on yourself."

"Can you show me how to flirt with women?" Gabi blurted, surprising Annika and making her choke on her beer.

What the fuck? Gabi thought to herself. Where had that come from?

"Show you? You want to watch me flirt with someone?" Annika clarified when she'd stopped coughing, eyebrows raised in surprise. "Damn, girl, who knew you had a voyeuristic streak."

"That's not what I meant!" Gabi exclaimed. She swatted at Annika's arm and knew she was blushing furiously as nervous sweat broke out along her hairline.

"I meant, like, give me tips on how to do it," she continued and looked down into her beer bottle, let her hair fall in front of her face to hide her embarrassment. "I've been having such a hard time on dates figuring out if we're flirting or just being friendly."

"Ah yes, the eternal sapphic struggle." Annika nodded sagely.

She cocked her head, hummed thoughtfully, and said, "Maybe I *should* demonstrate for you."

Annika kept regarding her, almost as if she was evaluating Gabi for weaknesses before an attack.

"I, uh, okay," Gabi stammered.

Annika's face broke out in a devilish grin.

Gabi was filled with instant regret. This was a terrible idea. Annika in her normal mode was already nearly too hot for Gabi to handle.

Annika looking at her like she wanted to swallow her whole? Brain-melting.

Annika was one of her best friends' sisters. They were Maia's co–maids of honor, Gabi reminded herself. If things turned to shit between them, a whole host of awkwardness would ensue.

But her hormones, the alcohol in her system, and that sweet-edged tension she'd been riding all night egged her on, begged her to keep that grin on Annika's face, to see if it would lead to where it seemed to promise her it would.

"Well," Annika said. She positioned her body so she could give Gabi her full attention and rested her hands on the table mere inches from Gabi's own. "The key to flirting is maintaining lots of eye contact."

Gabi's eyes locked with Annika's. In the half-light of the bar, the brown of her irises was like molten lava cake, rich and warm and decadent.

"Okay," Gabi said, voice suddenly shaky. "What else?"

"Physical touch," Annika replied.

Gabi's mouth went a little dry, and her stomach flipped as Annika's hand touched her forearm gently but still firmly enough that she felt the heat of Annika's skin through the wool of her sweater.

"A compliment doesn't hurt," Annika said in a low husk of a voice, her head tilted to let her hair fall behind her shoulder and reveal the pale skin of her neck.

"Mm-hmm," Gabi replied, gaze still stuck on Annika, body so focused on what she might do next it felt hard to breathe, let alone speak.

"I might say something like, you have the most amazing hair," Annika continued. Her fingers trailed up and down Gabi's forearm lightly, sending tingles up her spine with the featherlight touch. "So curly and gorgeous. And your skin is so smooth. What moisturizer do you use?"

Her fingers crept under the end of Gabi's sleeve, tracing over the skin of her forearm.

"CeraVe." Gabi gasped as the tingle traveled farther and farther south. "My derm friend told me it's the best drugstore brand."

Annika kept brushing her fingers over Gabi's skin and gave her a one-sided smile, flashing the hint of teeth as she bit gently at her lower lip.

She said, "I love that you take care of yourself," in that same rich voice, and Gabi needed to press her thighs together beneath the table. She prayed Annika didn't notice.

"It's all about the tone of voice you use," Annika said, still speaking in that deeper register that coursed along Gabi's nerve endings like electricity-laced honey. "See? I can make anything sound suggestive when I talk like this. Like, tell me more about that vulva boil you lanced earlier." Annika smiled a lazy, indulgent smile. Her free hand pushed her hair back over her shoulder and caressed her own neck as she surveyed Gabi beneath lowered lashes.

Holy fuck, she's good at this, Gabi thought wildly to herself. Her whole body pulsed with the need to lunge across the table and seal their mouths together.

"I need to go to the bathroom," Gabi shouted as she jumped up and nearly sprinted from the booth.

Thankfully, there was no line for once, and she was able to lock herself away in the cramped, Sharpie-graffitied single stall right away.

Leaning against the sink, she took in her flustered appearance, eyes a bit glassy from the beers she'd had and the lust she felt pounding through her veins, the wetness she suspected she'd find between her thighs.

For Annika.

All for fucking *Annika*.

Annika, who had just been *pretending* to flirt with her, who had asked her about lancing a cyst, for God's sake, in that voice. That awful, delicious, midnight voice that made Gabi want to mount her on the spot and shove her tongue down her throat.

No wonder she got so many women to date her.

"Get a hold of yourself, Dr. Mendon," Gabi said sternly in the voice she used for insurance companies who refused to approve a procedure for a patient. "You're just reacting to a woman's attention. It's not necessarily that it's Annika that's doing it."

But she thought about Annika sprawled out in the booth, tattoos on full display. Thought about the way Annika's little grin looked around the top of a beer bottle. The way her hair shone loose and messy around her face. How her little compliments and attention had been sparking flutters in Gabi's belly all night.

"Fuck," she breathed and let her head thunk against the glass of the mirror.

"I think I'm going to call it a night," Gabi said when she returned to the booth five minutes later. "I'm working the twelve to twelve shift in emergency gynecology tomorrow, and I should probably get some sleep."

"Oh yeah, okay," Annika said, nodding faintly. "Do you need an Uber?"

"No, I walked here. It's only about a twenty-minute walk," Gabi replied, and she took her coat from the hook.

"Let me walk with you," Annika said abruptly and sprang to her feet.

"Sure, I guess," Gabi said as she put her coat on. "We are heading in similar directions."

They said their good-byes to Vanessa and a very tipsy Mindy, who hugged Gabi so fiercely Vanessa had to physically disengage her arms from around Gabi's back.

"She's much stronger than she looks," Gabi said. She rubbed her shoulder as they walked along the dark and quiet streets.

"Ha, yeah. Yoga teacher, remember?" Annika said, kicking at something with her scuffed Chelsea boots. "Listen, I want to apologize if I went too hard with the flirting thing earlier. If I made you uncomfortable at all—"

"You were fine," Gabi cut in. "I did ask you to show me, after all."

"Yeah, I just…" Annika trailed off with a sigh. She paused as they waited for a stoplight to change and leaned back against a telephone pole. "I got a little carried away. You were looking at me like that, and you, you know, look like you."

She gestured at Gabi's whole body with a sweep of her hand.

"Look like me?" Gabi said. She crossed her arms over her chest and cocked her head to one side.

"You know," Annika hedged and looked down at her feet, kicked her right heel against the toe of her left boot.

Gabi peered up at her down-turned face, and gasped.

"Annika Silberberg, are you blushing?" she crooned, as a swoop of something hot flared under her breastbone.

"Shut *up*," Annika whined and blushed deeper. She pressed off the pole and pushed Gabi lightly.

Laughing, Gabi grabbed her wrists to keep herself from falling, tripped backward on a crack in the pavement, and somehow ended up against the wall of a building, Annika's hands braced on either side of her head.

It felt like such a simple thing, in that moment, to tip her chin up to Annika, to lightly fist her hands in the open front of Annika's jacket as she continued to laugh.

"You are so beautiful," Annika said on an exhale, her face close enough to Gabi's that she felt the words gust over her skin. "That's what I meant. So, so beautiful."

She brushed a curl back from Gabi's face, and her fingertips glided gently over her skin, settled at the back of Gabi's neck. She tipped Gabi's head up a fraction more so that Gabi stared Annika full in the face, and her breath ghosted over Gabi's suddenly sensitized lips.

Gabi's heart felt like a racehorse charging down the final stretch of track, her pulse pounded in every inch of her body, every nerve ending alive and on alert, but her head was shockingly silent. Like a held breath, like the second before a favorite band began to play, anticipation mounted until it felt nearly unbearable.

"I'm sorry we didn't find you someone to kiss tonight," Annika said, her face somehow even closer, angled just a little bit more to the left. Her eyes were fathomless dark pools Gabi could feel herself on the edge of drowning in. "I mean, *I* could kiss you, just so you get it out of the way."

"Maybe you should kiss me," Gabi said, voice nearly a whisper in the space between their faces.

Annika huffed a laugh, and her eyes dropped away from Gabi's face for a second.

"I was joking," she said, but didn't move away. "That would be a really bad idea, Gab."

But to Gabi, who at this moment operated purely on alcohol and lust fueled instinct, it sounded like the perfect thing. She slid her hands down to Annika's hips and tugged her an inch closer.

Despite her words, Annika let herself be pulled in.

"It is," Gabi agreed, nodded, but her gaze dropped down to Annika's mouth. So close now. It looked so soft she almost wanted to cry. She watched Annika's tongue glide over her lower lip, eyes locked onto Gabi's, and knew she had her. "It's kind of the worst idea."

Annika swallowed and said, a bit hoarsely, "Truly fucking terrible."

And then they both rushed in, bridged that final crucial inch between them. Their lips met, and Gabi's whole body, whole spirit, whole world exploded.

Annika's lips were even better than they looked. Her body pressed Gabi into the rough stone of the building behind her, softer than she'd ever imagined it could be. Annika's body molded to hers, and warmth permeated every inch of her.

Their lips came together and slid apart and came together again. Gabi heard a whimper only to realize that she had made it. Her hands glided around Annika's back and gripped into her shirt. She pushed her breasts into Annika's midstomach. Her nipples were hard and ached already, and she wanted to get even closer still.

Annika's tongue flicked at her lower lip, and Gabi opened her mouth to her, tasted beer and bar peanuts and Annika as their tongues met.

She felt one of Annika's hands tangle in her hair, tug slightly to get her to move her head so she could kiss her deeper. The other dropped to her waist, pressed her more firmly against Annika's body until Annika was nearly wrapped around her.

Gabi's hand slid under Annika's jacket and then fit itself just below the waistband of Annika's jeans. She touched the warm, silken skin of Annika's lower back and felt Annika shiver as her fingers caressed her.

Then a car horn honked.

"That's right, ladies," a young male voice called out, "get it!"

"Fuck off!" Annika yelled back. She turned to flip off the car of college students as it drove out of view, breaking their kiss and bursting the moment.

Gabi stood against the wall feeling dazed. She brought her hand to her lips, skimmed over the kiss-swollen surface, and watched Annika's dark hair ruffle in the breeze from the harbor as she turned back toward her.

They stared at each other for a long second, and then Annika opened her mouth.

"Gab," she started and reached out her hand to her.

"I need to go," Gabi said in a rush. "Thanks for a fun night, Annika, I'll talk to you later."

"Wait," Annika called after her, but Gabi was already power-walking away, like the coward she was.

CHAPTER THIRTEEN

W hat the fuck, Annika?" she muttered to herself as she walked the rest of the way home, taking a less direct route to avoid catching up with Gabi. "You couldn't keep it in your pants for one night?"

It was more than that, she knew. More than just alcohol and hormones and proximity.

She had been primed to kiss Gabi for weeks now, if she was honest with herself. Had nearly done it on her sister's couch only days before.

But she hadn't thought Gabi had wanted her to, wouldn't have made a move anyway because Gabi was so new to exploring her identity, and her sister's oldest friend, and a million other valid reasons.

But then Gabi had complimented her on her hair and Annika had thought, hmm, this is kind of flirty.

And Gabi had looked *so* fucking good tonight. Those curves in those tight jeans, and her boobs, *holy shit* her boobs, in that sweater. And Annika had never been good at resisting her impulses when she saw something she wanted.

Gabi'd been so awed by a run-down little bar like The Clam Shack, so wonder-struck at the clientele, that it made Annika feel all melty inside.

And Gabi had vibed with Vanessa and Mindy, laughed at Mindy's absurd drunken answers and Vanessa's caustic wit in turn. Annika had never taken a girlfriend to trivia before, had rarely introduced them to her friends, preferring to keep her romantic and personal lives separate.

She'd never stopped to think how nice it could be to have someone round out their little trio. To have someone to shoot glances at when Vanessa and Mindy were being extra mushy, someone to sit with when they went off to socialize and she needed a quiet moment. Someone who was on *her* side before anyone else's.

And then Harley, of all fucking people, had shown up and clearly thought Gabi was Annika's latest fling, and it had made her feel…good, to think of Gabi being there with her in a more than friendly capacity.

Annika let herself into her studio apartment, filled a glass of water from the fridge, and collapsed on her couch, one end occupied by this week's laundry still waiting to be folded, Vera Wang perched contentedly on top of it.

She took a long sip of water, placed the glass on the coffee table, and let her head fall back against the cushions.

Can you show me how to flirt with women?

God, why had Gabi asked her that?

Why had she agreed to do it?

Did Gabi truly just want a demonstration?

And she seemed to *really* be into it when Annika flirted with her. Annika had hit on many, many women in her life. She could tell when someone was responding to her advances. She knew she'd turned Gabi on with her little display and couldn't even feel that bad about it.

Gabi was so easy to fluster. All it took was a little eye contact, a little light touch, and Annika had her shifting in her seat, her breath coming a little more quickly.

The skin of Gabi's forearm under the sleeve of her sweater had been the softest thing she'd felt, like real satin, fine cashmere, and so warm. She'd wanted to run her hand that lightly over Gabi's whole body, see if she blushed that lovely pink everywhere.

You can be a real horny asshole sometimes, she scolded herself.

She closed her eyes now, though, and allowed herself to relive kissing Gabi.

The moment she thought it was going to happen, when she ended up bracketing Gabi against the wall of that building after she'd tripped.

The moment she knew it was going to happen, when Gabi had agreed with her about what a bad idea it was and pulled her closer by the hips.

The moment it happened, and it felt like all the air was punched out of her lungs. All she could think was get closer, touch more.

And oh, that little whimper Gabi made.

It had been sweet heat to her system, like a shot of mezcal. She couldn't help herself from wanting to taste it on her tongue.

Gabi had liked kissing her, she knew she had. The way her body had responded to her, drawn her against her, opened up for her. The way her hands gripped in the back of Annika's shirt and slid onto her skin.

What might have happened if not for those assholes in the car heckling them? Would Gabi have let her kiss her neck, graze that skin with her teeth?

Would she have—

Enough, Annika scolded herself. She tilted forward to rest her head in her hands, her hair falling around her. She sat up, pushed it out of her face, and started to pace.

Why had Gabi run away from her before they could talk about what had just happened? Was it too much? Was it because she realized Annika was Maia's little sister, realized the truth about how colossally bad an idea them hooking up would be? Did Gabi think she was taking advantage of Annika? That somehow, Annika hadn't *wanted* to kiss her?

Should she call Gabi? Text her?

Gabi might think of her as some confident, suave lesbian of the world, but the truth was she hadn't felt this type of feelings, crush type feelings, for someone in a long while, and it drove her a little wild.

Her phone chimed at that moment, and she grabbed it, nearly fumbled and dropped it in her haste, to see a text from Gabi.

❖

"*Made it home safe. Thanks for a fun night, tomorrow's shift is going to be brutal lol,*" Vanessa read out loud the next morning at Something New, in a lull between customers.

"I mean, how do I reply to that?" Annika asked as her hands twisted a paper clip so violently it split in half. "It seems like she wants to ignore that we made out. So do I also pretend it didn't happen?"

"Walk me through it again," Vanessa said, and she peered down at the phone's screen.

"We were walking home, both of us a little tipsy, but definitely not, like, *drunk* drunk. There'd been sort of a vibe all night—"

"As a third-party observer, I second the vibe," Vanessa interjected with an authoritative nod.

"Thank you," Annika said with emphasis, "I admit, I *maybe* stepped over the line with the whole flirting demonstration shtick, but she seemed into it, like, *wicked* into it. But then she came back from the bathroom and wanted to go home so I was, like, okay, maybe she wasn't so into it. Then we're walking home and joking around, and I end up sort of pinning her to a wall." Annika grimaced and scratched her undercut sheepishly as Vanessa raised her eyebrows.

"And I tell her she's"—Annika buried her head in her hands. Her actions seemed worse and worse in the sober light of day—"beautiful and then said how I'm sorry she didn't find anyone to kiss her and made a joke about how I'd kiss her, and then she asked me to kiss her and so I did."

"Describe the kiss to me," Vanessa said.

Annika swallowed and looked up at her. "What do you mean?"

"I mean, was it just a peck, lips closed but lingering, was there tongue?" Vanessa rattled off.

"There was major tongue," Annika said, "and maybe a little groping."

"Hoo boy," Vanessa said with a shake of her head, "you're in deep shit, my man."

"Literally, what the fuck, Ness, that is not helpful." Annika groaned. She dropped her head to her sewing table and said, "How do I respond? It's too late to just like it and call it a day."

"Yeah, that would be weird," Vanessa agreed. "Hmm, well, if she's keeping it light, you keep it light. Sometimes friends just get tipsy and make out. You had that whole thing with Sadie three summers ago where that was literally all you did."

"But that was different," Annika replied.

"Why?"

"Because Sadie was Sadie, and I was twenty-five and an idiot." And now I'm twenty-eight and an idiot, Annika thought ruefully. "Gabi is my sister's oldest friend. I have to see her this whole year until the wedding, at least. And she's a baby gay," Annika said.

"As far as you know, maybe that kiss made her re-examine everything, and she's going back to men," Vanessa said, and she dropped Annika's phone on the table with a dull thud.

Annika glared at her.

"Seriously, I thought you would be more helpful with this," she said with a groan.

"Why? I've literally been with Mindy since I was eighteen," Vanessa said. "Plus, you've never needed my advice with women before."

Annika picked her phone up again and sighed.

"Glad you had fun, hope today's shift isn't too bad. Upside-down smile emoji," Annika dictated as she typed. "And…send."

"That's my girl, avoid the whole thing you were just panicking over completely," Vanessa said, patting Annika on the shoulder.

Annika flipped her off.

For the rest of the day, she checked her phone for a text that never came.

Part Four

Bridesmaid Dress Consultation

December

CHAPTER FOURTEEN

Gabi hadn't spoken to Annika in nine days.

She'd texted her when she got home on Thursday, fully freaked out, and gotten her chill response to her falsely nonchalant message on Friday.

Then radio silence.

They didn't even exchange turkey emoji on Thanksgiving, although she did get a text from Maia, which read, *Thankful for you today and every day, babe *kissy face heart emoji* *turkey emoji* *pie emoji*.*

A small twinge of guilt flared up as she read it.

Not only had she kissed a woman, but it had been a life-affirming, heart-pounding, panties-wetting kiss. It made her whole body perk up in a way she'd never experienced before. Her hands shook from adrenaline and lust the whole way home, and she'd needed to make herself come *twice* before she felt calm enough to even think about going to sleep.

Annika had made her feel like that.

Annika—sweet, funny, sexy, experienced—had kissed her within an inch of her life, and she had *loved* it.

Annika, Maia's little fucking sister.

Now she felt stuck. The person she'd usually go to for advice on this topic was Annika, which was obviously off the table. But she didn't know how to approach Annika, despite the urge to text her twenty-four seven.

How did you pretend you didn't know the way someone's tongue felt in your mouth? The way it sounded when you moaned into their lips, their body crushed against yours. The little hitch in her breath when your fingers first touched her skin.

Were you supposed to pretend at all, or laugh it off as some silly thing you did while drunk once, and move on? Was that even what'd happened?

Could she shove her attraction to Annika back into the little box she'd tried to keep it in, now that she had acted on it?

Unfortunately, she couldn't avoid Annika forever.

"Hey, babe, don't forget to bring your fine ass to Something New today after your shift. Niki's keeping the boutique open late to take your measurements so she can start working on the bridesmaids' dresses. Okay, byyyyyyyeeeeee!" Maia's voice chirped from the voice note she'd sent her at lunch.

Gabi had, in fact, forgotten about her consultation. Her own personal crises wiped it clean from her mind.

The last thing she wanted to do after a grueling twelve-hour shift was drive twenty minutes out of her way, hunt for parking, and then have to talk to Annika about dresses, all while she pretended she wasn't thinking about the way it felt to have Annika's lips on hers.

By some twist of fate, she found street parking down the street from the boutique, which she took as a good omen.

"Okay, Dr. Mendon, you can do this," she said to herself as she checked out her reflection in the mirror.

She looked like she'd just worked a twelve-hour shift in emergency gynecology.

Her skin was parched and gray, her eyes had dark circles under them, and her lips were chapped from the cold weather. The best she could do was shake her hair out of the bun it had been in all day, her curls frizzing from the static of the dry heat that pumped from her vents, and spread some tinted lip balm over her lips before she left the car to head to Something New.

She'd walked past the store many times before but had never really taken it in. Now that she knew Annika more, her personality clashed violently with the interior decorating of the store. It had sage-green walls and plush mod furniture, a clear acrylic coffee table, and curled cursive letters that spelled *bride* on the wall behind the couch.

In fact, the only thing that said Annika at all to her was the wingback green velvet armchair that sat opposite the couch.

"Annika?" she called out and hung her puffy coat up on the rack by the door.

The weather had plunged below freezing in the last few days since Thanksgiving, and Gabi hadn't quite adjusted to it yet. Her ungloved hands smarted in the warmth of the boutique.

"Yeah, hi, one minute." Annika's voice came from an open door to the right of the three-paneled mirror that took up the middle of the small shop.

Gabi walked to the door and peeked through to Annika's domain.

Two rows of hanging garment bags lined one side of the little room. The floor was wood, the walls a plain eggshell white, hung with pictures of gowns and suits and jumpsuits of all lengths and styles. Several dress forms in different sizes, with breasts and hips and without, sat in a semicircle before Annika's workspace like an audience watching her as she sewed.

There was a desktop computer on a desk off to one side, but pride of place went to the table that held the sewing machine that Annika currently sat behind. She looked frazzled and fully absorbed in the task before her, bangs clipped out of her face, messy bun studded with a pencil and a pen and hanging lopsidedly off her head.

Annika bent over a sketch pad, muttered to herself, drew a line here, added a small squiggle there. She stood up to survey her sketch, rested her hands on her hips, and pursed her lips, brow furrowed in thought.

Despite the chaos of her appearance, the ratty old flannel and black leggings she wore, Gabi thought she was gorgeous. That determined and captivated light in her eyes transformed and animated her face in a way Gabi had never seen before.

"Tough crossword today?" Gabi joked, hoping to head off the awkwardness she was afraid would be between them.

Annika blinked up at her as if coming out of a daze.

"Oh, it's you," she said blankly, and Gabi felt her smile fall. "Shit, no, I didn't mean it like that," Annika said. She came out from behind her work table and approached Gabi in a rush. A tape measure dangled from around her neck and a pincushion in the shape of a—

"Is that a vulva pincushion?" Gabi said incredulously.

Annika glanced down at her wrist and said, "It is. It's the one I keep back here for my own personal use. I usually don't show it to the clients."

"I love it," Gabi said and felt her heart flip over at the slow smile that spread across Annika's face. "Although, as a queer gynecologist, I am *kind* of obsessed with vulva themed items."

Annika came to a stop in front of her, not quite close enough to touch.

"I'll keep that in mind for Chanukah," she said. "Also, I think that's the first time I've heard you call yourself queer. Mazel for that."

Gabi grinned and knew her cheeks were pink. She wished she didn't blush so damn easily.

"So," Gabi said, "what were you working on?"

Annika waved her hand dismissively. "Just trying to figure out a way to sew pleats into taffeta in a way that won't look awful," she said.

"Is that possible?" Gabi asked, wrinkling her nose.

"Not without making you look like a circus clown, but the client is convinced this is what she wants." Annika rolled her eyes.

This wasn't too bad, Gabi thought. They were having a normal conversation, and she wasn't thinking at all about how good it had felt when Annika had scraped her teeth over her lower lip.

"Do you want to do it in here, or out there on the couch?" Annika asked, hands on her hips.

"Wh-what?" Gabi spluttered, mind still fixated on Annika's mouth.

"The consultation," Annika said, and she raised an eyebrow as something heated to a low simmer in her eyes. As if she knew exactly what Gabi had been thinking about. "The reason you're here at seven forty-five after working for twelve hours instead of at home unwinding with *The Emperor's New Groove* and a glass of chardonnay, or something."

Wow, that was actually eerily close to what she'd thought of doing when she got home. When had Annika gotten to know her so well?

"It was actually going to be *Mulan* and a pinot noir—I fell asleep after 'I'll Make a Man Out of You' last night, and I need to see her save the emperor before bed tonight," Gabi replied, a smile tugging on her lips.

"Ah yes, Mulan, Disney's gender-fluid icon queen," Annika said, nodding. "Makes sense you'd be into her."

"I'm not *into* Mulan," Gabi said, and she crossed her arms over her loose wool sweater.

"No?" Annika teased. "She fits your criteria, doesn't she? A femme with an edge?"

Gabi swallowed, and the reminder of trivia night made her squirm inside.

"Let's go out to the couch," she blurted, thinking that putting a coffee table between them would be a good idea.

Annika shrugged and said, "Okay, I'll meet you out there."

Gabi turned on her heel and fled to the couch, waving her palm to try to cool her cheeks. How could Annika act like nothing had happened between them? Or *had* anything happened between them? Maybe it was nothing to Annika, maybe she made out with women on street corners all the time.

"Would you care for some tea? Water?" Annika said in a lilting, high-pitched voice. "We aim to please here at Something New."

Gabi smiled at her nervously.

"No, but seriously," Annika said, "do you want some water? Or a snack? Have you eaten since work ended? I have some ziti in the fridge in the back room if you're hungry." Annika gestured over her shoulder with her thumb. "Full disclosure, it was my lunch, but I forgot to eat today, so it's yours."

"I'm fine, Niki," Gabi said, and tenderness spread through her chest like melting butter, a feeling she didn't particularly want to look at too hard right now. "How do you forget to eat your lunch?"

Annika shrugged.

"I was working," she said simply. "Vanessa usually reminds me to take breaks, but she had clients all afternoon, and before I knew it, you were here."

"You really love what you do, huh?" Gabi remarked.

"Mm-hmm." Annika nodded. She took a seat on the armchair and crossed her legs in front of her, then clasped her hands around her right knee and leaned back. "Don't you? You must, otherwise you wouldn't have spent all your life and money on going to school for it."

"I do," Gabi agreed and laughed. "God help me, but I do. I love helping people and problem solving, and *birth*? Girl, that shit never gets old."

Annika asked, "Even when your patients poop on you or have, like, the grossest, nastiest discharge you've ever seen?"

"Yeah," Gabi said, "*especially* then. I don't know much about what I want in life, clearly, but I know I love being a doctor."

"Seems like a pretty big thing to have figured out, to me," Annika said.

They smiled at each other, an ease settling between them.

Then Annika clapped her hands together, looked down at the pile of materials in her lap, and said, "Okay, so. Dresses. Do you have a style you like? Maia wants us to be in satin, and the other four plebeian bridesmaids will be in organza or taffeta, so it's visually clear who is a maid of honor and who isn't."

She stopped to dramatically roll her eyes at her sister's whims.

"Um," Gabi said, "honestly, I haven't had time to think about dresses."

"I figured, since I haven't heard from you since before Thanksgiving," Annika said, not meeting her eyes as she shuffled a few of the materials in her lap.

Gabi swallowed, that easiness gone between them now.

"Yeah," she said, "I…needed to sort some things out."

Annika nodded but didn't say anything. After a beat, she picked up a black tablet from the coffee table and handed it to Gabi.

"There's a catalog of sample dresses on there," she said. "Flip through it and tag the ones you like. I'll draw up a sketch and send it to you for your approval. I'll just need to take your measurements tonight so I have them on hand."

Her fingers brushed Gabi's when Gabi took the tablet from her. Gabi glanced up to see Annika's eyes darting away, her hands balled into fists in her lap.

"I'll, um, let you scroll through on your own if you want," Annika said and stood, a bit awkwardly, swinging her arms at her sides.

"You can stay," Gabi said quickly, not wanting Annika to go. She hadn't texted her, hadn't seen her in nearly two weeks, and she suddenly realized that she'd missed her. "I might have a question about something."

Annika sat back down across from Gabi, and Gabi started scrolling through the catalog. Models in dresses of various styles flicked across the screen, but she barely took in any of their details.

She glanced up at Annika, who seemed to be staring unseeingly past Gabi's left shoulder.

"Are you okay?" Gabi asked, and Annika blinked rapidly.

"Sorry, sometimes my brain is moving so fast I kind of go on screensaver mode," Annika replied. She waved her hand in front of her face and shifted in her seat.

"What were you thinking about?" Gabi asked, placing the tablet on the cushion next to her.

"That your dress should have a portrait neckline and a cinched waist with a looser skirt, to emphasize your curves. A slit in the skirt to make your legs look long and so the skirt doesn't overwhelm your short stature. Since the fabric itself is so luminous, you don't need any fancy frills when it comes to shaping or cut. No, you're simple and elegant, a touch sexy but in a classy way. You'll probably wear your hair up, knowing Maia, so the neckline should dip in a smaller vee in the back to show off your neck," Annika said in a soft voice, eyes unfocused like she was picturing the image fully formed in her head.

Gabi scooted closer to the edge of the couch.

"That sounds perfect," she said in a soft voice.

She reached out and touched Annika's hand, made sure she met her eyes as she said, "I trust you."

Annika turned her hand over so she held Gabi's, her thumb stroking idly over the back. They stared at each other across the table for a moment, hands linked.

"Measurements," Annika said suddenly, voice a touch hoarse. She cleared her throat. "I need to take your measurements."

She sat back and pulled her hand away from Gabi's. Gabi's hand registered the loss of her touch immediately.

"Right," Gabi said and tried not to feel stung. "Um, okay. How do you want me?"

Annika grinned at her choice of words, and Gabi grimaced internally.

"If you could strip down to your least bulky layer and stand with your arms out to the sides and your legs a little more than hip distance apart, that would be best," Annika said, all business now. She stood up from her chair and pulled out a notebook.

Gabi shucked off her wool sweater so she stood in just her black leggings and a white T-shirt, leaving her arms bare.

She moved to a clear patch of carpet next to the couch and spread her arms out and legs apart.

Annika whipped the measuring tape off her neck and set to work, taking her measurements in quick, efficient movements.

This version of Annika was so different from the teasing, smirking woman who liked to rib her sister and knew every nineties female pop icon's discography by heart. She was serious and professional, all business.

Gabi had to admit she found her just as sexy. It made her wonder what it would be like if Annika turned that intense focus on touching her.

Neither of them spoke. Standing far enough away from Gabi so that their bodies didn't touch, Annika measured Gabi's wingspan and her height from floor to neck, then scribbled the numbers down in her notebook.

She then measured from the back of Gabi's neck to her tailbone. Her fingers gently swiped against Gabi's nape to move her hair out of the way, and it sent a shiver through Gabi's body, set her nerves on notice. She measured her back from armpit to the dip of her waist on each side, Gabi's body now on high alert for the slightest touch.

"You can drop your arms for a second," Annika murmured before she walked slowly around to face Gabi.

"Up again, please," she said, motioning for Gabi to raise her arms.

"This is a workout," Gabi joked, just for something to say.

Annika smiled politely, then paused. She surveyed Gabi, fingers tapping against her hip.

"I need to measure your bust," Annika said. Her eyes dropped to Gabi's breasts, and a flush crept up her neck.

Gabi could feel her heart rate accelerate under Annika's gaze.

"Okay," she said.

"Okay," Annika echoed and nodded.

Then she leaned forward, wrapped her arms around Gabi's back, and spread the measuring tape around her torso. The back of her fingers glided against Gabi's body as she moved along the tape.

Gabi's breath went shallow, her senses dialing up from Annika's proximity. Alert for even the barest hint of her touch over Gabi's T-shirt.

She swallowed and looked up at the ceiling, tensed her thighs against the tingle that had started between them.

Annika leaned back to bring the end of the measuring tape to meet the other side to get her measurements, and her knuckles grazed the sides of Gabi's breasts, dragged over her nipple slightly.

It was possibly an accidental touch, but Gabi couldn't help the hitched breath she let out, the way her back arched involuntarily.

She glanced up to meet Annika's gaze and found it intent on her face, lips parted slightly.

"Sorry," Annika mumbled. She placed her right thumb over the score marks on the measuring tape to mark the number, but Gabi saw a tremor in her fingers. And her eyes were still locked on Gabi's.

Neither of them moved.

Gabi's chest rose and fell like she'd just climbed four flights of stairs, bringing her breasts in contact with the back of Annika's hands on every inhale. As if of its own accord, her hand wrapped itself around Annika's wrist, keeping her in place.

"Gab—" Annika began, but Gabi cut her off.

"I have been thinking about that kiss constantly for the last nine days," she blurted, mouth dry. She licked her lips and watched Annika's eyes dip to her mouth.

"Yeah," Annika said, "me, too."

Gabi nodded.

"What I've been thinking is…" She trailed off, feeling suddenly shy about being so forward. But she reached for that zinging energy between them and leaned into it. "Is how much I want to kiss you again."

Annika's eyes widened and she said, "Really? You weren't writing it off as a drunken mistake you were embarrassed by, and because I'm your best friend's little sister, how could you ever face me again knowing that you regretted it? That wasn't why you were avoiding me?"

Gabi felt guilt well up in her stomach at Annika's words, but also a dash of awe that she could make confident Annika Silberberg doubt herself like this. She wasn't used to Annika being anything less than wholly self-assured.

"No, fuck no, Niki," she replied. "I was a little overwhelmed by my reaction to kissing you, and I needed space to process it."

A familiar devilish grin spread across Annika's face.

There she is, Gabi thought.

"Oh yeah?" Annika took a step closer, pushed into Gabi's space so she had to lift her chin slightly to keep eye contact. The hand that still gripped Annika's wrist clenched harder in response.

Gabi nodded and said, "And I had no idea what to say to you. If I was supposed to pretend it didn't happen because, let's face it, us hooking up is a truly terrible idea for a number of reasons. So I sent you that text that made it seem like I was unaffected by it and—"

"You got in your head about it, and just decided that the best action was no action until we were forced together again," Annika finished for her.

"You know me so well," Gabi said as a smile stretched her lips, her eyes fixed to Annika's mouth now, too.

"Mm-hmm," Annika said. She took another step closer and slid the hand Gabi wasn't gripping into the back of her hair, tugged slightly so Gabi's neck bent back, leaving her tantalizingly at Annika's mercy, just as she'd done the first time they'd kissed. "I seem to remember you needing to be kissed so thoroughly you would stop thinking so hard."

Gabi's pulse was a thousand hoofbeats through her body, her whole being poised on the edge of a precipice waiting for Annika to close the distance, to tip her over it.

Her hand came up and gripped the front of Annika's flannel, pushed their stomachs together so that their bodies were flush. Every part touched now except their mouths.

"Yes," she said, and her voice came out shaky, nearly a moan, "please, do that."

Then Annika's mouth crushed to hers, and all thoughts of Maia and weddings and anything else in the universe besides kissing Annika, touching her, getting *closer closer closer*, fled her mind.

CHAPTER FIFTEEN

K issing Gabi was as good as Annika remembered.
Better even because the haze of alcohol blurring everything at the edges was gone. She wasn't any more clear on what this meant, only that Gabi wanted her seemingly as much as she wanted Gabi, and that was enough for now.

Gabi swayed into her when Annika grazed her neck with her teeth and bit the sensitive skin beneath her jaw lightly. She gripped Gabi's hair tighter, angled her so she could kiss her deeper, flood her senses with her.

Gabi's fingers scrabbled with the buttons of Annika's flannel shirt until she could pull it apart and slide her hands up Annika's stomach. Annika felt her muscles tense under Gabi's touch.

Gabi tasted like peppermint gum with a hint of stale coffee beneath, and Annika didn't care. She wanted to fill her mouth with Gabi until she couldn't tell what was herself and what was Gabi. Wanted to crawl under Gabi's skin and live there, burrow as deep inside her as she could get.

If she was honest, she was a bit overwhelmed by her reaction to kissing Gabi as well. She had never not enjoyed kissing a beautiful woman—their sweet scents and soft skin and lush, pliable bodies—and she had kissed her fair share.

But this.

This was another thing entirely.

She felt like her whole body was too small and too big at once. That she needed to go faster, taste and touch more of Gabi as quickly as she could, but also needed to linger, to never let their lips leave each other.

Gabi's hands slid up and down the thin white cotton tank top she wore beneath her thick flannel. She stroked a line from the dip of Annika's waist along her ribs to beneath her breasts. Her thumbs rubbed circles as her hands traveled and set sensations spiraling out through Annika's body like she caressed skin. Made Annika desperate for that to be true.

"You can touch me," Annika panted against Gabi's lips, "wherever you want, you can touch me."

Gabi let out a little whimper at her words, and Annika felt her hands begin to shake.

"I-I don't know," Gabi stammered, clearly frustrated at her own nervousness.

"Shh…" Annika stroked her sides soothingly. "No thinking, remember. Just follow what feels good."

Gabi opened her mouth to reply, but Annika ducked down and slid her teeth over her neck again before she sucked on it lightly, turning whatever words Gabi had been about to say into a breathy moan.

At the same time, she gripped Gabi's wrists and moved her hands to cover her own small breasts. She placed her palms flat against the back of Gabi's hands, encouraging her to touch however she wanted.

"Oh," Gabi exclaimed as her hands squeezed and rubbed at Annika's chest, clearly not minding their smaller size. Annika sucked harder at Gabi's neck in response, knew it would leave a mark, but didn't care, beyond caring now. "Wow, they feel so nice."

Annika smiled against her skin and said, "You touching them feels nice."

She stooped to kiss down to Gabi's collarbone, and Gabi laughed. Her hands slid up to Annika's sternum when she had to bend down low to reach the collar of Gabi's shirt.

"I'm too short," Gabi whined, and Annika huffed out a laugh against the skin over her collarbone. She straightened up and kissed Gabi's mouth again. She let her hands reach down to palm Gabi's ass through her leggings.

"This is an incredible butt," Annika said, panting, and she pulled Gabi closer again, pressed their hips together with her grip.

"Not as incredible as yours," Gabi said, and one of her hands left

Annika's chest to squeeze at her ass in return. "It was the first thing I noticed about you at Queer Climb night, how good your ass looked in your leggings."

Annika groaned, suddenly overwhelmed by the idea of Gabi checking out her ass, Gabi being into her, even then.

Gabi went up on her tiptoes, cupped Annika's jaw with her hands, and kissed and kissed and kissed her until Annika's legs felt weak. She spun them around, collapsed onto the couch, and encouraged Gabi to climb into her lap.

They paused for a second. Both of them breathed harshly as they gazed into each other's faces, Gabi's arms around her neck, and Annika's hands bracketed Gabi's thighs below the curve of her ass, her leggings soft beneath Annika's hands.

"How are you doing?" Annika asked quietly. She lifted her head to graze her lips against Gabi's teasingly.

"I—I'm so fucking turned on right now," Gabi said, panting, and her voice sounded surprised and maybe a little awed. Her hips shifted restlessly in Annika's lap, and Annika could feel how her hands shook as they ran over her undercut.

"Good," Annika said, lips curling up in a sultry smile as she craned her neck up to place small glancing kisses under Gabi's jaw. Gabi tipped her head to one side to give her better access to her skin.

"I've never felt like this before," Gabi continued, voice high, punctuated by a little moan when Annika's mouth found a spot that made her grind her hips against Annika's stomach. "God, you make me so fucking crazy just from kissing. Is it always like this with girls?"

No, Annika thought, no, it isn't.

It rocked her, that thought, rang clearly through the haze of lust in her mind, so she pulled back and rested her forehead against Gabi's sternum. She felt Gabi's hands card through her hair, strands falling wildly around her face as her bun came loose. Gabi's fingers were gentle, so gentle, at odds with the hammering of her heart Annika could hear through her shirt.

"Your skin smells amazing," Annika murmured, head still pressed below Gabi's collarbone, breathing heavily.

"I smell like hospital and sweat," Gabi said incredulously.

"You smell like you," Annika replied and surged up to kiss her again, wild and deep.

After a minute, she pulled back and rested her forehead against Gabi's, closing her eyes. She said, "We should probably stop before we end up fucking on the couch in my store."

Annika felt Gabi shiver at her words.

"Why?" Gabi asked. Her nails scratched at Annika's undercut, slid up to grip the longer hair above it, and tugged lightly so Annika would look at her.

"For one thing…" Annika said. She lifted her head but kept her eyes closed. She knew the second she looked at Gabi it would be over, that this brief moment of control and clarity would be lost in the beauty of her. "The lights are on, the windows are right behind us, and they face the street."

"Huh," Gabi said, "I didn't even notice that."

Annika opened her eyes to see Gabi looking at the windows thoughtfully. The sight of her punched through Annika even harder than she thought it would.

Fuck, she looked so beautiful. Hair mussed, lips swollen from kissing, pale cheeks flushed with warmth. Annika marked the red patch halfway down her neck left by her own teeth, and swallowed down a dizzying wave of want, trying to keep her tenuous grasp on rational thought for another moment.

"For another," she rasped, voice hoarse from desire, "it's your first time with a woman. Are you sure you want it to be like this?"

With me was the silent question beneath her words, but she knew Gabi heard it because she turned her focus back to Annika and, after a moment of thought, leaned down to kiss her again. It was slow but open-mouthed, tongues dancing in a way that made Annika's brain melt into a puddle in her skull. She'd lost control of this situation, somehow.

After a few more moments, they were both moaning and rocking against each other desperately, Annika's hands fisted into Gabi's clothes to pull her flush to her body.

"Does that answer your question?" Gabi panted and pulled back only far enough to see Annika's face.

Annika nodded almost frantically and said, "Uh-huh, definitely clears that up for me, thanks."

Then, "I could turn the lights off and close the blinds," Annika's mouth said before she could stop it.

"Yeah, why don't you do that," Gabi agreed with an enthusiastic nod.

Annika scrambled up to lock the boutique's front door, flipped the sign to Closed, pulled the blinds down, and flicked the lights off as fast as she could.

When she turned back to the couch, Gabi had reclined with her back on the far arm of the couch with her shirt off. She was illuminated by the streetlamps and the light from Annika's office, and the rays that filtered in played over her skin tantalizingly.

"Holy shit," Annika exclaimed on a gusting breath. She slammed her mouth shut before anything else embarrassing could come out.

But seriously, there was only so much she could do in the face of Gabi half naked.

Gabi grinned at her slack-jawed expression. She lowered her left leg to the floor, bent her right, and rested her elbow on it, twirling a curl around her finger. She looked like one of the pinups on the walls of The Clam Shack—small waist and sloping curves, breasts lush and high on her short torso.

Annika was in awe of how Gabi could go from a stammering, fumbling, overthinking mess one minute to this, this vixen temptress before her, in another.

She had a clear shot of her soft stomach, her skin even paler there, a mole on the top of her left rib just below her breast that called to Annika. She wore an unlined nude bra, plain and everyday, and yet the hottest thing Annika had seen in a long, long time.

"Gabi," Annika said. She took a deep breath and tried to steady herself, tried to think through the fog of want pounding through her, wanted to make sure Gabi was really ready. "Are you sure you want this?"

"You're the one who told me I've been overthinking everything when it comes to dating, that I should quiet my mind and just listen to my body. Well, my body is telling me that right now, I really want you to take your shirt off and come kiss me," Gabi said.

"Just kiss?" Annika asked. "Because it's totally cool if that's all you want. I love a good shirtless make-out."

She wasn't even lying. The idea of pressing her bare chest to Gabi's and kissing her until her lips were raw sounded like heaven.

The twirling of Gabi's fingers paused, the temptress act slipped, and Annika saw her swallow, all nerves once more.

"N-no," she stammered.

"No?" Annika repeated. She took a step closer and slid off her flannel shirt, tossed it on the armchair. Gabi's eyes went immediately to her right arm, traced her tattoos. Her tank top followed the flannel, and then she stood in just her black cotton bralette. Her hair shifted against the sensitized skin of her back, making her shiver.

"I-I want you to make me feel good," Gabi said quietly.

"What was that?" Annika said, enjoying teasing her as she squirmed to put her desires into words.

"Come and touch me, Annika," she said louder, with more confidence. "I need you to."

Well, Annika didn't need to be told twice.

She walked over to Gabi, enjoying the way Gabi tracked every swish of her hips, every swing of her arms.

When she got to the couch, she placed her hands on either side of Gabi's shoulders, her knees on either side of her hips, surrounded her with her body. But she didn't quite touch her yet, waited for Gabi to reach for her first, to adjust.

She watched Gabi inspect her mostly bare torso up close. Her fingers ghosted over her collarbones, the small strain of her breasts against the cloth of her bralette, the hint of muscles in her shoulders and biceps and forearms and wrists.

"Have I told you that I love your tattoos?" Gabi said. She ran her left hand up and down Annika's arm, thumb swiping gently against the inside, drew absent-minded circles like her whole body was restless to touch *more more more* of Annika.

"I guessed that, yeah," Annika said as she watched Gabi raise her head up from the arm of the couch and kiss the black ink that twined around her forearm. Each brush of her lips over Annika's skin sent jolts of pleasure fizzing through her body.

She'd had lovers and girlfriends in the past who enjoyed her tattoos, who found them hot, but their attention had never felt like this. Like there was a direct line between the nerves on her forearm and the spot between her legs where a throbbing ache grew.

Gabi pushed herself up on her elbows to reach Annika's biceps, and her tongue flicked out to trace the vining leaves inked there.

"They're kind of like a metaphor for your personality," Gabi murmured. "From a distance they look tough and cool, but when you get close, they're really lovely and delicate."

Annika couldn't deal with how those words hit her in the tenderest spot of her heart, so she let her hips lower to Gabi's, their bare stomachs coming together as their mouths reconnected. They both moaned at the first touch of skin on skin.

Then they picked up right where they'd left off.

Annika slotted her thigh between Gabi's legs, and their hips rolled against each other, their mouths and hands hungry.

Annika rested her hand on Gabi's stomach, slid it up to cup and palm her breast through her bra. She moved the cup to the side, left Gabi's mouth to kiss down her neck, over her sternum, nuzzle the silken, rounded flesh of her breast. Gabi made a noise of protest at the absence of Annika's mouth before she saw where Annika was headed, her eyes glued to her as she took her nipple into her mouth and sucked.

The whimper Gabi let out then was high and sweet, and Annika knew she would be playing it over and over in her memory for years to come. She kissed her way across Gabi's sternum, but before she reached her other breast, Gabi sat up and unhooked her bra, granted Annika uninhibited access to her chest.

She happily took it, leaned down to suck Gabi's other nipple, scraped it with her teeth. Drew it out and soothed it with her tongue. Gabi snaked her hands into Annika's hair, pulled and tugged in response to Annika's motions. A constant stream of moans burst from her mouth, and her hips moved rapidly, circled, sought friction.

"Holy shit," Gabi whimpered, face scrunched in pleasure, head thrown back, "*holy fucking shit.*"

Annika watched her face, lingered there for a long moment, and enjoyed the sounds Gabi made, the sight of her lost to pleasure. The taste of her skin on her tongue, salty with sweat from a long day at work, as delicious as any gourmet meal. Felt Gabi's writhing body beneath her as it got more and more frustrated.

"Niki," Gabi finally pleaded, "Niki, *please.*"

"Mmm," she said and lifted her head from Gabi's breast, brain and hips stuttering at the sight of Gabi spread out beneath her, hair wild and chest heaving and pink from her attention. "Please what?"

Gabi groaned and cried, "Niki!" again, voice full of irritation.

Annika laughed smugly.

"Please touch me," Gabi said after a beat. Her eyes flew open and peered at Annika through heavy lids.

"I am touching you," Annika teased, and she ran her hand up and down Gabi's stomach and sides in soothing strokes. "I'm touching you, like, a lot."

"You bitch," Gabi whined when Annika went back to lavishing attention on her tits, and her hands stayed firmly above her waist, waiting for Gabi to tell her exactly what she wanted.

She knew, from what Gabi had told her and her own idea of Gabi's relationship with Matt, that Gabi was used to focusing on her partner's pleasure. Used to waiting to be told how to please them. She wanted Gabi to feel absolutely lost in sensation with her, to be so focused on how Gabi's body was feeling that she couldn't help but break apart, leave her head as quiet as she could.

Focusing on someone else like this was one of the few circumstances when Annika's own head was locked in on one task, not wandering or dreaming or drifting into space.

Gabi's hips bucked into Annika now, ground on her thigh. Annika thought she could get Gabi off like this given enough time, but she didn't want to.

No, the first time Gabi came with a woman, with *Annika*, she should know that it had been because Annika had made her, because she'd wanted to drive her there.

"Can I take these off?" Annika asked, rubbing her fingers over the roundness of Gabi's lower belly beneath the waistband of her leggings.

Gabi nodded frantically and lifted her hips to help Annika take them and her cotton thong off, then fling them to the floor.

Annika sat back, surveyed Gabi spread out naked beneath her on the couch in her store. She looked like a Renaissance woman with her plump thighs and round stomach and lush breasts, the light from the streetlamps filtering in through the blinds illuminating her so she glistened like an oil painting.

"You're so gorgeous," she said on an exhale, her gaze fixed between Gabi's legs. Her hands stroked up her calves, her knees, her thighs, spreading them a little more.

"No one's ever looked at me like that before," Gabi said, and she widened her legs for Annika.

"Like what?" Annika asked as she crawled back over Gabi.

Gabi craned her neck up, head on the arm of the couch, and watched Annika settle over her, eyes dipping to her still covered breasts.

"Like they're hungry for me," Gabi said before her hands glided up Annika's back and unhooked her bralette, sliding it down her arms.

I'm starved for you, Annika thought as Gabi held her rib cage to keep her still and delicately, so delicately, raised her lips to Annika's chest to place ghosting kisses over the small rise of her breasts, her nipples, the skin between.

Annika closed her eyes and just felt, let her mind and her body fully inhabit this wonderful, extraordinary moment she'd fantasized about but never dreamed would be a reality.

"I thought…" Annika stopped as a full body tremor took her when Gabi ran her teeth along her nipple, growing bolder and imitating what Annika had done to her. "I thought," she started again, "that you wanted me to touch you."

"I took a little detour," Gabi replied, her lips still on Annika's skin.

"I'm not objecting," she said, and Gabi continued to explore Annika's breasts, her mouth spiraling that ache in Annika's core tighter and tighter.

But the urge to touch Gabi, to hear her crying out in absolute pleasure, was overpowering.

So she dropped her hand to Gabi's lower stomach again, slid it down between her legs, touched her with the lightest caress of her fingertips.

At the first light touch between her legs, Gabi's body shuddered, and she let out the loveliest sound yet. She buried her face between Annika's small breasts, forehead rested against her breastbone as Annika's fingers continued to run over her gently.

Annika increased the pressure, the tempo, focused in on the spots that made Gabi keen until she vibrated with tension, body taut and hips rising from the couch.

Then Annika slid her fingers lower and in, gave Gabi the heel of her palm to grind against.

"Oh my God. Oh, my *fucking* God!" Gabi cried out when Annika entered her.

She tossed her head back against the couch cushion, thighs

quivering as Annika felt her clench around her fingers. Gabi's hand gripped her right forearm like it was a lifeline, nails pricking her skin.

Annika kept going and going until, with the help of her mouth on Gabi's nipples again, she finally pushed Gabi over the edge. Worked her through and past and into another wave of ecstasy, her limbs quaking and shaking, wordless moans roiling from her throat in long cries, one after another, eyes squeezed shut and color high on her cheeks.

This was what Annika loved, what she found addicting, the high she kept chasing relationship after relationship, partner after partner. For her, there was no greater accomplishment than making a woman come undone so completely, no dopamine rush purer, no validation more clear.

Gabi went boneless after the second time, and Annika laid her own body flat against her, pressed her into the couch and soothed her with sweet kisses on her sweaty cheeks and temples, the corners of her eyes. She smoothed Gabi's sweat-damp hair back from her face as Gabi caught her breath.

"What. The. Fuck," Gabi stated when her breath evened out. "Has sex been like that this whole time?"

Annika laughed and rolled to the side so she didn't crush her. Her hand still stroked Gabi's sides, her stomach. She rested her head against her fist, and her hair fell in a curtain against her sweaty back, her bangs stuck to her forehead, as she watched Gabi raptly while she recovered.

"Pretty much, yeah," Annika said. "It's actually kind of amazing when you're into it."

Gabi squeezed her eyes shut again and shoved the heels of her hands against them.

"Fuck," she repeated.

CHAPTER SIXTEEN

G abi was not about to cry.

She lay naked with Annika Silberberg after earth-shattering sex that had quite literally tilted her whole world and everything she'd thought she'd ever known about herself on its head, Annika's fingers still tracing light patterns against her skin, and she was *not* going to cry.

Absolutely would not because that would ruin what was arguably the best sexual experience of her life, and the fact that Annika had done that to her, *Annika*, made it even better. Would she ever not be surprised by her intense attraction to her, by the way she kept her on her toes with her teasing?

And, oh, how she'd teased her. Worked her until the tension had built to an amazingly excruciating tightness inside her, frustration forgiven by what had followed.

Two times! Had she ever come twice in a row with a partner before? Usually, she was lucky if she finished at all when she had sex with Matt and the other men she'd hooked up with before him. She'd always been focused more on if she was performing well enough to please them, if her body looked okay in the position she was in, too in her head to fully let go despite their best efforts.

She'd written herself off as someone who didn't need sex, didn't crave it the way other people seemed to. That sex served a purpose in her life beyond providing her pleasure.

But now, nearly drunk from satisfaction and the feel of Annika's bare skin on hers, she felt that craving build under her skin again.

She *wanted*.

She wanted Annika, wanted to make her feel the same way Annika had just made her feel. Wanted to know what she looked like and tasted like and sounded like when she lost all control.

And yet…

"I can't help thinking," she started.

"Gab," Annika said, "if you're thinking right now, then my job isn't finished."

Annika's fingers slid lower, caressed lightly between her hip bones.

Gabi laughed, felt arousal start to build again, hips moving with the drag of Annika's fingers. "That's the fucking problem. It was…"

She lowered her hands and turned her head to see Annika looking down at her, a little wrinkle of concern between her brows. Annika's hand came to a stop and rested against her skin, a warm, soothing weight.

Gabi reached out a shaking finger and smoothed that wrinkle out.

"It was amazing, Niki," she said. "It was so amazing, I think I astral projected into a different dimension for a minute. But…it's…I can't…"

Gabi fumbled for her words for a second, flailed to articulate this sense of profound understanding and profound loss she was experiencing.

She'd wasted so much time. So many years of her life doing what was easy, what was expected of her. Not investigating the little thrill she felt when she got attention from older girls at camp, the way she was always so careful not to let her eyes wander in lockers and dressing rooms and when she changed into her scrubs at work.

After a moment, Annika's face filled with comprehension, and she settled down on the couch, stretched out alongside Gabi, wrapped her arm around Gabi's bare waist.

Gabi turned into her warmth, tucked her face into Annika's neck as Annika's arms nestled her closer.

"You're here now, Gab, that's what matters," she whispered into the tangled mass of her hair. "Not how long it took you to get here, not where you stopped along the way. You're here, with me, and I had a fucking *incredible* time having sex with you," Annika murmured as Gabi squeezed her eyes shut again, breathed in lungfuls of her smell, finding comfort in her nearness. "And I really, really, *really* hope we can do it again."

Gabi laughed wetly, the tears she had tried to stop falling freely into the crook of Annika's neck.

"I barely even touched you," she protested. "You didn't finish."

Annika shrugged. "But you did."

For some reason, that made Gabi cry harder. And still, Annika held her as she wept, giving her the space she needed, not even sure what it was she was crying for.

Maybe she was mourning her old life, the person she had been for the last thirty years, who had seen life as a set of tracks she had to run on, who thought easiness was the same as happiness and comfort was the same as love.

Who thought sex was at best nice and at worst a bit of a chore to be gotten through.

But I'm here now, she thought. I'm here now and that's what matters.

And I don't ever want to leave.

With that thought, her tears dried, and something settled in her chest.

She pulled back far enough to look at Annika's face, surprised to see her own eyes a little bright.

"I'm definitely a lesbian," Gabi whispered, and Annika smiled tenderly at her. She lowered her head to kiss her gently and ran her palm up and down Gabi's spine in long strokes as Gabi kissed her back.

These kisses were different from the lust filled frenzy of before. They were kisses for the sake of kissing, of being close, not as a means to an end.

Gabi felt like she was floating in a safe, warm bubble as Annika brushed her lips over her cheeks, her chin, beneath her jaw. Her eyes began to close, and her breathing deepened, as exhaustion from the long day at the hospital, and the long nine days of indecision and second-guessing and yearning for Annika's embrace crashed over her.

"Gab," Annika murmured after ten minutes that felt like an eternity.

"Hmm." Gabi nuzzled her jaw sleepily against the soft skin of Annika's shoulder.

"I know you're, like, wicked cozy right now, but you can't pass out here for the night. Not only will it be *kind of* awkward when Vanessa comes in in the morning to open the store, but the heat is set to go off from eleven to seven," Annika said, and she shifted so she hovered over Gabi.

Gabi groaned and stretched. Her gaze flitted down Annika's torso, and a pinch of arousal flickered through her at the sight of bare skin despite the sleepy fog in her brain.

Annika watched her stretch with interest, eyes stuck somewhere around her breasts. Gabi arched her back lazily, enjoying the attention.

"Looks who's teasing now," Annika grumbled, hand trailing up her ribs to palm lightly at Gabi' left breast. "Fuck, you are so hot."

Gabi, who had been inches away from true sleep mere seconds ago, found herself now wide awake. Wide awake, and *turned the fuck on*.

She reached up for the back of Annika's head, craned her neck to reach her lips, and gave her a deep, slow kiss that made Gabi's toes curl and Annika whimper.

"I thought you were tired," Annika mumbled against her lips.

"Things change." Gabi shrugged, and her hands dragged down to grip Annika's waist, pull Annika's hips flush against her, and, following some instinct, wedge her bare thigh between Annika's still covered legs.

Annika's hips ground down on her with added pressure as the kiss turned hotter. Gabi ducked her head to suck at her nipples, switched between them as Annika ground herself against Gabi's leg. Annika gripped the arm of the couch for support and panted, moaned, swore as her hips picked up pace and Gabi's mouth got rougher on her breasts.

"I—I want to touch you, too," Gabi said against the skin of Annika's chest and felt nerves start to bubble in her stomach.

"Yes, please," Annika said, neck bent forward to watch Gabi, hips still rolling and circling.

"I don't know what I'm doing," Gabi replied, hands shaky as she slid them down her stomach and into Annika's leggings, pausing in the thatch of coarse hair she felt beneath her fingers.

"I'll show you what I like," Annika said.

She moved off and away from Gabi for a second to shove her leggings down before she returned to her former position over her on all fours.

"Wow." Gabi looked down at a bared Annika hovering over her and tried to decide where to touch first.

"Step one," Annika began, voice raspy and low, "kiss my neck. I like a bit of teeth, so don't be scared to bite me."

Gabi swallowed and did as she was told.

"Oh, that's good, Gab, that's really good," Annika said, voice high-pitched and breathy as Gabi caught skin between her teeth and tugged. Gabi could listen to Annika say her name like that for hours.

After a moment, Annika continued, "Step two..." She captured Gabi's wrist and guided her hand to her breast, encouraged her to squeeze and pinch at her nipple.

"Step three," Annika said a minute later, breathing harsh, eyes closed, and cheeks and neck flushed as the effects of what Gabi was doing began to show.

She reached down to guide Gabi's right hand between her thighs. She pressed her fingers over Gabi's and showed her what and where and how to touch.

When her fingers made contact with Annika's body, Gabi was amazed at the heat and silken softness of her.

"*Ah*..." Annika cried out as Gabi hit a particular spot, "fuck, stay there, Gab, don't stop, just like that."

Gabi glanced down their bodies at their hands twined together between Annika's legs, and bit back a moan. It was the hottest thing she'd ever seen. Annika was naked and flushed above her, hips circling against their fingers, taking pleasure from Gabi's touch.

Annika's hand left hers and came up to grip the cushion of the couch to stabilize herself, leaving Gabi's hand to play on its own. Annika grabbed some of Gabi's hair in the process and pulled, but Gabi didn't care. She couldn't, because Annika was unraveling and it was all because of Gabi's fingers, her lips.

She captured Annika's nipple again in her mouth, and her left hand stroked down Annika's back to touch her ass. She gripped one cheek tightly as she continued to touch Annika between her legs, pacing and pressure picking up. Gabi saw Annika's stomach clench and her head drop, felt her hips twitch wildly as she came, moans falling from her lips like precious stones.

Annika collapsed on top of her, and it was Gabi's turn to stroke her naked skin from her shoulders to hips and back.

"You're *really* good at following directions," Annika said, her words garbled from the way her mouth was mashed into the side of Gabi's neck.

Gabi laughed. "I've had years of practice."

Annika laughed, too, a bit helplessly.

Gabi turned her head to bring her lips back in contact with Annika's. She couldn't help it. She needed to kiss her, even though she'd been kissing her for what felt like hours.

Would she ever get enough of her? The sweet taste of her mouth, the magical feel of her skin against her own.

After another few minutes of languorously making out, Gabi felt the sweat cool on her body and shivered. Annika stirred to hoist herself off Gabi, and Gabi immediately missed the warmth of her body.

"When can we do this again?" Gabi blurted out before she could overthink it.

Annika paused in the middle of putting her tank top back on and turned to look at Gabi over her shoulder.

"You want to do this again?" she asked.

"Are you fucking kidding, Niki? If I'm honest, I actually want to throw you down on this couch and have my way with you again *right now*," Gabi said emphatically, and Annika laughed, her cheeks pinking at the intensity in Gabi's voice. "I never, *never*, knew that sex was supposed to be like that, that *kissing* was supposed to be like that."

Annika's eyes softened, and she reached out to hold Gabi's hands where they rested in her lap, giving them a squeeze.

"Listen, tonight was, quite frankly, unexpected, and also the best thing to happen to me in a long time," Annika said, and she ran her hand through her hair, pushing her bangs off her forehead so they stuck up.

They were frizzy from sweat and rumpled from Gabi's hands, the rest of her hair a wild tangled mass of waves. She still was one of the most beautiful women Gabi had ever seen, skin glowing with drying sweat and eyes bright with the aftermath of sex.

Gabi squeezed Annika's hand back.

"I sense a *but* coming," Gabi said, and Annika sighed.

"Well, us hooking up again is still kind of a bad idea. I mean, beyond the Maia of it all, you're still exploring your sexuality."

"If anything, us hooking up could help me do that," Gabi replied hopefully, not even sure what she said, just knowing that she needed, *needed*, Annika to agree to fuck her again. "No, listen," she said in response to Annika's raised eyebrows, "I trust you, I feel comfortable with you, and I'm insanely attracted to you, obviously. You're experienced, and as I learned tonight, you don't mind coaching your sexual partners. I think that this is the perfect arrangement."

The left corner of Annika's lips tipped up. "Oh?"

"Unless you don't want to fuck me again?" Gabi said with a shrug, quirking her brow back at Annika.

Annika did a quick sweep of Gabi's still very naked body and bit her lip.

"I very much do want to do that," she said almost solemnly.

"So," Gabi said.

She scooted closer to Annika and pressed herself against her side, wrapped her arms around her waist, and rested her chin on Annika's shoulder. Annika turned her head to peer down at her. Gabi said, "Why shouldn't we hook up again? I think it's, like, your responsibility as my lesbian guru to help me get as comfortable as possible with lesbian sex."

"I've created a horny little monster," Annika said, groaning, and she dropped her head back.

Gabi nodded, took advantage of her position to graze her lips against Annika's neck, and felt Annika's skin break out in goose bumps beneath her lips.

"You're really not playing fair, Gab," Annika said as Gabi took her earlobe between her teeth and pulled. "My sister would be so mad if she found out we're hooking up."

"So we won't tell her," Gabi said. "We're adults, we don't have to tell anyone what we do, right?"

"Can't argue with that logic," Annika replied and turned her head to capture Gabi's mouth with her own. "And I *do* still need to get the rest of your measurements."

Gabi's lips stretched into a wide smile as she kissed Annika again.

CHAPTER SEVENTEEN

I had sex with Gabi Mendon last night, Annika thought as she stared at herself in the mirror while she brushed her teeth the following morning.

She thought it as she ate breakfast, remembering the press of her lips on Gabi's soft skin, the way she arched her back and tossed her head when Annika played with her gorgeous breasts, how her hips moved restlessly against Annika's thigh.

Thought it as she drove to work, eyes unseeing, mind full of the sounds Gabi made, the way it felt when Gabi's hand had slipped between her own legs.

Thought it as she unlocked the door and glanced over at the sitting area, pictured Gabi posed like a pinup girl against the arm of the couch.

She sat at her sewing machine all morning, neglected the garments around her and the clients in the store, and replayed the events of the previous night over and over in her head, thighs pressed firmly together.

After two hours of this, she fished her phone out of the pocket of her loose jeans and opened her thread with Gabi.

Annika: *You've broken my brain. Us having sex in my place of work is having surprisingly negative affects on my concentration, which was not that great to begin with. I can't look at the couch without picturing you naked on it.*

Last night before they had said good-bye on the sidewalk outside the store, they had agreed to hang out Saturday after Gabi's shift at the hospital. Annika had thought she'd regret it, fucking Gabi, agreeing to do it again, when she woke up this morning. But the wonder and thrill that had filled her during and after their time together had yet to leave her.

Gabi replied to her text fifteen unproductive minutes later.

Gabi: *I haven't been able to stop smiling all morning. One of the nurses asked me if I took something.*

Gabi: *That really happened, didn't it?*

Annika couldn't stop the grin that stretched over her lips as she read Gabi's texts.

Who was she kidding, pretending to be reluctant to hook up with Gabi again? So what if they were her sister's co–maids of honor? If Maia would be so pissed at Annika if she found out that she was hooking up with Gabi?

It wasn't like they were dating. They were just friends who were deeply attracted to each other and occasionally gave in to that attraction.

Besides, Gabi made it very clear she was in this for the self-discovery, not to develop something romantic with Annika.

She was sure that they would both lose interest in each other sooner rather than later. That Gabi would want to move on to explore other women, and Annika would grow bored and look for the next thing to chase. Then they could laugh about the couple of times they'd had sex when Gabi was first figuring herself out.

No harm, no foul.

And, *fuck*, did Annika want to have sex with her again. She had told Vanessa she wasn't into the whole baby gay thing, but showing Gabi how to touch her had been *hot*. And Gabi's reaction to it? How could she not feel good about herself when she had rocked her world so thoroughly she'd cried?

Granted, she was hoping she didn't make Gabi cry *every* time, but it had definitely been an ego boost for Annika.

Not being able to see each other didn't stop them from texting all day long, though. The Tuesday after they'd slept together for the first time, Annika was surprised to find a text at two p.m. from Gabi.

Gabi: *Your friendly neighborhood gynecologist stopping in to remind you to eat your lunch. Gotta keep your energy up for all your after work activities *winking emoji*.*

Annika ignored the way this text made her heart flip-flop around in her chest.

It became a routine. Gabi texted her sometime between one and two to remind her to look up from her work and take a break. She found herself looking forward to this little notice that Gabi was thinking about her. Which surprised her, since she usually found concern like this from the woman she was seeing to be stepping over a boundary. That it implied that she couldn't take care of herself and needed them to do it for her.

But these texts, the joking, teasing way Gabi phrased them, made her feel...cared about, not coddled. Like Gabi saw her independence and wasn't trying to take it from her.

By Saturday evening, the anticipation coursed so thickly through Annika, she vibrated with it.

"Dude, what is up with you today?" Vanessa asked.

She poked her head in the back room after Annika fumbled her container of pins and sent them crashing to the floor for the third time in an hour.

She hadn't told Vanessa about hooking up with Gabi and had made sure to delete the security footage of the floor of the boutique from that night. It had captured a rather spectacular account of that night's events that Annika had been tempted to save to her personal hard drive.

They had decided not to tell anyone, and Annika knew if she started telling Vanessa, she was more liable to blurt it out to Maia the next time she saw her. She had made it through Shabbat dinner at her parents' house the previous night by the skin of her teeth, making sure to keep her phone out of Maia's sight so she wouldn't see Gabi's messages.

She'd even changed her name in her phone to Gyno, which was technically true. Gabi was a gynecologist, just not *her* gynecologist, although she sure seemed to know her way around Annika's female anatomy.

"Must have had too much caffeine," Annika lied. She picked up her pins and managed to only poke herself twice in the process.

Vanessa gave her a steely look before she hitched on her most winning showroom smile and headed back to the client.

"Sorry about that, a little mishap in the tailoring room. How are you feeling about this one? Isn't the beading just *darling?*" Annika heard her say to the client.

Annika checked the time on her phone. The white digital numbers seemed to mock her as she read five forty-five.

Gabi's shift was over at seven.

They had made plans to research things to do in Nashville around eight at Annika's apartment.

She rushed through her closing tasks, left several items to be tailored for the morning, hands too shaky to hold the fabric straight anyway, and waved a hurried good-bye to Vanessa as she sped to her car.

Why was she so nervous? She'd been calm as the bay on a clear morning with Gabi on Monday.

Maybe it was because then, she had expected Gabi to say they should forget that first kiss had happened. She'd been ready to shelve her attraction to Gabi forever, ready to pretend she didn't want to rip her clothes off her every time she saw her.

But now that sex was on the table, she wanted it to be as good for Gabi as she could make it. Partly because she wanted her to keep coming back for more. But mostly because, in her opinion, Gabi had over a decade of pleasure to make up for, and it was now Annika's solemn duty to help her get it.

She raced home and parked her car hastily in the lot. Slammed her apartment door too hard when she got into her unit.

She surveyed her L-shaped studio with her hands on her hips. The secondhand navy couch from her parents' house, the cushions perfectly worn in from a decade of Annika and Maia tussling and flopping and jumping on them, sat in the living room portion of the open space on top of an oriental rug she'd gotten at a yard sale in Falmouth. The coffee table made from a giant piece of driftwood she'd found on the beach and dried in the sun one summer and topped with an oval slab of glass. The TV anchored to the opposite wall.

Grabbing up random clothes off the couch and the floor in the living room, she rushed into the bedroom section where her queen-size bed took up the whole of the back wall opposite the only windows in the unit. She hurriedly picked up other detritus she'd left marooned around the place as she went, until her arms were full.

"Okay," she said to herself as she padded into her kitchen in her bare feet and pulled an open bottle of red wine off the counter, poured a glass, and took a swig, "it'll be fine. Gabi is coming over, and you guys will chat and have some wine, and then you'll kiss and maybe have sex, but it's not a big deal. You've had fuck buddies before. Just because it's your sister's best friend who you maybe have a little crush on doesn't mean it's any different, right?"

She felt sweat break out on her lower back and took another big slug of wine. Maybe she should take half an edible to chill out? But she didn't know how Gabi felt about hooking up with people on substances, and she didn't want to be too out of it when she got here.

She took a couple of deep calming breaths just like her ex Fiona, the social worker, had taught her and tried to halt the growing panic that was about to climb out of her stomach.

Ten minutes later, Annika buzzed Gabi in and waited what felt like an interminable amount of time for her to climb the stairs.

You're the cool, confident lesbian guru, Annika said to herself as she took deliberate steps to the door when Gabi knocked on it. *This is your space, you're the one in control.*

"Hey," Gabi said when Annika opened the door. She wore a black puffer coat that fell to her shins and a blue beanie over her dark curls, both damp from flakes of snow. She looked so adorable Annika wanted to wrap her arms around her and squeeze.

She smiled widely at the sight of Annika leaning against the doorjamb.

"Hey," Annika returned and felt an echoing smile stretch her own lips. Her whole body seemed to sag at the sight of her, all the whirring in her mind and body going quiet. "Happy Chanukah."

"Happy Chanukah to you, too," Gabi replied, and they grinned at each other like fools for a second before Gabi stepped forward and said, "You going to let me in or what?"

Annika moved out of the way and held the door open for her to walk through.

"Boots there," she said and gestured to the rubber tray by the door where she kept her winter boots. Gabi tromped over and bent to untie her snow boots. She still wore her coat, which blocked Annika from ogling her ass, unfortunately.

"Coat there," Annika said, pointing to the coat rack next to the refrigerator in the square slice of the room that had been retrofitted with dollhouse-size kitchen appliances.

"Come here," Gabi said, once she was free of her outwear. She reached her hand out to Annika who took it and pulled Gabi close.

She was miniscule in her socked feet, a tiny curvy package all wrapped up in a brown turtleneck sweater and high-waisted boyfriend jeans. A Chanukah gift Annika couldn't wait to open.

She took Gabi's face in her hands and bent to kiss her, meant it to be soft and slow, just a kiss hello. But the second their lips touched, the longing for this woman she'd felt since the moment they said good-bye on Monday washed over her, and she found herself using her hold to angle Gabi's mouth to deepen the kiss almost immediately.

Gabi whimpered at the change and wrapped her fists in the fabric at the sides of Annika's sweater, hauled her body up against Annika's, and pressed her breasts into Annika as her tongue flicked into Annika's mouth.

So much for the talking and the wine, Annika thought, as she spun and began to back Gabi the short distance to her bed. Both of them tossed their sweaters and shirts and bras on the floor in quick succession, and their hands roamed over the newly bared skin hungrily.

"Today was so long," Gabi said, panting as she took a seat on Annika's bed and raised her hips to pull down and kick off her jeans. Then she was only in a black cotton thong and her wool socks, a look Annika found deeply sexy. Annika knelt between her legs, her own socks and pants already discarded somewhere on the floor behind her. "I kept glancing at the clock to see how long it was before I could be with you."

Annika ignored the way the sound of the words *be with you* made her heart sing. *She just meant like this, naked, bodies on bodies and lips on lips*, she scolded herself.

She straightened out Gabi's leg and slid her sock off slowly. Then she ran her lips over the arch of Gabi's foot, her calf, the inside of her knee, repeated the process leisurely with the other leg, luxuriating in the impossibly soft, smooth skin of Gabi's legs. She looked up to see Gabi collapse backward on the bed, watched as Gabi's hands rose to knead her own large breasts.

"Mmm," Annika said and rose to kneel more firmly between

Gabi's plump thighs to lavish kisses on the sensitive skin. "Someone is really worked up."

"No teasing, please, Niki," she whined, her breath already harsh. "Not tonight, I need you too much."

And God, if Gabi that desperate for her wasn't the hottest thing Annika had ever heard. She nipped at the skin of Gabi's stomach and slid her hands up to take over tweaking Gabi's nipples. Gabi's arms fell against the bed by her head with a thunk.

"Ah, shit!" Gabi cried out, high and sweet, as Annika tugged her nipples lightly with her fingers.

Her head dropped down to mouth at Gabi through her underwear, and Gabi said, "Fuck, that's *so good*, Niki."

"I love your tits." Annika groaned and spread her hands flat to touch more of them, the soft flesh molding to the grip of her fingers as she squeezed. Gabi's back arched into her touch, and her hips shifted as Annika sucked at her inner thigh. "They're incredible, Gab."

Annika expected her to make a joke about how she made them herself, but Gabi was clearly too gone for that.

Gabi groaned and then pushed Annika back by the shoulder. Before Annika could ask her if something was wrong, Gabi sat up and tugged off her underwear frantically, tossed it onto Annika's floor, and then flopped back on the bed, thighs spread, an open invitation.

Annika grinned and slotted her shoulders between Gabi's legs. Her left hand gripped Gabi's right thigh and lifted it to hook over her shoulder.

She spared one second before she got to work to glance up. Gabi had pushed up on her elbows and stared, rapt, round cheeks flushed and chest heaving with her harsh breaths, as she watched Annika dip her head and lick a slow stripe from the bottom of her slit to the apex of her thighs.

"Oh my God," she cried. Her head dropped back in pleasure and eyes squeezed shut as Annika settled into her task. "Oh my fucking God, Niki."

Annika felt herself clench at the sound of her name like that but focused all her attention on Gabi. Then she lost herself to the musky taste of Gabi on her tongue, the unbelievable heat and slick of her when she slid first one and then two fingers inside. Gabi's moans grew in pitch and frequency as Annika worked at her until she nearly screamed.

Gabi's back arched and her stomach clenched, and Annika had to pin her hips to the bed with a forearm so she could keep her mouth on her as she writhed and whimpered. When she'd stilled and collapsed, Annika placed gentle kisses along her core as little quakes of pleasure tensed through her.

"See, I can be efficient," Annika said, voice low, and she crawled her way over a limp Gabi. She collapsed at her side, fingers trailing over Gabi's plush stomach, up around and over one breast and then down her side in soothing repetition as Gabi came back into herself.

Gabi threw an arm over her face and huffed a laugh.

"What?" Annika asked as she looked down at her and continued to stroke her skin.

"I thought it was only so intense the first time because I hadn't been with a woman before," Gabi answered. "But now, I think it's just a *you* thing."

Annika felt her whole body glow.

"I *have* had a lot of practice," Annika said smugly. Gabi punched her arm weakly, opened her palm, and let her hand rest there, as if she needed to hold on to Annika in any way she could.

After a minute of deep breathing, Gabi lowered her arm and met Annika's eyes.

For a brief second, Annika thought Gabi might sit up then, might make some excuse to leave.

But then, without warning, she swung her legs over Annika's hips and pushed her into the bed, making the bed frame squeak.

There was a loud meow, and a streak of dark gray fur shot out from under the bed.

"That's just Vera Wang," Annika said. She waved one hand, and the other gripped Gabi's round hip to keep her where she was.

"Excuse me?" Gabi said, and she raised her eyebrow.

"My cat," Annika murmured as Gabi leaned over her. "Vera Wang, patron saint of wedding dress designers."

Gabi grinned down at her and lowered her head to capture Annika's mouth in a kiss like a slow blazing fire and pressed their chests together tightly.

Annika, already turned on from going down on Gabi, reached her hand between her legs for some relief as Gabi's right palm rubbed teasingly light circles on her nipple. But Gabi grabbed her wrist to stop her.

"My turn now," she purred, a wicked gleam entering her rich brown eyes as she gazed at Annika.

"Are you sure, Gab? You don't have to," Annika said to her softly.

Gabi gave her a disbelieving look.

"Are you kidding me? I mean, look at you," Gabi said, and she gestured at the length of Annika's body, a move that encompassed everything from her longer legs and the dark curls that peeked out around her underwear, to her flat stomach and small breasts. "I have been fantasizing about licking your pussy all week."

Annika swallowed thickly, heat cascaded through her at those words, and the pressure between her legs grew nearly distressingly heavier.

She had always felt more comfortable being the one to give pleasure rather than the person receiving it. Not that she didn't like women fucking her, *of course* she did. It was just easier to get out of her head when she was in control, to feel less vulnerable.

"Is that okay with you? I don't have to—"

"Gab, *please* go down on me," Annika cut in, a sentence she'd never thought she'd say. She shoved her own underwear off and scooted up to rest against her pillows, bent her legs at the knees, and spread them wide.

Gabi smiled and licked her lips, gaze falling between Annika's legs.

"So beautiful," she murmured mostly to herself. Her hand glided over Annika's thigh and gripped right below her hip where her thigh met her body. Her thumb brushed against Annika's core lightly.

Annika drew in a sharp breath at that first touch as rivulets of pleasure trickled through her, honey sweet.

She closed her eyes as Gabi passed her thumb over her again in a broad sweep, lingered a bit at the top, rubbing a slow circle that had Annika's hips moving with it.

"You're so wet," Gabi said wonderingly as she ran her thumb over her again and again.

"Uh-huh," Annika moaned, her hips pressed into the tauntingly light touch.

She heard Gabi let out a shaky breath, then felt the mattress shift as she got into position. She opened her half-lidded eyes to see Gabi, long curls pulled back behind her head in one hand, stare intently at her pussy like she was imprinting the sight of it onto her brain and bite her lip.

The sight was so hot she had to squeeze her eyes closed against it.

And then Gabi slid her tongue over her, and she was gone. Went zooming off into another dimension where all that existed was the slide of Gabi's mouth on her slick skin.

Gabi was hesitant at first, tested and tasted and took her time. Annika didn't care.

After a little while, Gabi pulled back and said, tentatively, "Is this okay?"

The shyness and uncertainty mingled with the lust in her voice twisted something a little raw in Annika's chest.

"*More* than okay, Gab," she gasped out. She was so turned on it was almost painful now.

"Can you give me some tips?" she said, voice still that intoxicating mix of ingenue and vixen.

"I can barely think straight right now," Annika said, panting. "Just…just, go a little harder and maybe try sucking a bit."

Gabi nodded and leaned back down, applied Annika's advice to great success. Annika's hand speared into Gabi's hair when she hit that spot that had her hips arching, tangled her fingers in the strands to ground herself as Gabi reached the perfect speed and pressure.

"Holy shit holy shit holy fucking *shit*," she chanted as she came, as her hips rose and twisted, thighs shook around Gabi's head. Her hands nearly tugged Gabi's hair from the root as she thrashed. Gabi's mouth stayed on her all the while, tongue and lips gentle when she came down.

"Good?" Gabi asked when she was finished.

Annika nodded and felt Gabi crawl up the bed and curl up next to her. She flung a thigh over Annika's waist, a warm weight that settled her back into this reality.

Felt but not saw because Annika's eyes were still squeezed shut as she tried to piece herself back together.

"How was that for my first time going down on a woman?" Gabi asked after a moment, clearly looking for reassurance.

"A-plus work," Annika said. She peeled one eye open to peer down at Gabi, whose head was nestled against her shoulder as her hand stroked Annika's still twitching stomach lightly.

"Hmm, really? Because I think I need some more practice," Gabi replied, and her hand now danced over Annika's sternum, slipping lightly between her breasts, making her shiver.

"I mean," Annika said, "there's always room for improvement."

PART FIVE

Bachelorette Planning Session #2 and First Fitting

January–February

Chapter Eighteen

G abi had never really seen herself as a sexual person.

Sure, she liked sex just fine. Liked the slide of skin on skin and the way kissing could send her blood thumping through her body. But she and Matt had never had what you might call a robust sex life. Most of the time she did what he wanted because she felt bad she wasn't more sexual and he clearly wanted her to be.

And she'd find it fine, nice even. But she never craved his touch, even when they first started dating. Sex was just another expected thing they'd do together, like move in or get married eventually.

But ever since her first kiss with Annika, it felt like her body had woken up from some long slumber and was now hungry—no, *ravenous*—for sex. Particularly sex with Annika Silberberg.

Over the next six weeks, Gabi saw Annika at least twice a week. They had to work around both of their jobs and menstrual cycles, but Gabi made sure she never went more than a few days without Annika's skin on hers.

She was sure, at some point, one of them was going to cut this off to pursue a real relationship. But what they had for now was miles better than anything Gabi had had before. If she could manage to see Annika more often, she would.

For the sex, obviously.

Definitely not because being with Annika made her feel seen and held and safe to open up. Not just to express her sexual desires, although Annika seemed game to try just about anything Gabi might suggest. But other things, too. Her fears about finding a job postresidency. How she worried her friends were leaving her behind now that they were marrying and having kids. She found herself spilling it all to Annika. Via text on the nights they didn't see each other, or as she lounged in Annika's bed, body and mind loose with the pleasure Annika always wrung from her.

It had nothing to do with the fact that distractible Annika paid just as intent attention to her when they talked about her day or the latest show she was watching on Disney+ as she did when Gabi lay spread out naked before her. Took as much care and consideration with her when she systematically destroyed her with pleasure as she did when she fed her a midnight dinner of grilled cheese in Gabi's still barren apartment.

"Aren't you the one that's always checking in on me to see if I've eaten?" Annika teased, as she flitted through Gabi's tiny kitchen in just her bralette and undies one night at the end of January, hair tossed carelessly in a loose, messy bun on top of her head.

"Yes, but it's only a problem when *you* forget to eat. It's called having back-to-back appointments and procedures, and needing to catch up on charting when *I* do it," Gabi called from where she sat on her couch. She enjoyed the simple pleasure of watching Annika move erratically about her space.

Annika turned to her, spatula in hand, and braced on her hip at the waistband of her underwear, and rolled her eyes.

"Ah yes, everything is more virtuous when a doctor does it," she said.

She was just so…ugh.

Gabi couldn't even put it into words.

There was the physical, of course. Annika was a gorgeous woman with a body that broadcast her love of climbing and hiking. Those tattoos that decorated her right arm still made Gabi go weak in the knees. And her ass, good God, Gabi could spend all day just thinking about it.

But it was more than that, too. The way she mercilessly teased her, in and out of bed, but held space for her emotions, talked her through her anxieties, listened to her fears about the future, held her while she cried.

Annika was silly and serious, creative and compassionate. Could sit still at her sewing machine for hours on end but barely sit down through a whole thirty-minute episode of TV. She was a puzzle that Gabi couldn't quite solve. And Gabi, who was used to having and expected to have all the answers all the time, was captivated by her.

In the six weeks since they'd started this routine of having sex and hanging out, Gabi had seen Annika in various states: blissed out, torturously intense, absent-minded.

But she loved Annika like this best, loose and languid, joking with her as they cuddled and watched a movie on one of their couches, or talked together in bed postsex. Annika going on excitedly about one of her various hobbies, of which Gabi was learning there were many.

One time, Annika jumped out of bed butt naked with half a joint sticking out of her mouth to search through a pile of pulpy fibers to show Gabi the paper she'd made before work earlier that morning.

Another time she went over to Annika's after work, tense and ready for Annika to take her apart, only to have Annika yell, "It's open!" when she knocked and found her elbow-deep in a big glass bowl of milk.

"What the fuck are you doing?" Gabi had said, eyeing Annika. She was in just a sports bra and leggings, bangs streaked with white as she mixed the substance with her hands.

"Making mozzarella," Annika said as if this was a perfectly normal thing for a twenty-eight-year-old Jewish dressmaker to say at eight p.m. "I'm trying to form the curds into a smooth ball, but it's harder than it looks. Want to help me?"

And the wild thing was, even after working twelve straight hours swabbing cervixes and doing pelvic exams and breaking the news that a girl's cheating ex had given her chlamydia, Gabi did want to help her.

Despite having come over *strictly* for sex, she ended up spending an hour helping Annika form and package the cheese and then wipe down every inch of her kitchen. They laughed as the slippery curds squelched through their fingers and squirted milk at each other, exchanging kisses over the bowl, hands full.

"Thanks for that," Annika had said, taking Gabi's face in her soggy hands and kissing her lightly on the lips once the kitchen was clean.

"I can't believe you were making mozzarella at eight thirty at night," Gabi murmured and giggled with a shake of her head.

"I had an urge," Annika said with a shrug that turned into a wicked grin. "Speaking of urges, want to join me for a shower?"

She wasn't falling for Annika, couldn't be. But she couldn't deny that her feelings for her had grown past friends-with-benefits territory.

"Why have you still not decorated your apartment?" Annika said now as she collapsed on the couch next to her and handed Gabi the grilled cheese. Gabi's stomach grumbled at the smell, and Annika shot it a pointed look.

"I don't know," Gabi said, and she took a bite. The cheese oozed perfectly into her mouth. "At first it was just because I was so busy—"

"Being gay, yes, I remember." Annika nodded, and Gabi swatted her with the hand not holding the grilled cheese.

"But now"—she turned to survey her naked apartment—"it just doesn't feel permanent, I guess."

Annika watched her, an almost wary look in her eye. "You're not thinking about moving back in with Matt, are you?"

Gabi burst out laughing, spraying grilled cheese crumbs from her mouth.

"Oh my God," she said. She coughed and took a sip of water. "Fuck no, Niki. I have *no* desire to go back to him. You've more than shown me the errors of my ways."

A light crept into Annika's eye, and she grinned, self-satisfied.

"Good. Just wanted to check," she said.

"What I mean is…" Gabi paused and chewed her sandwich thoughtfully, watching Annika pinch a bite off from the plate in her lap and pop it into her mouth. "I moved here out of necessity. It was the first place I could afford on my own. I don't know if you know this, but debt really fucks up your credit score."

Annika snorted. "Please, I'm a small business owner who went to fashion and design school, of course I know that."

Gabi smiled and shimmied her shoulders to nestle deeper into the couch cushion, swiveling to rest her feet in Annika's lap. Annika's hands were on her instantly, like she couldn't hold back a moment more from touching her. She stroked her calloused fingers up Gabi's arches, gently massaged her tired feet.

"This place, it just doesn't feel like mine. And I keep waiting for something to click. Maybe it's because I've never lived alone. I mean, I went right from rooming with Rachel to rooming with my med school classmates to living with Matt," she mused.

"I love living alone," Annika said, her hands now stroking Gabi's calves idly. "No one there to interfere with the way I do things. I can be as messy as I want, and no one can say shit about it. Sew in the middle of the night if I can't sleep, and not have to worry about waking someone up—"

"Make mozzarella at eight thirty at night," Gabi cut in, and Annika pinched her calf but laughed to take the sting away.

"Exactly," she said. "I shared a room with Maia until she went to college, and I swear it's the reason we fight so much still."

The mention of Maia caused a pang in Gabi's chest. She'd seen Maia twice one-on-one since she and Annika had started hooking up and had felt horrible when Maia asked her how dating was coming along.

"Speaking of my darling sister," Annika said, breaking the swirl of Gabi's guilty thoughts, "we have her second bachelorette party planning sesh tomorrow. Are you going to be able to keep your hands off me in front of her?"

She said it jokingly, but there was an undercurrent to her words that needled at Gabi. Annika had agreed they shouldn't tell anyone about their…arrangement, but a part of Gabi hated keeping her a secret. Annika was so wonderful, so vibrant and a touch dark, so empathetic and giving, in bed and out, and she deserved someone who would and could show her off to the whole world. One day, she was going to figure that out for herself as well.

Not for the first time, she also thought about how no one had been able to capture Annika's heart for long. She wondered how much longer Annika would be amused by her before she got bored and moved on like she did with all her hobbies.

But it was only right, because Gabi didn't want to take up more room than a hobby in Annika's life and heart, even if she was becoming increasingly intoxicated with her.

"Oof," Gabi sighed exaggeratedly. "You know, it will be wicked hard, but I think I'll be able to just manage not to ravish you like a horny teen in front of your sister."

Annika grinned back at her and took the now empty plate from Gabi's lap, fingers brushing her bare thighs beneath the big T-shirt Gabi wore.

"Look at you, saying *wicked* like a native," Annika nearly growled as she crawled up Gabi. She settled her legs in between and outside of

Gabi's, rucking up her shirt with her movement until their bodies were pressed skin to skin from the stomach down.

"I am from New Jersey," Gabi said. Her breath was labored, and her heart kicked up at Annika's proximity. Despite how often Annika touched her and kissed her and lay naked with her, her body didn't seem to get used to her.

"Absolutely not New England," Annika murmured just before she kissed Gabi and pressed her deliciously back into the couch with her body weight.

Gabi's hands slid to her favorite spots, one on Annika's breast and the other on her ass. She dipped beneath the fabric of Annika's bralette to rub her palm against her, her nipple peaked and stiff against Gabi's hand, as Annika kept melting her mind with her kisses, with the movement of her body.

"That's right," Annika crooned into her ear, hips circling against Gabi's, "get it all out now before tomorrow night."

"Like you're going to be so calm and collected the whole time. Maybe I'll wear a V-neck sweater just to tease you," Gabi retorted, undercut by her slight moan as Annika sucked at the spot on her neck she loved.

Annika pulled back from Gabi and stared down into her face, eyes suddenly intense, mouth tipped down at the corners.

"I'm going to be dying to touch you the whole time regardless of what you wear, Gab," she said, and Gabi felt her heart lurch, not unpleasantly.

Rather than responding, though, she surged up to capture Annika's mouth, letting her body speak what her mind was denying.

CHAPTER NINETEEN

Annika was so fucked.

Like, even more fucked than the time she decided to clean up her own undercut and accidentally shaved half her head.

Or the time in ninth grade when she'd borrowed Maia's expensive sweater she'd just bought with her hard-earned babysitting money without asking, and a pen exploded on it.

Or the time she'd accidentally sewn shut the armholes on a jumpsuit made from a delicate French lace, and taking the stitches out had ripped the expensive fabric.

The list of her various mishaps went on and on—that was life when your mind flitted from one thought to the next to the next like a hummingbird searching for nectar.

But none of those scenarios came close to the level of fucked as this one.

She was having regular—and plentiful, and soul shatteringly good—sex with one of her sister's oldest and dearest friends and lying to her about it. After they'd had sex on the couch the night before, rubbed against each other as their kisses grew furious, hands grabbing at hips and backs for leverage until they both cried out in pleasure, capturing their sounds between their sealed lips, Annika had gotten up and gotten dressed and left Gabi luxuriating in the afterglow on the couch.

They had yet to have a full sleepover and seemed to have come to an unspoken agreement that they could hang out after sex, but eventually they would go to sleep in their own respective beds.

"I'll see you tomorrow night, then," Annika said as she leaned over to place a good-bye kiss on Gabi's lips.

Gabi, slowly drifting into sleep, had gazed at her beneath half-lowered lids and smiled up at her. Annika had wanted to snuggle back into her warmth and stay there forever.

"Try not to look too hot, okay? A girl can only handle so much," Gabi had mumbled drowsily, and Annika had grinned but turned quickly to the door to hide the truth she was sure was plain in her eyes.

And that truth was that Annika was into Gabi, big time.

Like quicksand sinking, heart skipping every time her name showed up on her screen, daydreaming about holding her hand as they walked along the harbor, watching her while she slept and thinking her snoring was cute into her.

She'd felt the first prickle of it the fourth time Gabi had come over to her apartment. After they were done, Gabi had followed Annika into the tiny kitchen to get a glass of water, both of them disheveled and dressed only in T-shirts. They had teased each other and chatted about nothing in particular. A sense of rightness had bloomed beneath Annika's breastbone as she gazed at Gabi in the low kitchen light.

She found herself wishing every night could be like this, Gabi coming over and being with her, being in her space. They didn't even need to hook up, they could just lie on the couch together and watch TV or chat. She almost never wanted the women she slept with to be with her like that, preferred her personal space and time to herself.

But she'd nearly asked Gabi to stay that night as she kissed her good-bye, the urge to do it so strong it shocked her.

Over the following two weeks, she'd catch herself gazing off into the distance and thinking about Gabi's smile, her laugh, her calming, steady presence. Wondered what her day was like, who she was talking to, what she was eating, wanting to catalog her every habit like she was a naturalist and Gabi was some exotic species she'd discovered.

Once, Gabi fell asleep on her after they'd had sex, her body a living weighted blanket, and Annika had played with her curls and watched her face, relaxed and peaceful in sleep. She was mesmerized by every little twitch of an eyelid, every small puff of air she let out that blew gently over the skin of Annika's neck like a summer breeze.

I could lie like this forever, Annika thought, fidgeting limbs quiet, in no rush to have her apartment to herself.

But reality slammed into her moments later.

Gabi was not hers to lie with for hours.

Gabi didn't *want* to be hers, period.

This whole situation was temporary, and Annika knew it would shatter her heart when it ended, but that was her own fault for finally catching meaningful feelings for the one person who had told her not to.

But rather than put a stop to it and some distance between them, Annika picked at the scab over her heart, let Gabi in deeper and deeper. She *needed* to kiss her, needed to make her come in a way she had never felt before. Wanted to, one day, hold her through the night as she slept in her arms.

"Fuck," she groaned forlornly as the thread got jammed in her machine the day after midnight grilled cheese with Gabi. "Fuck!"

She smacked her sewing machine with her hand and then immediately regretted it.

"I'm sorry, Greta, it's not your fault," she apologized to her machine, stroking its flat side with her hand.

"If you're assaulting Greta, something really must be up," Vanessa said, swinging her long blond braid over her shoulder as she straddled the back of the chair at the computer desk and crossed her black clad arms over the top of the seat.

Annika sighed.

"I've really fucked myself over, Ness," Annika said. She rested her elbows on the sewing table and her chin in her hands.

"Mmm, let me guess," Vanessa said and swiveled the chair slightly side to side with her hips. "It has to do with a certain tiny yet hot gynecologist who keeps texting you, and who you made out with after trivia back in November."

Annika clasped the sides of her face and glared at her. The expression was short lived, however, as she dropped her head and her hands to the table and groaned.

"I like her *so* much," Annika whined to the floor and saw Vanessa's black leather slides scoot into view as she wheeled the chair to sit opposite Annika at the table.

She felt Vanessa's hand pat her hair.

"Now you know what it's like to be on the other side of dating someone emotionally unavailable," Vanessa said sympathetically.

Annika sat up, dislodging her hand.

"First of all," Annika said, and she stuck up her index finger, which still sported the little rubber protectors she wore while she was working, "we aren't dating, just, like, having sex regularly and then hanging out after."

"Dude, that's dating. That's literally all dating is," Vanessa said, giving Annika a look.

Annika rolled her eyes.

"No, but, we don't, like, go on dates. We don't really do activities together, except that one time she helped me make mozzarella, or that time I made her dinner, and we watched a movie."

"Both dates," Vanessa interjected enthusiastically. She lifted her finger to emphasize her point.

"Or just things friends who have sex do together," Annika argued. It was Vanessa's turn to glare at Annika's stubbornness. "Also, who ever said I was emotionally unavailable?"

This made Vanessa cackle, actually tip her head back and let out a deep, throaty laugh that seemed to come from the center of her chest.

"Dude, I love you like family, but you are one of the most emotionally unavailable and guarded women I've ever met," said Vanessa.

"What do you mean?" Annika said indignantly. She sat back in her chair and crossed her arms over the chest of her favorite forest-green hoodie, slumped down like a petulant child.

"Every time a woman starts getting close to you, you panic and find the smallest little reason to dump her," Vanessa said. "Back me up here, Maia."

To Annika's horror, her sister appeared—perfectly coiffed as always in a black puffer coat with a fur-lined hood over a gray wool sweater dress and brown leather riding boots—in the doorway of the workshop.

Maia said, "You do exhibit traits characteristic of those who are afraid of vulnerability, leaving you closed off to true emotional connection, Niki."

"You've read, like, *an* infographic on love languages, and now you're suddenly a psychologist?" Annika shot back at her sister.

"I do work in the psychological field," Maia retorted. She crossed her arms and leaned her weight into her right hip.

"You're an HR rep for a start-up," Annika said, annoyed.

"I *have* a degree in psychology," Maia said.

"Yeah, a BA. Vanessa has a BA in psychology," Annika said as she flung a hand out to her friend.

"Whoa, leave me out of this." Vanessa held her hands up defensively before her chest.

Maia rolled her eyes and said, "Why are we talking about this anyway? As far as I know, you haven't dated anyone in months. Which, actually, are you okay? That's a wicked long time for you to go."

Vanessa opened her mouth, and Annika kicked her ankle under the table.

"Just doing a little midday introspection," Annika replied and sat up in her seat. "What are you doing here, Mai?"

Maia looked at her like she was clueless and then pointedly shot a glance at the clock on the wall.

"Um, hello? I'm here for my fitting, obviously," she drawled, hands on hips.

Annika glanced at the clock on the wall which did indeed read two thirty, the time Maia had said she'd come today for the first fitting of her gown.

They had, finally, decided on a design about a month ago, a sweetheart ball gown made from a sturdy silk fabric patterned subtly with sunflowers. There would be a tasteful five-foot train for the ceremony that would hook up to one of the thirty tiny pearl buttons that secured Maia into it and would take Annika about three hours to affix by hand. The back would arc down beneath Maia's shoulder blades, showing off her slender neck and spine.

They were still stuck on whether or not to add off-the-shoulder straps—Maia for, Annika against—but the rest of the design had been finalized. Then they had hugged and cried and reminisced about how Maia had once pretended to marry their friend Shy from temple with a paper towel on her head when she was eleven.

"Yes!" Annika said now, springing up from her chair, "Okay, yes. Ness, take her to the dressing room."

She grabbed Vanessa's arm when Maia had left the room.

"Don't mention anything about a certain tiny-yet-hot gynecologist," Annika whispered. "She doesn't know about me and Gabi."

Vanessa gave her a sympathetic look.

"Oh, honey," she said, sighing.

Annika shoved her away. "I don't need that shit right now, Vanessa."

Vanessa put her hands up placatingly and left the back room.

Annika turned to the dress rack at the back of her office and flipped through dresses and suits and jumpsuits in garment bags, looking for Maia's name.

Grabbing the correct garment bag, she walked to the dressing room, two stalls partitioned by flimsy drywall with a dusky-rose-colored fabric that acted as doors.

"Here, Mai," she said and handed the garment bag to her sister through the curtain. "Just remember, it's only half done. I'll add the buttons and final details once we know how this fits you. We still have six months until your wedding date, so there's plenty of time to get it perfect."

"I know, I know," Maia called impatiently.

Annika chewed her thumbnail as she and Vanessa waited in the salon for Maia to emerge, Annika studiously ignoring the couch and the memories associated with it.

"Just so you know," Maia called from the dressing room, "I think it's great you're reflecting on your emotional availability even if you're not dating someone."

Annika shot Vanessa a glare over her shoulder as she leaned against the register, and Vanessa sat on the stool behind it.

"I know you don't like talking about it, but women with ADHD can have a harder time sustaining romantic relationships in adulthood," Maia continued, and Annika rubbed at her temple with her right forefinger and thumb.

"Mai, can we not talk about this during your fitting," Annika grumbled.

"I'm just saying," Maia said, and she pushed the curtain aside as she strode out in the half-made dress, "it's good to talk about these things. I'm happy to help you find a therapist if you ever want to give counseling another shot."

"Okay," Annika said, ignoring the final part of her sister's sentence. She was doing just fine on her own, thank you very much. Besides, her ADHD didn't seem to be as much of a problem since she'd left school. "Up on the pedestal, please."

"I love this shape," Maia said. She smoothed her hands across the bustline on her slim chest, conversation abandoned. "Makes me look like I actually have boobs."

"For once," Annika agreed and circled her sister, vulva pincushion on her wrist and fully stocked. "Can you breathe with the bodice the way it is?"

Maia took a deep breath and nodded. Then Annika had her swish around, sit, bend over, and crouch just for good measure before she marked the changes she needed to make with pins and on the design sketch.

"Don't be late tonight," Maia said as she pushed open the door after she'd changed back into her clothes. A gust of frigid air from the harbor blew into their heated oasis as she did. Before she stepped onto the street, though, she turned back to Annika and let the door thunk shut behind her. "Dad gave me his credit card for booking the trip and told me to tell you not to worry about paying him back, he just wants you to enjoy the trip," she said.

Annika was acutely aware that her career was not the most lucrative, especially when Maia made an absurd amount doing what she did, and hated when it was brought up like this.

"Yeah, yeah, whatever." She waved Maia off.

"Oh, and I'm pretty sure Gabi's been hooking up with someone, so come prepared to grill her," Maia added with a sly slant of her eyebrow.

Annika froze.

"W-what makes you say that?" she choked out and pretended to cough to cover it up.

Vanessa shot her a look that let her know she wasn't fooling anyone.

"She's just been very…peppy the last few times I've seen her," Maia replied with an irreverent wave of her hand. "Oh, and I'm almost sure she had a hickey when I saw her after New Year's."

Annika, who vividly remembered giving Gabi that hickey while Gabi straddled her lap and rode her fingers, willed herself not to blush.

"Woah, really?" she stammered.

"You're being weird," Maia said, surveying her through the three paneled mirror with a skeptical eye.

"Just hungry. Forgot to eat lunch again, too focused on work," she said and patted her stomach with a self-deprecating laugh. "There's that old ADHD, I guess."

Maia shot her a big-sisterly look of reproval and sighed. "I have a granola bar if you want."

Annika shook her head, and Maia shrugged as if to say *I tried.*

"Well, anyway, I'll see you later," she said and turned to leave.

She paused in the door and turned back to Annika, eyes gone soft.

"The dress already looks amazing, Niki," she said, a quaver in her voice.

Annika smiled, and then she and Maia hugged, letting more wintery air into the shop.

"Enough sisterly affection, close that damn door," Vanessa whined from behind Annika.

They pulled apart after a moment, and both wiped their eyes.

"I have a four p.m. call, so I really need to go. Bye, Niki, bye, Vanessa," Maia said and fluttered her gloved hand in a wave as she headed out into the cold. The door banged shut behind her with a jingle.

Annika watched through the glass door until Maia'd turned left up an alley.

"Dude," Vanessa said, with feeling, "you really are fucked."

Annika let her head drop against the icy glass of the door and groaned.

Chapter Twenty

Gabi was, again, the last one to show up for this meeting of Maia Silberberg's Bachelorette Planning Committee.

She'd assisted on a very messy birth at the end of the day and needed to take a hot shower to thoroughly scrub herself when she was done. Then she'd had to diffuse her hair so it wouldn't freeze in the subfreezing temperatures of an early February day in Maine.

She might also have been stalling being with Annika and Maia in the same room. The last time they'd been together, the three of them, had been before Thanksgiving, before Annika had invited her to trivia.

Before they'd kissed.

Before they'd slept together.

Before Gabi began suspecting that she might be developing more than friendly feelings for Annika.

Gabi's hand shook with anxiety as she raised it to knock on the front door of Maia's apartment, the building as sleek and modern and upkept as Maia was herself.

"Okay, Dr. Mendon," she whispered to herself, "you can do this. Just pretend you haven't seen Annika naked."

But that was the wrong thing to bring up because now her mind pulled up selections from the dozens of images it housed of Annika without clothes and in very compromising positions.

She groaned internally and shook her head to clear it as the door opened, and then there was Annika in the flesh.

They stared at each other.

Neither of them said a thing.

Annika began to dip her head forward but then jerked it to a stop, like she had been about to kiss Gabi hello as she usually did when Gabi arrived at her apartment.

Gabi's own lips itched for that kiss. Even though she had seen Annika less than twenty-four hours ago and had had several satisfying orgasms with her, her body ached for her touch.

"Hey, Gabi," Annika managed, an awkward smile lurching across her lips as she forced her way through the tension.

"Hi, Ni—Annika," Gabi fumbled.

Annika seemed to visibly relax at the sight of Gabi's nerves. She sunk a hip against the metal doorframe and said coyly, "Long time no see."

She bit her lower lip, and Gabi felt a flush creep into her cheeks.

She opened her mouth to respond, but then Maia's voice called from behind Annika, "Is that Gabi? Let her in, you weirdo."

Annika rolled her eyes at Gabi and held the door open wider for her to step through. The elbow of her jacket brushed against Annika's stomach on her way in, and they both flinched.

Annika turned wordlessly and padded on socked feet into the living room while Gabi hung her jacket up on the wooden pegs Maia had installed by the door. She kicked her boots off onto the mat with Annika's sensible sherpa-lined duck boots, Maia's fur-topped lace-ups, and a pair of much bigger rugged-looking ones that must belong to Jonnie.

Taking a breath, she steeled herself to face the sisters.

They both turned their faces up to her when she walked in. Maia was perched once again on the floor, laptop and notebook spread out on the coffee table, bottle of red uncorked and breathing beside them.

Annika, in her favorite green hoodie and black jeans, sat tucked up in her habitual corner on the couch, munching on a bowl of pretzel thins and hummus. She looked just as soft and inviting as she had the last time Gabi had seen her seated on this couch.

Only now, Gabi's body knew intimately how lovely it felt to be pressed up against her side, the feel of Annika's hands traveling soothingly over Gabi's skin beneath her sweater as they made out slowly on her couch.

She was struck, as she often was, by how different the sisters were. Maia's sleek brown locks highlighted and slicked back into her signature high pony, upper lids lightly lined with brown eyeliner, skin dewy. Annika, her darker hair tossed up into a messy bun, bangs frizzing and undercut a bit grown out. One willowy and slim all over, one bottom heavy and athletically built.

But the expressions on their faces and in their identical brown eyes matched. Both faces of these women she...*cared* for were lit up by her presence.

"Hey, babe," Maia said and stood to give Gabi a tight hug. Gabi's gaze flitted to Annika over her shoulder. She raised her eyebrows in a private smile at Gabi as she crunched down on another pretzel.

"Hey, girl," Gabi replied as they pulled apart, and she smiled at Maia. She took the corner of the couch opposite from Annika and tried to scrunch in her already short limbs as tightly as possible.

Maia poured wine into glasses.

"Gab, there are some snacks in the kitchen. I had a late call so I didn't have time to prepare a full spread, but if you're hungry I can whip you up something," Maia said and handed her a glass of wine across the coffee table, "if you didn't get a chance to eat after your shift ended."

Her words conjured memories of midnight grilled cheese and Annika's body pressing her into her couch. She could tell that Annika was thinking along the same lines because she felt her shift at the other end of the couch. It took a greater force of will than she'd thought to keep herself from glancing at Annika.

She took a big gulp of the wine and said, overly bright, "I'm good, thanks, Mai. Let's get into these plans."

Maia nodded sharply once and began to sort through her notes, but then she stopped, eyes suddenly piercing into Gabi's.

"Girl," she said to Gabi, "are you hooking up with someone?"

Gabi spluttered and spit the sip of red wine she'd just taken back into her glass, coughing.

"What the fuck, Maia?" Annika exclaimed, reaching over to take a napkin from the stack on the coffee table and passed it to Gabi. "I thought you said you were going to ease her into the conversation."

Maia shrugged innocently and said, "I decided a more direct approach would work better. Less time for her to be evasive."

Gabi shot Annika a look as she wiped her mouth, confused why Annika would be plotting with Maia to interrogate her about her sex life, which Annika was a very large part of. Who was she kidding—her sex life *was* Annika. There had been no one else since they'd kissed the first time, no one who had even caught her eye.

Gabi knew what that meant, the dangerous game she played with her own heart, but she couldn't stop herself from playing it.

Gabi opened her mouth to respond but what came out was, "Mai, can you get me some water?"

"Of course," Maia said, and she shot to her feet and pranced to the kitchen.

Gabi immediately turned to Annika.

"What the fuck, Niki, you couldn't have warned me?" she whispered.

"I did," Annika emphatically shot back. "You must have missed my text."

Gabi nodded, knowing it was entirely possible.

She thought for a moment. Considered how awful it made her feel lying to Maia.

"I'm going to tell her," Gabi murmured and saw Annika's eyes go saucer wide, "not about, you know, us"—she gestured between her and Annika—"but that I am...*seeing* someone, but it's just sex."

Something in Annika's expression seemed to wilt and close off, but she nodded.

"Whatever you want, Gab," Annika said softly. She reached across to squeeze Gabi's hand once quickly.

What do you *want?* she was dying to ask Annika. *Are you bored of me yet?*

But then Maia returned with Gabi's glass of water, and Annika was back on her side of the couch, a safe distance away.

Gabi took a sip of water and, in typical Gabi fashion, blurted out, "I am seeing someone, but it's just sex, mostly."

Maia squealed and jumped up to engulf Gabi in a tackle hug. It made her feel awful for all the vital truths she wasn't telling this woman who'd loved her so much for so long.

"Ah! Gab, this is amazing," Maia almost yelled, voice high-pitched and girlish as she sat back on her heels on her spot on the rug and clapped her hands together, a gesture that reminded Gabi forcibly of Annika. "Okay, tell me everything. Who is she? How did you meet her? Is the sex good? What do her boobs look like?"

"What do her boobs look like?" Gabi asked with raised eyebrows.

Maia shrugged. "I don't know, I'd usually ask about his dick, but that doesn't apply here."

"And that's my cue to go get more snacks," Annika said, getting up from the couch, face obscured from Gabi's sight.

Maia rolled her eyes at Annika's back.

Gabi decided to tell her as much of the truth as she could handle.

"Remember when I went to trivia with Annika back around Thanksgiving?" she began.

Not strictly a lie, she reasoned with herself. She and Annika had kissed for the first time after trivia.

"Oooh," Maia crooned, "please tell me she isn't one of Annika's exes."

"God, no, that would be too weird," Gabi said, thinking hard. "She works at Annika's climbing gym."

"Oh my God, Melissa? That receptionist that flirts with everyone?" Maia said.

"Mm-hmm," Gabi continued, "we hit it off at trivia. We've been hooking up consistently since."

Okay, she reasoned with herself, there was enough of the truth in there for her conscience.

She hoped.

"And the sex?" Maia said. "I know you've never really considered yourself a sexual person. Is it different with a woman?"

"It's..." Gabi thought of the way Annika made her feel, like every light in her brain had turned on at once, flooding her with clarity. How alive and in her body she was in that moment right before Annika tipped her over with her fingers or her hips or her tongue. How obliteratingly good it felt when she fell. How making Annika come was the most powerful hit of confidence and connection she'd ever tasted. "Really, *really* different with a woman. In a very, very good way."

She felt her cheeks getting hot and took a sip of wine to steel herself.

Maia grinned at the look on her face and said, "Wow, Gab, you must really like this girl. I've never seen your face, like, *glow* like that before."

Of course, that was the moment Annika reentered the room.

"I, uh, I don't know about that," Gabi stammered. "Maybe it's just because someone is actually paying attention to *me* during sex for once."

"Orgasms are magical," Annika agreed, bun bobbing as she nodded her head and crunched into a baby carrot.

"God, Niki, did you eat at all today, or just shotgun a cold brew with a shot of espresso from Dunkin'," Maia asked.

Annika mimed zipping her lips together and took another bite from her carrot.

Maia turned to Gabi and jabbed her thumb at Annika. "I swear, I have to drag her into health, kicking and screaming."

Gabi—who knew by now every contour and rigid dip of Annika's lean muscles beneath the softness of her body, who had felt her strength when she'd suddenly flipped Gabi over onto her stomach to eat her out from behind, who had eaten meals Annika had made for her, sometimes elaborate, sometimes simple—thought this was an outdated view of the woman Maia's sister had grown to be.

But Gabi also knew Annika could be a little dreamy, erratic, locked in her own sense of the world, oblivious to time as it passed her by.

Annika flipped Maia off.

"Maybe I should start a *giving Annika unsolicited opinions on how she lives her life* jar, see how you like it," Annika said, an edge in her voice beyond the usual sarcasm, Gabi noted.

"I just want you to live long enough to meet my kids," Maia said, hugging Annika's shins and resting her head on her knees.

Annika rolled her eyes but placed a gentle hand on her sister's hair, stroking it lovingly.

Gabi looked at the pair with a pang in her chest. For all they fought, they loved each other fiercely, told each other everything.

It suddenly hit her. Not only was *she* lying to Maia, but she was making Annika lie to her sister as well.

And for what, because they had mind-blowingly good sex?

Deep down, Gabi knew that wasn't everything they were to each other, but she refused to look at that tender, mushy place too hard.

She couldn't stop thinking about it, though, as she listened to Maia and Annika bicker about restaurants and rental apartments and whether or not it was okay for a group of mostly straight women to go to a Dolly Parton drag show.

Annika was lying to her sister, and she was doing it for Gabi.

Starting this with Annika, giving in to her desire for her, had been a terrible idea.

"You've been quiet for the last hour or so," Annika said to her as they left Maia's apartment together. "Everything okay?"

Annika flexed her mittened fingers slightly so they grazed down the back of Gabi's bare hand. Reflexively, Gabi shoved her hand into the pocket of her winter coat and buried her face more firmly in her thick scarf, trying not to see the flash of confusion mingled with hurt in Annika's brown eyes.

"Listen," Gabi started when they were about a block away from Maia's place, "I don't think we should hang out anymore."

Annika froze on the spot and stared down at her, cheeks red from cold.

"What? Why?" she replied, her words puffing out in clouds of mist in the frigid night air.

"It's been so, so good, these last six weeks," Gabi went on, lips quirked up in a smile despite herself, "but I realized tonight that it's getting kind of...complicated."

"If you want us to stop hanging out because you don't want me anymore, fine," Annika said, and a sudden fire filled her eyes, a ferocity in her voice, "I can handle that, because I'm a big girl and I'll respect your wishes. But"—she took a step closer to Gabi, and her arm wrapped around Gabi's waist, their bodies obscured by their winter layers—"if you're ending this because you're trying to protect my relationship with Maia, or because you think you know better than me about the consequences of this thing between us, think again, babe." Gabi swallowed. "I don't need protection or someone thinking they know what's good for me better than I do."

Gabi knew Annika's anger was about more than just their relationship, but she persisted.

"We're lying to Maia," Gabi said in a small voice, and Annika's eyes went soft, fire banked for now. "I sat there, and I lied to her about hooking up with some other woman, and you were sitting *right there*."

"I was." Annika nodded, and then, to Gabi's amazement, she

grinned, pulled Gabi tighter against her. "And I heard you tell her the sex was very, very good."

"Oh my God, Niki," Gabi said. She raised her hands to slap her chest in annoyance but ruined the effect by resting them there. "That is not the point."

Annika cocked her head to one side, surveying Gabi thoughtfully for a minute before she spoke again.

"Let's say I agree with you. We stop hanging out," Annika said finally.

"I don't want to stop hanging out with you, Niki, you're my friend," Gabi said. The idea of excising Annika completely from her life made her ill.

Annika laughed and said, "Do you think the second we saw each other again, with Maia not there, we wouldn't be all over each other?"

Gabi tipped her head to Annika's chest in frustration. She knew if she saw Annika one-on-one, it would be impossible to resist the allure of her lips, her curves.

She groaned and shook her head against Annika's sternum.

"Yeah," Annika sighed out, "me either."

"Fuck," Gabi replied, head still buried in Annika's chest. "I just hate lying to Maia, and I hate you lying to Maia for me."

"Would it help if I said I like you, hanging out with you," Annika amended hastily, "more than I feel guilty about lying to Maia?"

Gabi felt her heart wiggle at the words *I like you* like a lovestruck teen giddy with a crush.

"It might make me the shittiest friend, but I like hanging out with you that much, too," Gabi said and raised her head to meet Annika's. She went up on her tiptoes, and Annika bent down at the same time. Their eager lips met in the middle and warmed each other's frosty faces.

"Besides," Annika murmured as she gripped Gabi's jaw with one mittened hand and held her flush against her with her other, "Maia thinks she knows everything and can read everyone. It will do her good to be kept in the dark for a little while."

"Cruel." Gabi giggled and then caught Annika's lips with her own again.

Even though they'd seen each other last night, Gabi was hungry for her skin. She didn't think about the ungodly early time she had to wake up the next morning, or the long day she'd had today. Only listened to her heart, for once paying attention to what it murmured to her.

"Come home with me?" she whispered to Annika.

"Yes," Annika gasped against her mouth, "absolutely."

Chapter Twenty-one

S orry," a sleepy voice murmured beside Annika in the dark as the sound of a phone alarm blared off to her right, "go back to sleep."

Annika rolled over to see Gabi, dressed only in a washed and worn sleep shirt, standing up from the bed. The outline of her short curvy legs was just visible in the light from the streetlamp as she stretched before padding softly over the hardwood floor to the bathroom.

Annika checked the time on Gabi's phone, five thirty a.m., and collapsed back with a groan. She nestled into the warm pillows and drifted off again.

"Niki, baby," Gabi murmured an indeterminate amount of time later, "I have to leave for work now."

Annika cracked one eye open to see a fully put together Gabi crouched before her, hand gently stroking her bare right shoulder where it peeked above the mountain of covers.

She grumbled sleepily, and Gabi grinned, then leaned in to press a sweet kiss to her forehead.

"You are adorable when you're grumpy," she crooned and kissed Annika's cheek, moved down her jawline lightly until their mouths met, and Annika was, if not wide, at least more awake than she had been a minute ago.

She fished her arms out from beneath the covers and wrapped them around Gabi, pulled her on top of her as Annika rolled to her back, and kissed Gabi deeper.

Gabi gave a brief shriek of surprise, which was quickly stifled by Annika's mouth.

"Mmm," Gabi said, eyes still closed as she pulled back, a smile gracing her face. Annika's heart swelled at the look of absolute happiness there. "That's a nice way to start the day. You should stay over more often."

"Okay," Annika croaked out immediately, surprising herself, and Gabi laughed.

"Ugh, despite how beautiful you look first thing in the morning, I do need to get to the hospital," Gabi said and stood up.

Annika let go of her reluctantly.

Gabi said, "You can stay in bed for as long as you want. There's coffee in the kitchen and the front door will lock behind you automatically."

"Okay," Annika croaked again, already halfway back to sleep.

Gabi leaned in for one more kiss and then murmured, "Bye, baby. Have a good day."

Annika turned over in bed to watch Gabi leave the room.

Then she flopped onto her back and stared at the ceiling while she listened to Gabi bustle around her apartment as she got ready for the day, waiting for the front door to slam shut.

She closed her eyes, intending to go back to sleep, not accustomed to being awake before seven thirty. But her mind was running and roaring right along now.

She was in Gabi's bed.

Where she had spent the night.

The *whole* night.

Doing things other than sex.

Cuddling things. Talking and laughing things. Gazing into each other's eyes until one of them fell asleep things.

They had kissed and kissed and kissed, both of them too tired to do much more, until Gabi had, almost shyly, asked her to hold her as she fell asleep. Annika had convinced herself she would sneak out once Gabi was out.

She had never slept well with girlfriends and lovers in the past, preferring to leave late for the comfort of her own bed rather than toss and turn fitfully in someone else's sheets. She loved her space, being able to sprawl across the mattress or cocoon herself into her blankets, Vera Wang curled at her feet or near her head, never worried about someone else's comfort.

But then, last night, as Gabi's body loosened with sleep, Annika's own breath had deepened to match Gabi's. Her limbs had sunk with exhaustion into the warmth of the bed, her own lids closing. She had spent the whole night wrapped around Gabi and had barely had a dream.

It was disconcerting.

Sure, an intense crush on someone she had agreed to no-feelings sex with was one thing. It was why she had never stayed over at Gabi's before, never asked her to stay at her apartment. She half dreaded what the morning might reveal.

But now that she'd done it, all she felt was an intense longing for Gabi to come back, for them to spend a lazy morning together. Gabi could read and drink her coffee while Annika sketched in her daily picture journal beside her, the whole day spread out before them, theirs to spend together.

A floorboard creaked, and Annika turned to see Gabi, her work bag slung over her shoulder and a travel coffee mug grasped in her hand, leaning in the bedroom doorway.

"I thought you were in such a rush to get out the door?" Annika said.

"I am," Gabi said, a soft smile on her lips. "I just wanted to get another look at you in my bed."

Annika felt an awful, gooey feeling flood through her at the words. As if she wasn't already freaked out enough by how waking up with Gabi had affected her.

She tossed a pillow at Gabi and said, "Scram, those vaginas won't heal themselves."

Gabi laughed and, with one final quick kiss to Annika's lips, left for work.

Annika lay back in Gabi's bed and closed her eyes again. Let the lingering taste of Gabi's kiss, coffee and mint toothpaste, slip over her tongue.

Then she grabbed a pillow, shoved it over her face, and screamed into it. It didn't help much since the pillow smelled like Gabi.

She needed to get out of here. Despite the outrageously early hour, she jumped up out of bed and threw her clothes on, ignored the half full pot of coffee Gabi must have made for her in favor of rushing out the door.

She drove distractedly to her apartment, took a quick shower, and then called Vanessa, hair still dripping onto the collar of her T-shirt.

"She called me *baby*," she said by way of greeting when Vanessa picked up, "when she woke me up this morning. Because I stayed at her house last night. And the worst of it is, I wanted us to go to a farmers market together, Ness, *a farmers market*."

"Whoa, whoa, slow down, man," Vanessa said, the sound of cutlery and clinking mugs filling the background. "I'm literally just having coffee now, how can you already be in a full-blown crisis?"

Annika pictured Vanessa, her long blond hair down around her shoulders, wrapped in the cobalt-blue terry cloth robe she loved, opposite miniscule Mindy with a cashmere pashmina around her shoulders, as they sat at their breakfast table together the way they did every morning.

"Start from the beginning and go slow," Vanessa said. "Also, I'm switching you to speakerphone because I don't want to repeat this all to Min."

Annika took a breath and then told them all about staying over at Gabi's. How it felt so good to hold her as she slept, to wake up to her in the morning.

"I was lying there, and I was thinking, Wow, I really want her to come back and spend the day with me. We could do nothing, read at home, go for a walk by the lighthouse—"

"Go to the farmers market," Mindy added excitedly.

"Yeah," Annika agreed with a wistful sigh.

"What's up with the farmers market? It's fucking February in Maine. The only thing growing here right now is icicles," Vanessa demanded.

"It's just an analogy for something tedious and domestic, love," Mindy supplied, voice sweet as honey for her cantankerous wife.

"Yeah," Annika agreed sadly. She dropped her head against the counter that divided her kitchen from her living room. "I want to wake up and do all sorts of silly domestic shit with her, like fight about how to load the dishwasher and send each other recipes to make for dinner."

There was a collective gasp from the other side of the line.

"That's serious, Nik," Mindy said gently. "I've never heard you like this before."

"I fucking *know*," she whined miserably. The cool surface of her Formica countertop soothed her inflamed cheeks. "What am I going to do, you guys?"

"Two options," Vanessa stated matter-of-factly. "One, tell her how you feel and let the chips fall where they may."

"Two," Vanessa said quickly before Annika could open her mouth to interject. Annika frowned at her phone where it lay next to her face on the counter. "Stop sleeping with her and get some distance. There's no reason for you to be around each other so much now that the bachelorette party is planned. You don't even have to talk to each other before the event starts."

Neither of those options sounded particularly good to Annika.

"There's no way for things to stay exactly as they are, but for them to suck less for me?" Annika asked hopefully.

The couple on the other end laughed loudly with each other.

She really needed to make friends with more single queers, Annika thought.

"Dude," Vanessa said when her laughter died down, "it's literally hilarious seeing you have real feelings for someone, finally."

"What my lovely wife means," Mindy clarified, an exasperated glare audible in her voice, "is that it's very mature of you to have allowed yourself to fall for someone, even if that someone is kind of not a smart choice."

"I'm plenty mature, I own a fucking business for fuck's sake," Annika muttered. She was pretty sick of people treating her like she was their inexperienced kid sister.

"That's not what we meant, man," Vanessa said. "We know you can handle your shit financially and businessly, I see it every day. It just seems like sometimes you're so concerned about getting hurt or rejected, you push away the person you're seeing before they even get the chance to know you. And you haven't done that with Gabi."

"Yeah, well, it hurts like hell," Annika mumbled. "I liked it better when I was an emotionally unavailable hyperindependent loner who dated people she didn't even like that much."

"Ha, yeah," Vanessa said, "that is the trade-off. When you let yourself feel, you feel *everything*. The good, the bad, the wicked ugly."

There was a pause and then Vanessa said, "So, what are you going to do, Nik?"

"I don't know yet," she replied dismally, then hung up the phone.

In the end, she chose neither of Vanessa's very sensible options, but a third, more unhealthy and masochistic one.

She kept hooking up with Gabi. Kept cooking her late-night dinners and holding her while they slept. Kept falling deeper and deeper down the rabbit hole of her feelings, leaving Gabi none the wiser.

Part Six

The Bachelorette Party

March–May

Chapter Twenty-two

Gabi knew she was in full denial when it came to this situation with Annika. Had known it since her birthday in March, her first single in eight years.

Her attending brought in a cake for her, and her residency friends took her out for after-work drinks to celebrate. Rachel sent her flowers and cupcakes from her favorite local bakery, which she didn't usually do. Gabi suspected this was motivated by her fear that Gabi would become immediately depressed by being reminded she was single on her birthday.

She thought that might be the extent of her birthday celebrations. Despite all the changes she'd made in the past year, thirty-one didn't seem that momentous an age. So, it took her a full half an hour to notice what Annika had done when she came home.

She was walking back to the couch with a glass of water in her hand, *Raya and the Last Dragon* cued up on her screen, when she glanced at the wall behind the couch and froze.

There on the wall, hung up neatly in its frame, was her favorite print. Gabi circled on the spot and then ran into her bedroom.

All her prints and pictures and posters had been taken from the box that had sat in her bedroom since the day she'd moved in, and hung throughout the apartment.

The place instantly felt homier, the walls no longer barren and white but filled with color and Gabi's personality.

Before she could wonder who had broken into her house and reverse-vandalized it, she noticed an envelope sitting on her kitchen table.

She opened it to find the confetti texture of homemade paper, the edges ragged fibers, the surface a bit lumpy. Her name was on the front in neat script, and on the inside *Happy B-day, Sex Friend* was scrawled in Annika's hurried handwriting. She wrote like she thought, like she had already moved on to the next sentence while she finished writing the previous one.

Beneath the message was a heart and Annika's name. Gabi traced the looping letters with her fingertips as she felt tears slip down her cheeks.

"Rach," she said, as soon as Rachel had answered the phone, "I have a huge problem."

"So, let me get this straight," Rachel said as she sat on Gabi's couch and cradled a mug of tea spiked with whiskey half an hour later. If her husband had complaints about her fleeing into the night to comfort Gabi, he hadn't voiced them.

"You've been having sex with a woman regularly for *three months*, and oh yeah, that woman happens to be *Annika Silberberg*, the little sister of your other best friend and co–maid of honor in her wedding. And to top it all off, you're lying to her about it."

Gabi winced. She'd come out to Rachel shortly after her talk with Maia, so the woman part wasn't a surprise. Who the woman was in particular was certainly a shock to her, though.

"It, uh, sounds pretty bad when you lay it all out like that," she said and stared into the depths of her own mug.

Rachel leaned forward and rested her hand on Gabi's forearm.

"None of it is bad per se," she hedged. "I mean, the lying isn't great. It's just a lot for you to be withholding from your supposed *best* friends."

"I know," Gabi said. "I swear it had nothing to do with me not wanting to confide in you and more to do with me not knowing *how* to confide in you."

"What do you mean? You think I'm some big homophobe or something?" Rachel said, affronted.

"Just because you don't hate something doesn't mean you understand it, Rach," Gabi said gently. "You're married to a man you've been in love with since you were twenty. You guys have a home and a baby together. You're moving into the next phase of adulthood, and I'm just starting out in this whole new world, dating again, trying to figure it all out with women."

"Sounds like you figured it out pretty well with one woman," Rachel retorted, and Gabi buried her face in her palms and tucked into her knees.

"Ugh," she groaned, "Annika…she just sort of happened. I went to her for advice, and then suddenly, I was daydreaming about kissing her. And then I was actually kissing her, and it felt amazing. Like my whole body came alive just from her lips on mine."

"That's some good kissing," Rachel said, and Gabi nodded emphatically in agreement.

"It's *unbelievable* kissing, Rach. She's just so *sexy*. Even the way she looks at me turns me on," Gabi said. "And she is so, so sweet, too. I mean, look at what she did for me"—she gestured at the poster that hung above the couch—"and I'm not even her girlfriend."

"Why aren't you her girlfriend, if you like her so much?" Rachel asked, taking a sip of her tea. "Because I got to say, babe, I've never seen you like this about someone. Not even when you first started dating Matt, but that kind of makes more sense now, retrospectively."

"For one thing, she hasn't asked me to be her girlfriend. We just keep saying we're *hanging out*," Gabi replied, using her fingers as air quotes. "For another, I don't know. I just was someone's girlfriend for eight years, and I kind of lost myself in it. I let him decide everything about our lives while I focused on school until one day I looked around and barely recognized anything."

"Yeah, but that was totally different," Rachel said. "You were young and in med school and you let Matt carry you along with him. And *he* let you be carried. Does Annika seem like she's going to let you be carried?"

Sometimes, it seemed like Annika was going to consume her in the storm of her, Gabi thought. But no, she wouldn't let Gabi just coast. She challenged her, made her think about who she was and what she wanted.

"She's always asking me what I want, giving me space to check in, letting me set the pace," Gabi said.

"So?" Rachel prompted. "Do you want her to be your girlfriend?"

Gabi looked around her home, at the art now hung on her walls, at the bralette she knew lounged in her laundry basket from the last time Annika slept over.

"I like her so much," she admitted, "but I don't know if I want something serious now."

"And she feels serious?" Rachel asked softly.

Gabi didn't answer the question, which was answer enough.

"I should probably stop sleeping with her until I figure myself out, huh," Gabi said, and Rachel nodded.

She didn't stop sleeping with Annika, though.

Obviously.

It was too good when they were together, too hot and sweet and silly all at once.

"Maia wants to invite you over for Seder next week," Annika said one night in early April. They lounged in Annika's bed, and Annika traced patterns along her bare back as a chilly spring rain pattered against the window.

Gabi was sleepy from sex and lulled by the warmth of Annika's presence beside her. "Oh?" she replied, her cheek resting on her stacked palms, forearms flat to the bed. She raised her eyebrows in surprise at Annika.

"Mm-hmm," Annika said. She shifted to place soft kisses along Gabi's back from hips to shoulders, making Gabi shiver, "She knows you can't go home for Passover because you have to work, and she wants to invite you to join us."

"Would it be okay with you if I went?" Gabi asked. She'd had Shabbat dinner with the Silberbergs several times since she'd moved to Portland and had always felt embraced by them like family.

"Gab, you know you don't have to ask me that," Annika said. She sat up and rested her hand on the center of Gabi's back lightly.

Because you're not my girlfriend rang like a gong through Gabi's head.

"You were Maia's friend long before you and I were ever anything. I don't want you to feel like what we have gets in the way of that," Annika said, her torso now pressed over Gabi's bare back, her lips mouthing along her jaw and ear.

The sensations swimming under Gabi's skin muddled her thoughts.

"It's so hot when you're considerate," Gabi said. She let out a whimper and bit her lip as Annika's hand slid down her stomach and ghosted between her legs.

"I want you to come," Annika whispered in her ear, and Gabi wasn't sure if she meant now or to Seder, but she didn't really care because Annika's fingers were inside her and the heel of her palm was pressed right *there*. Annika's body caged and surrounded and overwhelmed her as she drove Gabi's pleasure higher and higher with her fingers and soft words whispered into her ear, nipped bites at her neck and jaw. Gabi's hands gripped into the sheets, and she moaned and moaned, and her whole body clenched and shuddered and then finally, finally released.

"I love watching you do that," Annika murmured in her ear and placed tender kisses on Gabi's temple, soothed her body in sweeping strokes of her rough hands as Gabi panted, body wrecked.

Annika slipped to the side, cradled her from behind, and said, "Stay tonight?"

I want to keep you, Gabi thought as she drifted into sleep, Annika's easy breaths and warm body at her back.

Maia invited her to Seder the next day, and Gabi happily accepted the invite, showing up at the Silberberg residence at six o'clock on the following Wednesday, tray of matzah candy in hand.

"Gabi, shaina, it's so nice to see you." Annika and Maia's mom Nora greeted her at the door with a hug as tight as her slender arms could manage.

She was Maia in thirty years and after attending an Ayurvedic healing retreat. Sleek light brown hair gone gray at the temples hung around her slim shoulders and fell nearly to her waist, and she wore black stretchy pants and a flowy green velvet top embroidered with yellow roses.

There was something about her eyes, though, about the tilt of her mouth, that spoke of mischief. It made Gabi want to smile because it reminded her of Annika.

Maia and Annika were already bickering in the kitchen over bowls of peeled vegetables, Maia in a blue and white striped shirt dress and knee-high brown leather riding boots, hair parted in the middle and pulled back in a shiny bun at the nape of her neck. Pearl studs glinted in her ears and a simple gold chain with a minuscule *M* charm hung around her neck. Annika wore a sweater dress that Gabi recognized as belonging to Maia, and her dark waves were styled and fell loosely around her shoulders.

"Gabi, don't you think Niki looks nice with her hair curled?" Maia prompted as soon as Gabi walked into the kitchen, immediately recruiting Gabi to her side in the never-ending sisterly war.

"It looks very nice, yeah," Gabi agreed, though she secretly thought that Annika could be dressed in a potato sack with mud in her hair and Gabi would probably still want to kiss her. She wrapped her arm around Maia's shoulders and leaned into her friend's side in greeting.

Annika rolled her eyes at Gabi. Her face looked luminous and dewy, upper lids lined with a tasteful wing, cheeks rosy with blush—a polished and refined version of herself that sat heavily on her like a too-thick coat of varnish.

"My lovely sister insisted she give me a makeover for Seder," Annika replied snarkily as she plucked a carrot from the bowl and peeled it with efficient flicks of her wrist, "like I'm thirteen again."

"*My* lovely sister showed up wearing an oversized button-down shirt and black dress pants like she was a bar mitzvah boy that had to borrow his older brother's suit," Maia shot back.

"It's called fashion, sweetie, look it up," Annika drawled, then tossed her hair and vamped like a model with her peeler.

Gabi laughed, and Annika caught her eye, her grin growing wider. Maia shook her head exasperatedly and huffed, but the corners of her mouth tipped up.

Before she could respond, their mother called for Maia to come help her in the dining room down the hall.

"Coming!" Maia called back. "Gab, do you mind helping Annika finish up in here? We just need to, like, wrap up peeling and chopping the veggies for the salad and then whip up three cups of salt water for the karpas."

"On it," Gabi said. She took the peeler Maia had abandoned and sat down in front of Annika as Maia left the room, the heels of her boots clacking firm and precise against the wood floors as she went.

"I hate that she's always doing that to me," Annika muttered.

The more time Gabi spent with the sisters, together and on their own, the more she realized how complex their relationship really was. She only had brothers, and as much as she loved them, if either of them ever tried to dictate how she should live, like Maia sometimes did to Annika, she'd laugh in their face.

"She just wants what's best for you, Niki," Gabi responded quietly.

"I know, I just wish…" Annika began and then trailed off, staring out the window on the opposite wall.

Gabi reached out and placed her peeler-free hand over Annika's where it rested on the kitchen table. She said nothing, gave Annika the space she needed to get her thoughts in order.

Over the past months, Gabi had learned that despite her cool exterior, Annika felt things deeply and all at once. She kept so much of her emotions bottled up that in order to get to the deeper bits, Gabi had to allow Annika to ease open, rather than try to force her to.

It reminded her of when she'd first gone tide-pooling down the shore, and her brother Eitan had taught her to hum to periwinkles. You had to be patient, to allow the vibrations to coax it to poke its head out of its shell rather than bash the shell against the rock to force the soft vulnerable animal inside to show itself. If you stuck your fingers in and tried to pry it out, it would just curl up deeper and harder against the intrusion.

If she pushed Annika too hard or too fast, Annika would get overwhelmed and turn prickly, clam up and shut down and push Gabi away. But if Gabi was patient and waited, let her sift through the turbulent funnel cloud of her thoughts, Annika would come to her. She'd lay her head in Gabi's lap and let Gabi draw her out of her protective space.

It made Gabi wonder how many women had had that patience with Annika before. If Annika had ever even allowed them to try.

"I just wish she saw *me* rather than her idea of me, you know?" Annika mused after a moment's thought.

Gabi gave her a tender smile and squeezed her hand. Their gazes held a moment longer, and the tension in Annika's face melted as the moments passed.

I see you, Gabi thought to herself but didn't dare say. The phrase revealed far too much about her own feelings.

They broke apart when Maia bustled back into the kitchen.

The rest of the night, Annika was just out of reach. Nora sat Gabi across from a cousin and Annika far down the long rectangular table that stretched from the dining room into the living room. She watched Maia and Annika flit around, helping their mother and father run the Seder, while little kids fidgeted through the rituals and first two cups of wine.

When it came time to eat, though, everyone grew loud and boisterous. The family members swapped embarrassing stories that got progressively more ridiculous as the wine flowed. Annika and Maia's father, Saul, a small man in his late fifties with almost no hair, told a story about Nora from the early days of their relationship that made Nora spit red wine into her napkin, to everyone's amusement.

"Your family really loves each other," Gabi said to Maia as she helped collect plates after dinner.

"They're insane, but in a good way," Maia said, the sleeves of her shirt dress rolled up to her elbows and yellow rubber gloves on her hands, the diamond of her engagement ring sparkling in a small dish by the faucet.

"It's always amazing to me how, despite how progressive this family is in most other ways, we always end up like this," Annika proclaimed as she waltzed into the kitchen with an armful of brisket tray, "women in the kitchen, chatting and cleaning up. Men in the dining room, arguing about something."

Gabi looked around and noticed that it was true. The aunts and female cousins all crammed into the kitchen. Some plated dessert and made coffee and tea while others tended to children who were weeping because they didn't find the afikomen or the older kids were excluding them from their games.

"Even Jonnie, the most empathetic and feminist man alive," Annika added with a nod to her sister, "is in there lounging around while his beautiful fiancée toils away."

Maia didn't even look up from the plate she scrubbed as she said, "Bin."

"What?" Annika exclaimed and placed the brisket tray down on the counter with slightly too much oomph so it clanged against the marble. "That wasn't remotely wedding related."

"No, but it was a commentary on heterosexual gender roles, so it's adjacent," Maia said as she flicked excess suds back into the sink.

Annika huffed an annoyed breath and went back to clear another dish. Gabi took a container and began to scoop the brisket into it, thinking.

She'd never noticed things like that before. The way her straight friends often divided down the gender line. How the women flocked together to laugh and gossip and vent, and the men sat side by side, talking about nothing important.

She thought about the time she'd assisted on her first stillbirth delivery. How she'd lain in bed all night and sobbed while Matt patted her back and made her tea but still met up with his friends for their weekly jam session. How she'd never even considered asking him not to go.

She placed the brisket container in the stuffed fridge and remembered a night two weeks ago when Annika had come over and listened to her talk for an hour about her favorite patient. Let Gabi describe in detail how the woman had miscarried a much longed for baby a year ago, and was now pregnant again. The fear and hope and excitement Gabi felt for the woman and her partner.

Remembered how Annika had wiped her tears away with her thumb and told her she was incredible. How she'd kissed her and held her through the night. Annika had smiled at her in the dark of the morning, eyes bleary and barely open, over a mug of coffee before Gabi left for work the next day, awake hours early so they could have a little more time together.

Annika came back into the kitchen, her hair now tossed up in a bun. The soft curls Maia had put there had dissipated, and the bun made her look more like herself.

The urge to kiss her pounded through Gabi. The need to touch her in some way just for the sake of knowing she was there, feeling it.

Annika caught Gabi's gaze and smiled an abbreviated version of that lopsided grin, eyes bright as they met hers, and Gabi felt her heart swoon.

CHAPTER TWENTY-THREE

Not kissing Gabi tonight had been a physical feat.

Annika had watched out of the corner of her eye as Gabi listened patiently to Uncle Milton as he regaled her with every detail of his coin collection, and she wanted to kiss her.

Had felt her heart twinge and twist and stutter at the effortless way Gabi seemed to blend in with her family.

The way she laughed with her cousins and played with their kids. The way the table grew quiet as she talked about her job.

Annika had been overcome with the desire to let everyone in that room, everyone in the world, know that this woman, *this woman*, smart and strong and a little neurotic but gorgeously so, was *hers*.

She wasn't really hers, of course.

She was borrowing Gabi, teaching her the skills she'd need to cope on her own once she was ready to move on from Annika. Fostering her for some terribly lucky woman in the future to offer her a forever home where she'd integrate Gabi into her family and hold her hand in public and take her on dates, not just meet up at one of their apartments in secret.

After Gabi said her good-byes and headed to her car, Annika slipped out the back door of the house and nearly ran to meet her before she could drive off.

"Niki?" Gabi said, surprised to see her, before Annika had her hands on her plump cheeks and pressed her against the door of her car, bent nearly in half to kiss her.

"I just had to do that before you left," Annika murmured against her lips and pressed another kiss on her.

Gabi wrapped her arms around her neck, the wool of her peacoat rough against the bare skin at Annika's nape, and pulled her closer.

Gabi tasted like tart red wine, apple sweetness, and a hint of spice from the tea her mother had served with dessert. Annika wanted to drink her down to the last drop.

She pulled away after one final press of her lips against Gabi's and whispered, "Chag Sameach, Gab."

Gabi smiled, eyes a bit dreamy from their kissing.

"Chag Sameach, baby," Gabi replied, then blushed like the endearment had slipped out.

Annika secretly loved when she called her *baby* but had never made it a whole thing in fear that Gabi would stop doing it.

She watched as Gabi got into her car and pulled away from the curb, headed back to her apartment in Portland. She wrapped her arms around her middle to keep herself warm in the spring chill, and to keep that feeling, the one that swelled uncontrollably in her chest, from bursting loose.

Later that night, after her father had passed out on the couch with one of the long-haired cats her parents owned curled on his chest, and Maia and Jonnie had retreated to Maia's childhood room for the night, Annika wandered into the kitchen in sweatpants and a hoodie to find her mother gazing out the window with a mug of tea steaming in front of her on the kitchen table.

"Hey, Mom," Annika said softly. She took a seat opposite her mother and curled her legs up on the chair beneath her, rested her cheek against her knee.

"Hi, shaina," her mother replied and turned to look at her with a light smile on her lips.

"Tired?" Annika asked her mother, and she nodded.

"Wiped. Thank God your aunt does second Seder—I think I'd collapse if I had to do this two nights in a row," she said with a sigh.

Annika reached out and squeezed her mother's wrist, felt the papery thin skin there, so different from what she remembered from childhood. She didn't like to think of her mother as aging, but the signs were beginning to creep in at the edges these days.

"It was nice," her mother continued, "that Gabi came. I know Maia has been worrying about her since she broke up with Matt, not having his family as a support system. And with her family all the way off in New Jersey."

She shivered like New Jersey was as far away as Australia, and Annika smiled.

"Aren't you lucky neither of us ever really left the nest?" Annika teased.

"You and Gabi seem to be closer than I remember," her mother added, and Annika felt herself tense.

"We've just been spending more time together because of, um, wedding stuff," Annika said, tracing the rim of her mug with a finger.

It wasn't a total lie, they had been spending more time together because of wedding things. But that time together was negligible compared to the amount of time they spent in bed together, or texting each other, or talking on the phone nights when Gabi had a slow overnight shift and needed entertainment.

Her mother shot her a sly look before she said, "I didn't know kissing was a part of co–maid of honor duties."

Annika's jaw dropped.

"I saw you two," her mother said with a shrug. "I went to see if I could catch Gabi to give her some leftovers and a box of matzah because she mentioned she couldn't find any when she went to the store, and I saw you giving her something else entirely against her car."

"Mom!" Annika exclaimed, swatting her mother on the forearm.

Her mother laughed. "Does Maia know, about the two of you?"

Annika dropped her forehead to her knees again and groaned.

"No," Annika replied miserably.

"Certainly explains her breakup more. *And* why you haven't mentioned dating in months," her mom concluded with a nod to herself.

Annika hummed and ran her finger through some stray salt spilled on the table's surface, hands eternally restless.

"I know it's going to be complicated when Maia finds out, but I'm so happy you've finally found someone you obviously care about a great deal, Nik," her mother said affectionately. "It's all I've ever wanted for you."

"We're not exactly dating," Annika said hesitantly to her mother, cheeks burning. "It's just, ah, physical mostly."

But that wasn't strictly true either, and Annika knew it. Knew that ever since they'd started sleeping over at each other's places, things had taken on a different tenor. Lust filled, sure, but it wasn't as frantic, as desperate as it had been in the beginning. Now, they took their time with each other. They sat on the couch and talked about their days, legs intertwined, hands folded together. They kissed long and slow and often. Sometimes that's all they did before wrapping around each other in bed and sleeping, deep and easy.

When a bride was ecstatic with her suit, a tricky custom with epaulet-like designs shaped like flames that licked over the tops of her shoulders, made from an applique of three different fabrics and tiny beads that Annika had spent hours and days laboring over, hand-sewing sequins and crystal until nearly every inch of her fingers was covered in Band-Aids, she'd reached to tell Gabi before she'd spoken to Vanessa, or alerted her group chat with her mom and sister.

Gabi was her first thought in the morning and last thought at night even when she wasn't with her. Annika knew what it all meant, and it terrified her.

Her mother seemed to read her thoughts now and gave her a skeptical look.

"You don't sneak out the back door to give *just physical* a good-bye kiss like that, honey," her mother said firmly.

No, you certainly didn't, Annika thought.

She sighed.

Her mother picked up her tea and took a sip.

"I won't tell Maia what I saw, but you should figure out if this is something real before her wedding," her mother went on. "You don't want her bridal party to be awkward."

She cast Annika a pointed look over the rim of her mug.

Annika rolled her eyes and said, "You're right, that's the *last* thing I'd want."

"I think that's a dollar to the jar, honey," her mom said primly, sounding a hell of a lot like Maia, and Annika groaned.

She knew her mom was right, though. That the longer she and Gabi kept this a secret, the more hurt Maia would be when it inevitably came out. Especially as April turned to May and neither Gabi nor Annika seemed to be looking to end their relationship anytime soon.

"Should we…go out?" Annika asked out of the blue one rainy day. Gabi was tucked next to her on her bed and reading a giant medical book, which made Annika's skin crawl to just look at, as Annika reviewed the store's balance sheets on her laptop.

"Why would we when we could stay in?" Gabi replied, voice level as she turned the page.

Annika felt a stab of ice through her heart at those words but swallowed the ache away.

"Yeah, right." Annika relented and went back to her spreadsheet.

A second later, Gabi leaned her head against Annika's shoulder.

She didn't broach the topic again.

CHAPTER TWENTY-FOUR

"Mai, how much shit did you pack, we're literally going away for three days?" Gabi heard Annika grumble as she lugged her sister's wheeled suitcase from the trunk of the car and onto the curb at the Portland airport.

It was a Thursday afternoon, and Gabi, Maia, and Annika were flying down to Nashville to set up for the bachelorette weekend—Maia was far too type A to let her maids of honor handle that task on their own.

"Every outfit needs its own pair of shoes," Maia said, like this was the most obvious answer.

"Not to mention the hair dryer, straightener, and curling iron she packed, as well as what looks like her entire makeup cabinet," Gabi shot back, and Annika grinned at her.

Things had been a little...off between them the last week or so. Annika insisted it was because she was nervous to leave Vanessa in charge of the store and had to finish some last-minute alterations before they left and she hated rushing. They hadn't seen each other all week, and she was dying for Annika to kiss her, to hold her, to touch her.

Gabi suspected, though, that Annika was distancing herself on purpose. That her shiny newness had finally worn off and Annika had grown bored with her, pulling away to make their inevitable conclusion easier. It made Gabi feel desperate, made her want to cling to Annika even harder, wrap her in her tentacles and squeeze.

"Listen, I won't apologize for wanting to look my best," Maia said. "Do you know how many pictures are about to be taken of me? I need to be prepared for every possible scenario."

"That's my girl," Jonnie said easily as he smiled from the driver's seat.

"I guess opposites really do attract sometimes," Annika muttered as Maia flounced over to give Jonnie a farewell kiss through the driver's side window, his performance fleece clad arm wrapping around the waist of her athleisure set, high ponytail swaying as she leaned in.

Gabi glanced up at Annika's unreadable expression and snuck her hand out, interlacing their fingers and squeezing.

Annika shot a sharp look down at their hands and then met Gabi's eyes, something in her gaze softening.

They smiled at each other for a brief moment before someone honked at Jonnie. Maia pulled away from him and bounced back to them.

"It's my bachelorette, bitches!" Maia screamed as she tossed her arms in the air and shook her hips as she climbed the curb.

"Woo-hoo," Annika called out in a monotone. She untangled her fingers from Gabi's grip quickly and shouldered her own duffel, a plain forest green with nylon straps.

Gabi tried to hold on to the warmth Annika's fingers had pressed into her skin, but the chill of a Maine spring morning quickly drained it away.

The flight was uneventful. Maia, seated between Gabi and Annika, chattered their ears off about the itinerary for the weekend and outlined the dynamics of the women attending. Gabi listened, made the appropriate noises, and asked the proper questions, but half her mind was fixed on Annika, who gazed out the window on Maia's other side, seemingly lost in thought, fingers tapping restlessly against her armrest.

They landed in Nashville and took a rideshare to the house they had rented for the weekend. It was located outside of the bustling downtown, but near enough for the big nights out they had planned.

The house was made from light wood and looked like a cabin that worked in tech and had dedicated itself to a carnivore diet and weightlifting. A tall wall of windows looked over the pool deck and green of the flat backyard, which was bordered by a wooden fence made of the same material as the house. A gas grill was tucked into a corner. The appliances in the kitchen were stainless steel and new, the carpets a soft powdery blue spread over the polished hardwood of the floors.

Annika whistled.

"This place is actually nicer in person," she said, dropping her duffel bag on the tiles of the kitchen floor and flopping onto one of the couches.

"For once," Maia muttered, fiddling with her phone. "Hold on, I'm going to call Jonnie to let him know we made it."

"Tell his other girlfriend I said hi, and I hope he's enjoying his time with her," Annika called from the couch to her sister's retreating back. Maia ignored her and lifted her phone to her ear.

Gabi plopped down next to Annika, who lifted her ankles and placed her socked feet in Gabi's lap automatically. She couldn't resist the call to touch Annika anymore but limited herself to lightly circling the bare skin of Annika's ankle above her sock with her fingers.

Something loosened in Gabi at this small touch of Annika's skin on her own, a tightness she hadn't even known she had eased.

Annika knocked against her hand with her toes, just a small nudge.

"Hey," she said quietly. She leaned her head against the back of the couch, bangs falling into her eyes, and smiled at Gabi.

"Hey," Gabi replied, fingers still circling over her skin, "how was your flight?"

Annika laughed lightly and said, "You were sitting with me the whole time."

"Yeah, but Maia was between us," Gabi murmured. Her thumb slipped under the hem of Annika's joggers and dug slightly into her calf the way she knew she liked. "And you were looking out the window the whole time."

Annika grinned and said, "Are you saying you missed me from three feet away?"

The wild thing was that Gabi *had* missed her. Had missed touching her constantly the way they always did when they were together, no space between them.

Gabi opened her mouth to say something teasing, but then they heard Maia's steps coming back down the hall, and she jerked her hand away from Annika, who hastily tucked her legs up and adjusted her body away from Gabi.

"Okay, bride squad, let's get cracking," Maia cheered.

Annika moaned and mimed gagging, and Gabi couldn't help but laugh.

"Get it all out now, Niki, because when the rest of the girls get here, it's bride tribe time," Gabi said.

"You know that's right," Maia exclaimed with a swish of her hips and a snap of her fingers.

Gabi heard Annika's muttered, "Oh God," and covered her grin by bending over to open the package of streamers she'd brought.

Maia connected her phone to the Bluetooth speakers, and they got started decorating the house with pink and silver streamers, disco balls, a penis-themed photo wall that made Annika shudder so badly Maia made her pose with it for ten minutes to document her discomfort.

By the time they were done, Gabi was starving, a little tipsy from the bottle of prosecco the host had left them in the fridge, and brimming with need for Annika.

They ate pizza on the floor in the living room in front of Maia's favorite cheesy rom-com where a bad boy European prince enrolls in a college in Idaho and falls in love with a working class farmer's daughter. Maia swooned dramatically, reminding Gabi of when they were thirteen and had weekend visits. They'd stay up way too late eating junk and watching movies and prank-calling their crushes, and just before they'd drift off to sleep, they'd whisper a secret to each other and see if the other remembered it in the morning.

I think I'm in love with your sister, Gabi thought as she watched Maia and Annika start throwing popcorn at each other and devolve into fits of giggles. Maia tackled Annika to the ground and tickled Annika until tears were running down both of their cheeks.

"Okay, okay," Maia said, catching her breath and then beginning to gather up the stray kernels of popcorn, "let's get to bed so we can be well-rested for the festivities."

"I thought we were just hanging at the house tomorrow while everyone else arrives," Annika replied.

"We are, but I'm still tired, and I want to shower before bed, and you guys can't hang out and have fun without me this weekend. Also, you don't mind sharing a room, right?" Maia said. She stood and stretched, the tank top she wore emblazoned with *Future Mrs.* in rhinestones riding up her flat stomach with the movement.

"Uh," Annika said, and Gabi could practically feel how hard Annika wasn't looking at her. "No, that's fine."

"Cool, most of the rooms have doubles or bunk beds, but there are two queens—one for me and one for you guys," she said and rested her manicured hands on her slim hips. "Yours is in the basement."

"Sounds good," Gabi said and willed her cheeks not to flush. She'd been sharing a bed with Annika for months now, very often without clothes, but Maia couldn't possibly know that.

"Great," Maia said, "it's my fucking bachelorette, babes, and no one is allowed to have any drama."

She threw her arms around Gabi's and Annika's necks and then skipped off to take a shower upstairs.

"So, we're sharing a bed," Annika said calmly.

"Mm-hmm," Gabi said, a smile creeping over her lips, "and we didn't even have to scheme to get it."

Annika returned her grin, and this time there was nothing guarded in her expression.

The next morning, Gabi woke with Annika's right arm thrown over her waist, her head nestled in the space above Gabi's breasts, Annika's long hair loose and silky soft against Gabi's skin.

She smiled and traced her fingers along the bare skin of Annika's lower back where her sleep shirt rode up. Annika nuzzled closer with the touch and grumbled sleepily, then lifted her face and searched for a kiss like a newborn puppy with milky blue eyes.

Gabi grinned and kissed her. It was just a brush of lips at first, but Annika took control of the kiss as she became more alert until she pushed Gabi into the mattress with her weight. Gabi's legs wrapped around her hips, and Annika's hand palmed her breast through her shirt, hips rocking against hers teasingly.

"We probably shouldn't." Gabi moaned as Annika slipped her fingers down Gabi's pajama shorts and kissed her neck, grazed her skin with her teeth.

"Mmm…" Annika's lips trailed to the neckline of Gabi's sleep shirt. Her fingers caressed Gabi's slit lightly through her underwear, making Gabi shiver and bite her lip. "You're probably right."

She started to pull back, and Gabi let out an involuntary whine of protest.

Annika chuckled and sat back on her heels, and Gabi's legs fell from her hips.

"You can't have it both ways, Gab," Annika said, her eyes suddenly serious despite her teasing tone, and something shuttered behind her gaze. She got up and located a hair tie from beside the bed, tying her hair up in a bun as she walked to the bathroom.

Gabi looked after her, frustrated desire still coursing through her, Annika's words echoing in her head.

Chapter Twenty-five

Maia's friends began arriving for the weekend around noon. Each arrival elicited screaming and hugging and jumping from Maia and the women arriving. They all gushed about Maia's ring and Jonnie and how nice the house was and how fun the weekend would be, like they had been sent a script beforehand.

After three such conversations, Annika felt her skin crawl, so she decided to hunt down a climbing gym, the need to move pulsating through her.

"Hey guys, I found a climbing gym about fifteen minutes from here. Anyone want to join?" Annika asked.

There was a chorus of nos from the six women seated on the couch, all Maia's sorority sisters who were deep into their phone camera rolls and showing off husbands, boyfriends, fiancés, houses, and even a baby or two. Maia sat with them and sipped a mimosa, decked out in a white frilly romper and sash even though they didn't have plans to leave the house.

"I'll come," Gabi said, and Annika felt her heart leap in her chest.

This morning had been a mistake. Sharing a bed with Gabi was a mistake. She had decided it was time to start pulling away, for her own good. When Gabi had so callously brushed off her suggestion that they go on a date, she had finally realized that this wasn't working anymore.

Annika was in love with Gabi.

Head over heels, totally gone. Farmers markets and matching overalls and all that sappy shit in love with her. She wanted Gabi's boring mornings and her grumpy nights. Wanted to tear open her own seams and rip herself wide, every boundary and inch of boning exposed to Gabi, even if it meant she would leave her mangled and unwearable.

But Gabi didn't even want to be seen in public with her. Wanted only to hold her hand in stolen moments and kiss her in private, and Annika just couldn't do it anymore.

Except she also couldn't stop herself from doing it either.

So, she had been planning on a slow fade. Leave more and more time between their hangouts. Not respond as quickly to her texts. Sure, this was nearly impossible when they were staying in a house together for three days and sharing a bed, but she could keep herself from one-on-one time, couldn't she?

"Cool," Annika replied almost immediately, "let's meet back here in ten minutes and hit the gym."

The ride over was quiet, neither of them familiar with the song some country station was playing in the rideshare. There was a rainbow and trans pride flag in the window of the gym when they arrived, and Gabi shot Annika a look of relief. You never knew, down here.

They signed their waivers and rented their shoes and chalk bags. Annika missed the worn-in perfection of her own shoes as she stretched. She felt the weight of Gabi's eyes on her body as she moved through her usual warm-up routine but told herself not to look over.

"You look so hot when you do that," Gabi whispered to her as Annika rolled up her mat and returned it to the bin.

Annika couldn't help but flex her arms a bit. She wore just an electric blue sports bra and teal leggings, arms and stomach bare.

"Your ass in those leggings is driving me wild," Gabi went on. Her hands gripped Annika's waist, and her right palm slid down to lightly squeeze her butt.

"Dr. Gabriella Mendon," Annika scolded. She clucked her tongue and pressed closer. "No wandering hands, I'm a lady and I must protect my virtue."

She put on a Southern accent and held her right hand to the center of her chest over her sports bra. Gabi rolled her eyes and, before Annika could react, leaned up to plant a quick kiss on her lips.

Annika looked at her, stunned.

"Relax, Niki," Gabi murmured and smiled. "We don't know anyone here."

Annika felt her heart sink and then soar.

She leaned in and kissed Gabi again, long and lingering.

Sure, she knew she needed to distance herself for her own good.

But for right now, she could give herself a little more time to indulge in Gabi, to thrill at getting to kiss her in broad daylight *and* in public.

The gym was mostly empty on a Friday afternoon, so they spent an hour messing around.

Annika strained as she crouched and shifted her weight to propel herself across a four-foot divide between holds, launched herself upright and caught the hold she'd been aiming for. She heard a cheer and saw Gabi on the mat below her watching her climb.

As soon as she reached the ground, Gabi was there. She gripped Annika's hips and swept her eyes up and down her body.

"I know I say it all the time, but you're really so beautiful, Niki," Gabi said, her voice taking on a hint of that delicious breathy quality Annika knew well by now. "The things you can do with this body are astounding."

Annika grinned.

"You'd swipe right on me," she joked as Gabi's thumbs swept up the grooves of muscle cut into her soft stomach.

Gabi's eyes glinted with some emotion Annika couldn't read.

She teased, "Oh, I'd swipe right. And I'd take you out to a bar and give you lots of eye contact and touch your arm until you would be practically begging me to kiss you."

"Mmm, seems like the student has become the master," Annika said, her hands coming up to wrap around Gabi's hips and pull her flush against her own body.

"Yup, some might even say I've outgrown your tutelage," Gabi said as she leaned in to steal a quick kiss. She released Annika and walked away, then tossed her a grin over her shoulder.

Annika's heart lurched unpleasantly at those words.

"Maia is blowing up our chat," Gabi said as she fished her phone from the pocket of her leggings and checked the screen.

"Yeah," Annika croaked out of a suddenly dry throat. She cleared it and continued, "We should probably head back to the house."

On the drive home, Gabi's hand found hers where it rested on the seat between their thighs, a smile in her eyes as she wove their fingers together.

And Annika, God help her, smiled back.

CHAPTER TWENTY-SIX

Alright, ladies, welcome to the most epic weekend of your life as we help Maia go from girl to woman—"

"Niki, this isn't my bat mitzvah," Maia cut in through Annika's part of the welcome speech she and Gabi had prepared.

"And we all know Jonnie has already made her a woman *many* times," Gabi continued right on cue.

The rest of the bachelorette attendees whooped and hollered as Maia laughed, covered her eyes, and then took a sip of her drink from her plastic penis straw, the fringe on her white cowboy hat swinging with the motion.

"I did write that joke, but then felt gross saying it about my sister," Annika said quickly, flipping her note cards and blowing the pink feathered boa she had wound around her neck out of her face. "Now that the men are away, the ladies will play."

Annika winked exaggeratedly and tipped her pink cowgirl hat.

From her spot next to Annika before the seated crowd of tipsy women all dressed in their sexy cowgirl best, Gabi saw one of Maia's friends from college grin and tip her cup at Annika. A flash of something hot and spiky flared through Gabi's chest at the gesture.

"And we won't tell Jonnie how many times Maia flashes strange men when she forgets she can't do cartwheels in a skirt," Gabi added. She pushed the feeling aside and raised her own cup in mock salute to Maia.

"That was one time," Maia exclaimed, and everyone laughed around her.

"So, raise a toast to the woman we love and the guy who loves her," Annika said, raising her own pink plastic cup, a penis straw spinning wildly around the rim.

"To Maia and Jonnie," Gabi cheered.

"To Maia and Jonnie," all the ladies cheered back, clinking their plastic cups in the middle and taking long pulls from their straws.

"Alright, we've got seven minutes until Ramesh and Irvin arrive with our cars to the first bar, so everyone down your drinks and put the finishing touches on your looks," Gabi called, phone held in one hand and drink in the other as she tried not to stare too openly at Annika's ass in the tight denim shorts she wore.

She had taken Gabi's urging to go along with the weekend for Maia's sake to heart and was apparently leaning fully into it. Her hair was curled in soft waves, a pink sequined cowgirl hat sat on her head, and a pink sash that read *bride tribe* in flowery white cursive hung over her black tailored vest. She'd even gone so far as to let one of Maia's friends from college put glitter at the corner of her eyes and pink gloss on her lips.

The friend seemed to be a little too eager to apply the glitter to Annika, in Gabi's opinion. She kept shooting Annika furtive glances, giving her big smiles, and tossing her hair when Annika walked by.

Gabi herself was having a hard time keeping her eyes off Annika's toned legs, the peek of soft stomach and hint of the curve of her breast she flashed as she moved through the room, topping up drinks and double-checking the itinerary she and Gabi had created.

Tonight was their big night out on the town—three different bars, impersonators, music, dancing, a mechanical bull, the Nashville works.

"I think we're good to go," Annika said as she circled back to Gabi. The rest of the women chattered loudly around them, gathered wallets and phones and spare lipsticks into purses, downed shots in the kitchen, and slurped up the last of their drinks.

"Looks like it," Gabi agreed.

"Team bride tribe rides in three minutes, bitches," Annika called, blowing the clear pink plastic whistle she had brought so she could keep track of everyone. "I swear I'm getting more heterosexual by the minute. Next thing I know I'll be suggesting Mackenzie's sister do a balloon pop for her gender reveal next month."

She motioned over her shoulder to the same skinny blonde who had done Annika's makeup and toasted her during their speech.

"You can make a donation to the HRC in the morning," Gabi said with a smile up at her.

Annika gripped her arms and shook her slightly, her hands clammy and eyes bright already from drinking, but Gabi didn't mind, got a little thrill from Annika touching her in front of people. "That is the sweetest thing you've ever said to me."

She swept her eyes quickly up and down Gabi's body in the tight jean halter dress she wore. Her eyes lingered where the skirt clung to her hips and on the generous swell of her breasts as they pushed against the fabric. Gabi felt blood rush into her cheeks at the desire she saw kindled there.

Take that, Mackenzie, Gabi thought triumphantly.

Annika leaned in, inhibitions lowered. Her murmur was lost in the din of the other women's tipsy chatter when she said, "You look *amazing* in that dress, Gab. So sexy."

Gabi grinned up at her, their faces close but not touching, and bit her lip, drawing Annika's eyes to her mouth.

But before either of them could do anything they might regret, Gabi's phone vibrated in her hand.

"First car is here," she yelled, and the eight other women in the house screeched and scrambled.

She lost track of Annika then. They were separated in the rides downtown, which was probably good. It was going to be hard to pretend she didn't want to tear Annika's clothes off and kiss every inch of her body in front of other people, especially when she had been drinking and Annika looked like a smoking hot lesbian cowboy.

She remembered joking that she'd outgrown coaching that afternoon at the climbing gym. It was true, she realized. She didn't need Annika anymore to practice on or to make her feel confident in her sexuality, in herself.

But she sure as fuck *wanted* Annika. Wanted to crawl inside her skin and live there, wanted them to merge so closely that she couldn't tell where she ended and Annika began.

And, to be honest, it scared the shit out of her. She had never felt this mixture of intense lust and aching tenderness for someone before.

She had loved Matt in a way, had loved the stability he had provided her, and she had let him guide her along, the tugboat to her barge. This feeling for Annika, the one she was terrified to name, could so easily sink her and her newfound sense of independence, swallow it whole if she let herself give in to it fully.

She wanted to know what else, who else she might be on her own. What other long neglected parts of her might emerge if she gave herself permission to look for them?

For the rest of the night, Annika stayed tantalizingly out of reach. She danced with Maia and her friends, locked eyes with Gabi where she sat at their table as she swayed her hips and shook her head, hair stuck to the sweat coating her gorgeous body. Laughed as she tried to line dance, her usual Chelsea boots with their delicately embroidered flowers standing out amongst the cowboy boots and sneakers.

It was a sweet torture to watch her but not be able to touch her. Especially as Mackenzie, clearly hoping for a little drunken experimentation, shimmied her shoulders in Annika's direction. This unfamiliar urge, possessive and strong, to make Mackenzie back off surged up in her.

Was this...jealousy?

"She better not go home with some rando," Maia grumbled to Gabi as she sipped her vodka cranberry. They were taking a break after Maia had been flung from a mechanical bull. They both watched Annika laugh with Mackenzie as they waited for another drink at the bar.

"Or fuck one of my friends," Maia said, "although that would be just like her. Not thinking about the future consequences of her actions as long as it feels good now."

Gabi shifted slightly in her seat, her thighs stuck uncomfortably to the wooden chair beneath her, sweat trickling down her back and between her breasts from the heat of the bar.

They were at their last location of the evening, and everyone in their group was straight up drunk.

Gabi watched as Mackenzie touched Annika's biceps, the one with tattoos, the one Gabi loved, had spent hours tracing and kissing and studying by now.

She squinted as Annika glanced down at Mackenzie's hand, eyes widening. Mackenzie tilted her head and bit her lip as she gazed up at

Annika from beneath her fake lashes, and before she knew what she was doing, Gabi was on her feet and making her way to the bar.

Annika glanced over her shoulder and locked eyes with Gabi, and the rest of the room fell away. All that mattered to Gabi in that moment was that Annika kept her eyes on her and not stupid Mackenzie, that Annika forgot every other woman in the universe existed.

She heard Annika's voice in her brain say *You can't have it both ways.* But the alcohol in her system let her push that aside as she pressed in close to Annika at the bar, let her breasts graze her arm.

"Mackenzie, do you mind if I snag Annika for a moment?" Gabi slurred brightly as she curled her arm possessively through Annika's and, pressing her breasts more firmly against her, said, "Some maids of honor business."

Gabi saw Annika's eyes flick down to her face, then lower to the neckline of her dress, and felt a savage thrill spike through her.

Before either of the other women could respond, Gabi turned and nearly dragged Annika away.

"Are you going to pee on me now, Gab?" Annika said, amused, as Gabi pulled her along into the street, the cool night air welcome against Gabi's overheated face.

She felt her face grow hot again with embarrassment and spluttered, "Maia didn't want you fucking one of her friends this weekend."

Annika raised her eyebrows, and Gabi grimaced.

Then they both burst out into laughter, leaning into each other as they came to a stop in the alley beside the bar.

"You know, you're wicked cute when you're jealous," Annika said, voice taking on that smoked-honey timbre that went directly to Gabi's core. She grabbed one of Gabi's hands and reeled her in, Annika's back against the wall of the alley that Gabi had blindly led them to.

She let herself fall against Annika, boxed in by her longer legs as Annika leaned back and leveled their heights. She reached down and slid her hand over the downy hair on Annika's muscular thigh. Her thumb trailed under the hem of Annika's denim cutoffs and swiped back and forth.

Gabi knew they were being reckless, that anyone—that *Maia*—could wander out here and see them, but she was tired of fighting her need for this woman. Tired of hiding how she felt for her.

"Just so you know," Annika murmured, resting her forehead against Gabi's and letting out a long breath, "I wouldn't have slept with Mackenzie. I mean, me six months ago might have, she was a horny asshole. But me now wouldn't have."

Gabi swallowed, heart kicking up in something like panic, something like joy as Annika continued.

"I know we haven't talked about it formally," Annika said, brown eyes smudged with glitter and mascara, bangs stuck to her forehead with sweat, bun tilting haphazardly on the top of her head, but still the most gorgeous person Gabi had ever seen, "but I haven't been with anyone else since the first time we hooked up."

Even though she knew it, it felt like fireworks going off in her belly to hear the words tumble from Annika's lips.

"Fine, I *was* jealous," Gabi conceded as a grin split her lips. "You look *so* good tonight, and she was touching your arm, *the* arm"—Gabi reached out and traced her fingers over Annika's tattoos in emphasis—"*my* arm."

Annika's smile was almost sad as she kissed Gabi, tasting like tequila and lime and a sweetness all her own.

And Gabi couldn't stop herself as she melted against her. Her hands buried themselves in Annika's sweaty hair at the base of her skull and tugged slightly to keep her in place. Like if she could only kiss her hard enough, grip her tight enough, she could keep her from slipping through her fingers. She could keep everything exactly as it was between them, bridge that distance she'd been sensing.

The whole group stumbled into the house around two in the morning and changed into sweats and pajamas, some of the women raiding the kitchen for snacks, others falling immediately into bed.

Gabi went down to their room to change, a big glass of water and two ibuprofen in hand. She was halfway through unzipping her dress when Annika appeared, closed the door behind her, and leaned against it.

"Hey," Gabi said softly, "can you help me with this zipper?"

Wordlessly, Annika stood behind her; calloused fingers dragged the zipper down Gabi's spine and then trailed up her skin and unclipped the clasp around her neck. Gabi was about to step away, but Annika tangled her fingers in her curls and gently tugged her head back against her shoulder, baring Gabi's neck as she leaned down to graze her lips against her skin. Her free hand came up to cup Gabi's breast over her bra.

Gabi shivered and sighed. She let the dress fall to the floor so she stood only in her strapless bra and shapewear shorts.

She pulled away from Annika to wriggle out of her shorts and toss her bra to the floor.

"You next," Gabi said. She surveyed a still fully clothed Annika, who watched her, an almost wistful expression on her face as she glanced at the door and the stairs to the first floor beyond it, and then back at Gabi. A small struggle seemed to take place behind her eyes, but desire won out.

She lifted her hands to undo the buttons of her vest and slid it off her shoulders to reveal her beautiful small breasts to Gabi's hungry eyes. She tossed it to the floor where it was quickly joined by her shorts and underwear until they both stood naked before each other.

Gabi reached for Annika first, hands gliding from hips to ribs and down around to caress the length of her spine, lower to her glorious ass. Annika closed her eyes at the first brush of skin on skin, bit her lip, and dropped her head back in response.

"Gab," she groaned as Gabi dropped her mouth to nibble at Annika's breasts.

Annika tangled her hands in her curls, tugged her closer, and said, "My Gabi."

Hearing those words on Annika's lips made Gabi feel even more dizzy, drunk on the feel and taste of her.

Yes, mine, her heart whispered as she kissed her way up Annika's neck, rose on her toes to reach.

Usually, Annika was the one in charge, setting the pace for how they had sex, prioritizing Gabi's pleasure above her own. But tonight, Gabi wanted to drive her wild. Needed to show her how much she wanted her, how much she had learned from her. How precious Annika was to her, even if she felt too scared to give her everything.

"Get on the bed," Gabi rasped out, throat dry with desire and drink. Annika raised her eyebrows at her but said nothing, taking a seat on the edge of the mattress.

"Lie back," she instructed and then crawled over Annika's prone body when she complied, straddling her hips with her plump thighs.

She watched Annika's eyes go dark as she took in Gabi's breasts, the roundness of her hips and stomach and thighs around her, the dark thatch of hair between her legs.

When Annika reached for her, Gabi captured Annika's wrists in her hands, stretched over her to pin Annika's arms above her head.

"Be good and keep these here for me," she murmured in Annika's ear before she tugged her lobe between her teeth and listened to Annika moan softly, felt her hips begin to lift off the mattress. Gabi bit her neck, hard enough to leave a mark.

Let Mackenzie see it, she thought darkly to herself. Let her see it and know she belongs to me.

"Gabi," Annika groaned, voice gone breathless as Gabi made her slow way down her body, kissing and touching and tasting to her heart's content. Annika writhed faster, more helplessly as Gabi took her sweet time.

"Gabi, *please*." Annika begged *her*, for the first time.

Gabi felt a thrum of power and grinned wickedly up at her from where she mouthed at her hip bone.

Annika's eyes were half lidded and hazy from pleasure, her back arched slightly from her where her hands still gripped the bedspread above her head. She looked sexy and needy and full of an emotion Gabi couldn't parse as her eyes met Gabi's.

She felt suddenly so overcome with love for this woman that she had to duck her head between Annika's thighs to block it out. Had to busy herself with driving Annika over the edge of pleasure again and again with mouth and fingers until Annika had to muffle her noises in a pillow so the rest of the house wouldn't hear her.

When she was done, Annika lay limp and pleasure-drunk on the bed.

"What was that?" Annika whispered as Gabi stretched out beside her.

Gabi shrugged and grinned at her, threw her thigh over Annika's waist.

"I was just really into you tonight," she said, pretending nonchalance.

Annika laughed weakly.

"I should make you jealous more often," she said, rolling over to press Gabi into the mattress in the way they both knew she liked.

"Please don't," Gabi whispered as Annika bent her head to kiss her, palmed her breast slowly as her tongue flitted into Gabi's mouth, so good it made her whimper.

She set about taking Gabi apart gently. It didn't take long until Gabi's arms were tensed like iron bars across Annika's back as Annika worked her with her fingers, Gabi's face buried against Annika's neck to dampen her own cries.

"That's it," Annika cooed to her as Gabi felt herself start to go over the edge. "That's my girl. I've got you. You can let go now, it's okay."

Gabi squeezed her eyes tight against the tender note in Annika's voice but couldn't stop her orgasm from dropping her into an endless pool of pleasure where she floated, warm and satisfied, for long moments.

After, they lay in silence, limbs tangled together, gazes held in the dark.

Gabi watched Annika drift off. But despite being drowsy with pleasure and the remains of the drinks she'd had still sloshing in her system, her mind whirred, sleep kept just out of reach.

That, she thought as she listened to Annika's deep, even breaths puffing against her chest, was about much more than just sex.

Chapter Twenty-seven

Annika woke with gritty eyes and a dry mouth, a dull throb taking root in her temples.

Rolling over, she saw that Gabi's side of the bed was empty already and felt a pang in her chest.

Gabi's jealousy last night had been as sweet as honey barbecue. When Gabi had sauntered up to her at the bar, the round slope of her hips swaying in the little skirt of her denim halter dress, Annika had felt victorious. She'd been amused at Mackenzie's transparent attempts to get in a little queer experimentation before her thirtieth birthday but hadn't felt a single iota of temptation.

No, her heart, her body, every part of her belonged to Gabi.

My arm, Gabi had said, a nearly possessive hunger flaming in her eyes as she traced the lines of Annika's tattoos in the alley last night.

And then that sex when they got home.

Gabi nearly always waited for her lead. But she had taken charge, been fully in her own power, and it had been hot as hell. Annika'd had to bite her lip so hard to keep from screaming out her love for the woman between her legs as she came, she'd tasted blood. And she swore she saw an echo of that same emotion in Gabi's gaze when they had lain together after.

But in the cold light of day, frustration bloomed beneath her breastbone, prickly with thorns. If they both had feelings for each other like this, then what were they doing? Was Gabi embarrassed by her?

Annika rolled over again, pressed her nose into Gabi's pillow, and groaned.

"Fuck," she said, long and low.

"Yeah, that's about how I'm feeling this morning, too," Gabi's voice said, and Annika turned to see her in one of her oversized sleep shirts and tiny shorts coming down the stairs with two mugs in her hands. Her curls were piled in a haphazard bun on the top of her head, and there were smudges of mascara and eyeliner under her eyes.

Annika wanted to wrap her in her arms and bury her head in her neck.

"Here," Gabi said, holding out a mug of coffee to her.

"You are truly a mensch," Annika said with a sigh.

She sat up and took the mug, realized she was still naked when she felt the brush of her own hair against her breast, and got up to search for something to throw on.

"Almost everyone is still sleeping, except Gretchen, who's out for a run," Gabi said with a roll of her eyes as she settled back against the headboard and sipped from her own mug.

"Fucking Gretchen," Annika grumbled. She did marathons several times a year and ran every day with no exception.

Gabi nodded and looked down into her mug.

After a pause, she looked at Annika, who had settled next to her in bed, their shoulders touching, and sighed.

"Look, Nik, we've been…hanging out for five months now," she began.

"We have," Annika said warily, tucking her right leg under her, mug cradled in both her hands.

Gabi smiled and placed her hand on Annika's knee. "I don't want to end things."

Annika felt a tightness in her chest ease immediately at Gabi's words.

"But I feel like we should, like, I don't know, talk about our feelings? Because I think it's clear we're both having those."

"That would be the grown-up thing to do," Annika agreed with a nod. Her heart leapt at hearing Gabi hint that she had feelings for her beyond lust and friendship.

"So?" Gabi prompted.

"Me?" Annika said, pressing her hand to her chest. "Why do I have to start?"

"Because you're the one that said you hadn't hooked up with anyone else in five months," Gabi retorted.

Annika felt her heart sink into her toes and her stomach roil.

"Have you, um, been seeing other people?" Annika asked hesitantly, trying to keep the terror she felt out of her voice. She didn't know how Gabi would have done that. Between her work schedule and the multiple nights a week she spent with Annika, it didn't seem possible. But she was gripped by a sudden fear that maybe Gabi had been seeing someone else. Or that she didn't want to be exclusive.

"No," Gabi said hastily, squeezing Annika's knee reassuringly, "but you brought it up, so you should talk first."

Annika, too relieved to argue with that logic, ran a hand through her messy hair and felt her bangs, stiff with sweat from the night before, stick straight up.

She took a sip of her coffee while she got her thoughts in order and had just opened her mouth to respond when they heard footsteps on the stairs, and Maia appeared.

"Good morning, my beautiful Mohs!" she said, her hair in its classic, if more disheveled and off center, ponytail, dressed in a white satin pajama set with *bride* embroidered over the left breast in light pink writing. There were moisturizing patches under her eyes, and she had a tumbler of water, also white with *Mrs.* spelled in gold paint along the side, in her left hand.

"Mohs?" Gabi questioned.

"Maids of honor," Maia said as she dropped onto the mattress with a bounce.

"Right, because that makes so much sense," Annika said, and she laid her head in her sister's lap.

"Why are you guys huddled down here giving off serious conversation energy?" Maia asked, stroking Annika's hair and taking a long pull from her tumbler.

"Just going over the plan for today," Gabi said with a shrug. She tucked her legs up on the bed and rested her cheek on her knee, arms loosely held around her calves.

Annika met her gaze, and they shared a look.

Guess their conversation was on pause for now, thank God.

Maia did a little excited wiggle and said, "I'm pumped for the games you made! Right now, though, I need you to come upstairs and make blueberry pancakes."

She addressed the end of this sentence to Annika, who sighed. Her sister didn't trust her to do much, but she did trust her to make her hangover pancakes like she'd been doing since Maia's first hangover when she was sixteen.

"Okay, okay, but I'm not making them bride themed. No *bridal blueberry pancakes*, or making them in the shape of a ring, or any of it," she said, allowing Maia to pull her to her feet and lead her up the stairs. "Having to look at you in this outfit is bad enough."

She spent the next few hours making the women of the house breakfast and coffee, chatting with Maia's friends as they filtered into the kitchen and collapsed in a heap on the couches.

Gabi cleaned up for her, shooting her easy smiles as she did, and the sweet domesticity of it hit like a punch to the gut.

They spent the rest of the morning and afternoon lounging around the house, sipping on spiked seltzers and sodas and resting.

Annika found herself floating on a flamingo-shaped pool toy with her Portland Sea Dogs ball cap pulled over her face sometime in the late afternoon, not asleep, but not fully awake either.

"Hey, whose phone is playing music?" Maia called. "Can you unlock it so I can add some songs to the queue?"

"It's mine," Annika heard Gabi reply, and she zoned back out until she suddenly heard her name.

"Gab, why do you have a playlist that's called *Annika's Gay Little Music*?" Maia asked. "Who are these artists? I haven't heard of, like, any of them."

Annika felt her heart sink into her stomach and her stomach sink into her toes. That was a playlist she'd sent Gabi way back in December after she'd said she hadn't known most of the songs playing at The Clam Shack and wanted to be exposed to more queer culture. Annika had made a joke about exposing her to more of *her* queer culture and had—

"Oh shit," she said, trying to sit up so fast she fell off the floaty and into the pool with a splash.

When she surfaced, she saw Maia staring down at the phone with uncomprehending eyes.

"Gab," Maia said slowly as Annika frantically swam over to the other end of the pool, "why are my sister's tits on your phone?"

Annika reached the edge of the pool and hauled herself out of it, dripping all over the pool deck and Maia's and Gabi's feet.

Gabi stood there with her mouth opening and closing like a fish gasping for air.

"It was a joke!" Annika nearly yelled, answering hurriedly. "It was a stupid joke. I sent Gabi the playlist because she wanted some new music and—"

"And you made the cover art your naked chest because…?" Maia demanded.

"Because," Annika stammered, searching desperately for a lie, "because I made it for someone else and forgot that was the cover art I used."

She experienced one split second of triumph before Maia swiped and another picture of Annika, this time kneeling on her bed clad only in black panties, hand slid below the waistband and teeth dug into her lip suggestively, appeared on the screen.

Annika's jaw dropped open.

Oh, they were so, *so* screwed.

"Gabriella," Maia said, voice oddly firm and formal, "why do you have a shared album of what seem to be nudes of my sister labeled *for when you're bored at work* on your phone?"

"How did you even find that?" Gabi whispered. Her face was white as a sheet, eyes wide as silver dollars. Annika felt like she was going to throw up.

"I wanted to take a picture of Annika on the float and then add it to the bachelorette shared album, and when I went to look for it, I found this instead," Maia explained nearly clinically.

Gabi closed her eyes and grimaced like she was in pain.

"I can explain—" Annika started, and Maia held up a hand to silence her.

"I'll deal with you in a minute, but right now I want to hear from my oldest, dearest friend," Maia said, every inch of her prickling like a spooked porcupine, liable to throw spikes. Even in her white triangle bikini and ball cap she was intimidating, arms crossed tightly over her chest.

"I…uh," Gabi stammered.

"Because what it looks like to me," Maia went on, brandishing the phone like a bloody knife in a murder trial, "is that you've been hooking up with my sister and lying to me about it for *months*."

"It kind of just happened. She was helping me figure stuff out with dating women and giving me advice," Gabi began, words running together like they did when she was panicking.

"So fucking her was just practice for you?" Maia yelled and Gabi flinched.

Annika was dying to wrap Gabi up in her arms and breathe with her. But she couldn't move a muscle, couldn't do anything but drip on the cement of the pool deck and watch her sister shout at the woman she loved.

"Not exactly, no," Gabi said, voice small.

"I can't believe you *lied to me about sleeping with my sister*," Maia said, voice rising with each word.

The other women at the party now sat in shocked silence on the pool furniture arranged around them, watching the show the three of them were putting on with wide eyes.

"Mai," Annika tried again, but Maia wasn't done.

"How long has this been going on? Is this why you broke up with Matt? Were you cheating on him with her? Is this why none of Annika's relationships work out?" she demanded.

"God, *no*, Mai. We didn't start hooking up until, like, really recently," Gabi said, hurt still written on her features.

"How am I supposed to know that? You've lied to me about *everything*. How long?" Maia asked. "Are you dating or just fucking? Do you like her?"

"No offense, Maia, but that's not any of your fucking business." Annika cut in, finding her voice finally. She crossed her arms over her chest and sat into her hip defensively. Even though she desperately wanted to know the answers to those questions herself.

"It is my fucking business, Niki. It's my fucking business because you're my baby sister and I've been watching you fall in love with some mystery girl for months after years of not letting anyone get too close. Yes," Maia said quickly when Annika opened her mouth, "I could tell you were seeing someone because your whole demeanor was just *happier*, but I was waiting for you to bring it up on your own. And if you're just some experiment and it gets your heart broken and you refuse to open yourself up again, I'm going to have to murder my oldest friend, not to mention find a new bridesmaid because having an odd number would throw off the whole bridal tableau and I *really* don't want to do that." Maia concluded, throwing her hands up angrily in emphasis.

Annika gaped at her, at a loss for how to respond. She was only realizing now that she had been expecting Maia to take Gabi's side all along.

"And you," Maia continued, turning on Gabi, "I don't care that you've been hooking up with my sister. I mean, I do, I don't like it just on principle. And if you're just using her, I will hurt you. But you're adults and you can do whatever you want with your bodies and your time, I guess. The lying, though, Gab. Oh my God, *the lying*."

Gabi's shoulders hunched in on her, making her already small frame shrink. She looked fragile and young standing there in her hot pink scoop-neck one-piece, curls bound back in a long French braid, sunglasses perched on the crown of her head. The urge to protect her surged through Annika, but she didn't know what to do with it. She felt like she was standing on the other edge of the chasm of Maia's anger, which was stretched out between them.

"I know," Gabi said, and she let out a small, defeated sigh.

"The girl you've been hooking up with?" Maia said, sitting into her right hip and counting the lies off with her fingers, "Meeting her at The Clam Shack? The dates you went on right after you broke up with Matt? Was it all Niki?"

"No," Gabi exclaimed. "No, it wasn't all her. I did set up an app, and I did go on some dates with other women."

She swallowed hard, cheeks burning brightly under the sun. Annika moved to stand at her side, lending her support through proximity. Maia's eyes narrowed at the movement.

Gabi looked up at her, eyes brimming, clearly on the verge of tears. Annika gave her a gentle, encouraging smile.

"Annika was just helping me out at first," Gabi said slowly.

"And then…" Maia prompted, waving her hand to urge Maia to go on.

"And then, I realized how great she is," Gabi said with a shrug.

"Well, *I* know that." Maia sighed exasperatedly.

Annika shifted, felt embarrassed by all the praise.

Gabi nodded and kept going, "I went with her to that gay trivia back in November, and we, ah, ended up kissing after. And then we, like, kind of just started hooking up and hanging out."

"And that's all *this* is?" Maia asked, brandishing the incriminating pictures of Annika again.

"Can we maybe put the pictures of my boobs away now?" Annika asked.

She placed her hands over her black bikini top. Maia sighed and locked Gabi's phone, tossing it on the table next to the Bluetooth speaker.

"Well?" Maia prompted. "Are you guys just fucking around, or what?"

Gabi and Annika looked at each other.

"We kind of haven't talked about it," Annika said sheepishly.

"In five months? Oh my God," Maia said exasperatedly. She dropped her head back and exhaled to the sky. "Here's what's going to happen now. The rest of us are still going to go to dinner because I want barbecue and this is still my bachelorette. You two"—she pointed between Gabi and Annika with one manicured finger—"are going to talk. I mean, *really* talk. You will not, one, get drunk or use drugs."

Annika huffed and crossed her arms, thought longingly about the little bottle of edibles she had stashed in her suitcase.

"Or two, have sex to avoid talking. When we get back from dinner, you will pretend, for my sake, that none of this is happening and we will play my bachelorette games. When we get back to Portland, neither of you will speak to me for a week because I'm still really fucking mad at you. *Both* of you," she concluded, shooting Annika a glare, "although I will still see you on Thursday for my second fitting, Nik."

Annika resisted the urge to salute and bowed her head, nodding like a scolded child. Gabi crossed her arms over her chest and stared down at the pool deck.

"I'm really sorry for lying to you, Mai," she said to her toes.

Maia's eyes softened and she nodded.

"I know you are, babe. But it doesn't change what you did or how I feel about it," Maia said simply.

And with that she turned on her heel and made her way back into the house, flip-flops whacking against the pavement.

"Someone get me some wine!" she called, leaving Annika and Gabi standing there, their secrets almost all exposed to the world.

Chapter Twenty-eight

I guess we should talk now?" Annika said, scratching at her undercut. "Actually, give me thirty minutes, I don't want to have this conversation in a wet bathing suit."

Annika padded after her sister into the house, and Gabi, still in shock, sat down at the table and took a long gulp of her spiked seltzer.

Maia knew about her and Annika.

She dropped her head into her hands, mind so full it was blank.

Maia knew she was hooking up with Annika. And she was angry at her. Less about the Annika part, more about the lying.

Not that she blamed her, she had lied to Maia *a lot* and repeatedly. For months.

If Maia had done that to her, she had no idea how'd she forgive her.

Maia would forgive her, right?

She heard the bustle of the other women getting ready and leaving for dinner, the sky darkening around her, but she still sat there, mind fixated on that one thought.

Had she ruined her relationship with Maia for Annika?

And was it worth it?

Annika returned after everyone else had left, wet hair thrown up in a bun, dressed in spandex bike shorts and a baggy T-shirt.

"I know Maia said we shouldn't get drunk, but I don't think there's a way I can talk about my emotions without *some* substance," Annika said.

She settled a bottle of wine on the glass-topped table and plopped down across from Gabi, then picked up the bottle and swigged directly from it. A stray dribble ran down her chin, and she wiped it off with the back of her hand.

She held the bottle out to Gabi, who accepted it gladly and took a long sip.

"So," Annika said into the silence, "should we talk about my sister finding my boobs on your phone, or our feelings for each other first?"

Gabi started laughing, sharp in the stillness of the backyard, the situation suddenly hysterically funny to her.

Annika joined in, chuckling ruefully as she took another swig of wine, and leaned back in her chair, body sprawled out and slumped.

"Fuck," she sighed. "I knew making that shared album would come back to bite me in the ass."

Gabi glanced over at her, shoulders still shaking with mirth. "I should have hidden it better. Or at all."

And then she buried her face in her hands and burst into tears, the whole overwhelming concoction of emotions washing over her.

Anxiety at Annika pulling away. Jealousy from last night when Mackenzie had been all over her. The need she'd felt to pin Annika under her so she couldn't slip away when they got home. The tenderness that had swelled in her chest when Annika told her she wasn't seeing other people, when she gazed at Annika before they fell asleep. The ache in her heart for this woman who wasn't even officially hers. The pain of Maia's anger, now that she knew the truth.

"Oh, Gab," Annika said, voice gentle, and Gabi felt her rough hands circling her wrists, just like all those months ago when she'd come out to Annika at the Queer Climb night.

She let Annika pull her hands from her face, then replace them with her light touch.

"What if Maia never forgives me?" Gabi wept, leaning her cheek against Annika's hand. "What if I ruined our relationship?"

"You haven't, baby, you haven't. I'll make her forgive you," Annika said emphatically.

Gabi felt her heart hiccup. Annika never called her baby, even though Gabi had used the pet name more than a few times.

Annika rose on her knees to peer into Gabi's face, and oh, how Gabi loved her in that moment. Her wet hair perched at a precarious angle on her head, bangs stringy, and such a painfully raw look on her face, like Gabi's tears had scraped her open.

"I think we should stop this," Gabi blurted out. She saw hurt and confusion register on Annika's face as soon as she said the words.

"What? Why? You said this morning you didn't want to end things. Is this because of Maia?" Annika said, her hands still on Gabi's face, brow furrowed.

Gabi shook her head. "Not because of Maia. Well"—she paused and drew in a breath—"not *just* because of her."

Gabi took another deep, steadying breath and blew it out. She needed to get this out, needed to expel it like poison from her blood.

"I love you," Gabi said and saw Annika's eyes widen, joy sprouting in their depths, but she kept on going before it could take root, "but I'm not ready to give you what you deserve, the relationship you deserve. I lost myself in Matt, Niki, let him take the lead, and I'm just now letting myself learn those parts of myself I've been ignoring for most of my adult life. I didn't even know I'm gay, that's a huge thing to not have realized. What happens when I lose myself in you, too? And you, you're so amazing and I've seen how you give your all when you're focused on something or someone you love, but I just don't think I'm in a place to do the same for you."

Annika's eyes were wide as saucers as she listened to the words tumble free from Gabi's lips, Annika's hands still cupping her cheeks.

"Gab," she said softly, stroking Gabi's cheek with her thumb. Gabi saw the emotions warring in her face. Love and joy at being loved. Hurt and pain from Gabi's doubt in herself. Confusion at how to move forward.

"I feel so alive and safe when I'm with you," Gabi went on. She covered Annika's left hand with her right, pressed it into her cheek, "But I'm scared, too."

"You think I'm not scared? I'm fucking terrified, Gab," Annika said. "I love you so, so much it kind of hurts to think about. I want to wake up with you every morning and see your face before I go to sleep at night. I'm so obsessed with you I want to know what you're thinking every second of every day, who you've been talking to, what weird vaginal issues you've had to deal with at work. I want to go to the fucking farmers market with you, Gabi, and I *never* want to do that. I've never felt this way about anyone before. I've let you in in a thousand ways. Usually when it gets to this point, hell, even well before this point, I break up with a woman. But you"—Annika smiled wryly and shook her head—"you little gremlin, you buried under my skin and curled up in my heart, and I can't seem to get you out."

Gabi let out a watery laugh and leaned into Annika's touch, let it ground her. She wanted that, too, all of it, with Annika, but there was a gate around her heart that she couldn't quite break through.

"I want that, too, Niki. I just…" She took in a deep breath and rested her forehead against Annika's. "I can't do it right now."

"And I can't keep going on like this," Annika whispered into the space between their faces. "So where does that leave us?"

"Niki." Gabi sighed, sat forward and let their lips brush. "You know where that leaves us."

Gabi let herself kiss Annika, soft and slow, her hands in her hair, the short spikes of her undercut and the long tendrils of the rest of her hair a beautiful contradiction, like everything this woman was.

She let Annika cling to her, let her deepen the kiss until they were grasping at each other with feverish hunger. Then Gabi pulled back, and Annika's head dropped into her lap, tears falling freely down Annika's cheeks now.

"I know," Gabi murmured to her, stroking her hair. "I know, Niki."

They sat like that for a long time.

And Gabi finally let herself acknowledge the full extent of her emotions for the woman before her.

She loved every part of her. Her erratic moods and eccentric hobbies, the way she gave herself over to the things she enjoyed, devoted herself fully to the people she loved. The way she could make Gabi feel like the most beautiful, treasured, and sexy woman in the whole world while still giving her room to be vulnerable, to be herself.

"I wish…" Gabi started and sighed. She wished so many things. That she'd allowed herself to admit her sexuality to herself a decade earlier. That she had broken up with Matt years ago, had already dated around before kissing Annika. "I wish I'd had a girlfriend before I kissed you. That I was a more experienced queer lady."

Annika looked up at her, tear tracks on her beautiful, beloved face.

"You know I don't give a shit about that, right?" she asked, brown eyes luminous in the light from the setting sun.

"No, I know. It's more…It's more that I wish *I* felt more confident in my queer identity."

"And being in love with me, having sex with me, a woman, for months doesn't make you feel that way?" Annika asked, scrunching her face up adorably. The bridge of her nose was freckled from spending the day in the pool, and Gabi wanted to count every new speckle on her skin.

"I know it sounds absolutely bonkers, but I *am* a scientist, and in order to come to a proper conclusion, I need more data," Gabi said. She brushed stray hairs off Annika's face and wiped her tears away with her thumb.

"So go kiss more girls," Annika said with a shrug. "Get your data points, draw your conclusions."

Despite what she'd just said, the idea struck Gabi as deeply unappealing.

"And you'll, what, be there by my side, waiting for me when I come home?" Gabi asked, a tiny bead of hope gathering in her chest.

But Annika shook her head.

"I know myself, at least that much. Like you said before, it takes a lot to hold my attention, but when I'm in on someone, I'm all in, no sharing. You're either with me and just me, or you're not," she said simply. "If you want to explore, you should. But I can't be a part of that, not anymore."

Gabi nodded, a few more tears leaking out.

"So that's that, huh?" she said, sniffling.

"I mean, you could always say fuck it, let's be girlfriends and spend every day together, and I would happily agree to that," Annika said, half teasing, half painfully hopeful.

Gabi smiled at Annika and wiped her eyes, placing one last soft kiss on her lips.

"I think…" Annika said. She still knelt with her head on Gabi's thighs, eyes shining with vulnerability and tears. "I think I need to not see you for a while, after this weekend. We have two months before Maia's bridal shower, and I don't think we should speak until then."

Gabi felt her heart crack like an egg, sadness filling her chest, thick and soupy as yolk, but she nodded.

"Okay," she rasped, voice hoarse from crying, "that sucks, but okay."

Annika stood, took her bottle of wine, and went into the house.

Gabi watched her, selfishly wanting her to come back and sit with her, for everything to be the same as it was three hours ago.

You can't have it both ways she heard Annika saying in her mind again.

PART SEVEN

Bridal Shower

May–July

CHAPTER TWENTY-NINE

Somehow, Annika had made it through the games she and Gabi had come up with weeks earlier, laughing and giddy, getting distracted by kisses.

She pulled the cards from the cardboard cutout of Jonnie's face, asked Maia's friends trivia about her sister and her fiancé, and doled out points.

She avoided eye contact with Gabi but kept up a smile and a steady stream of teasing patter for Maia's sake. Everyone pretended that the bride and her maids of honor weren't fighting.

Maia let her sleep in her bed that night, no questions asked, only shot her a look as she curled up for the night.

Annika barely slept, thinking of Gabi two floors below her, lying in the bed they'd shared just the night before. How this morning she'd woken up to a kiss from Gabi and now there'd be no more, despite the fact that they loved each other.

Feeling emotions is awful, she thought as the hours ticked by and the thoughts kept swirling. She wondered if Gabi was asleep, if she felt even a fraction as horrid as Annika did.

"You were right," Annika said when Maia came into the room to find her awake the next morning. "I never want to be emotionally intimate with someone I'm dating again."

Maia just smiled sadly and crawled back into bed beside her, sitting up against the pillows.

"I take it your talk with Gabi didn't go great," she said.

"What tipped you off?" Annika said sarcastically, crossing her arms over the cover and glaring at the ceiling, tear tracks now etched into her cheeks from the amount she'd cried.

"Actually, it was the fact that Gabi left on an early flight this morning," Maia said gently. "She sent me a text around five saying she was off to the airport, that she loved me and never meant to hurt me, that she's sorry for lying to me, and that she hopes I can forgive her."

Annika squeezed her eyes shut and said, "Mai, I'm so sorry I lied to you. If I fucked up you guys' friendship. I know how much you two love each other."

Maia sighed.

"First of all, you did nothing on your own. And I *am* still pissed at you," she said, tucking a strand of her loose hair behind her ear, "especially because this turned my bachelorette weekend into a clusterfuck and created tension between my Mohs. But I'm also impressed with the amount that you were able to keep a secret. You've *never* been able to do that before. Usually, you blurt it out to the first person you see."

Annika groaned.

"It was actually wicked hard," she said. "Ask Vanessa, I literally reached a breaking point and ended up just spilling it all to her."

She leaned her head against Maia's slim shoulder and said, "I really love her, Mai."

"I know, I could tell. And I'm so proud of you for letting your heart open to someone, even though it got smashed. But before I kick her ass for breaking your heart and then shake her for lying to me and *then* eventually forgive her because she's my best and oldest friend and I love her like a sister, give me the full rundown," Maia said. "Why is she on a plane to Maine and you're here?"

So, Annika told her. How Gabi wanted to find herself before getting involved in something serious again, how she needed to trust herself to stand in her identity, how she loved Annika, but she just couldn't be with her right now.

"Basically, she tricked me into loving her and then told me she loved me, but it wasn't enough," Annika finished, picking at a loose thread in the duvet cover.

I wasn't enough, she thought miserably.

It was this thought that she returned to again and again in the weeks that followed, when she sat staring forlornly out the window at her sewing machine at work, or out her window from her couch at home, remembering the times Gabi had lain there with her, had kissed her and touched her there. The nights she'd gone to sleep with her in her arms and woken to her smile.

A month after the bachelorette party, Annika spent most days just going through the motions. She missed Gabi like a physical ache in her chest, like she'd taken a spoon and carved out the chunk of her heart that Gabi had taken up residence in.

She realized how much time they had spent on each other. The texting during the days and Gabi's shifts, the weeknights and weekends spent together. Despite never having gone on a real date, they had embedded themselves in each other's lives in a way Annika didn't know how to pry out without serious damage.

Despite never having been her girlfriend officially, Gabi sure had given her a real broken heart.

She stopped climbing, stopped going to trivia with Vanessa and Mindy, rebuffed all of their lovingly transparent attempts to get her to hang out. She was even finding it hard to get her work done. Listening to brides cry about their dresses or gush about their fiancés finally got to her, especially when the couple was queer. It tore open that aching gap in her heart a little more with each appointment, each time she had to take a measurement and fake a smile.

It hit a low when Vanessa found her crouched behind her desk and sobbing one afternoon after an appointment where the bride had mentioned she wanted to look like Elsa singing "Let It Go," a fact that would have previously horrified her. But anything remotely Disney just reminded her of Gabi now.

Gabi and her whimsical, childish streak that made Annika melt. She thought about the time she'd watched her dance and sing off-key to the *Tangled* soundtrack, loopy from lack of sleep. Remembered hanging Gabi's copy of the original *Mulan* poster behind her couch for her birthday and how knowing it would make Gabi smile had made her heart glow like a jar full of fireflies.

"My guy," Vanessa said now, "I know you've been trying to keep her out of it, but I'm calling Maia in as reinforcement. You're clearly not doing well."

"What are you talking about," Annika deadpanned, flopping onto her back on the tile floor and staring at the white painted ceiling. "I'm in peak form."

Vanessa raised her eyebrow wryly.

Maia came to get her and brought her home soon after. She tucked her into bed and made her tea, petted her hair as she sobbed into her pillow.

"Niki, I'm so sorry," Maia whispered. "If I had known this is how it would go, I probably *would* still have made you talk to each other because open communication is the hallmark of a healthy relationship, but I'm still sorry your heart is hurting so much."

"Yeah, thanks for that," Annika said, voice muffled by her pillow. "We could have blissfully gone on as we were if you hadn't been controlling and scrolled through her pictures."

Even as she said it, Annika knew this was a lie. She herself had known what they had was untenable. But it felt good to blame Maia, rather than face the truth. That Annika hadn't been enough to make Gabi stay, that she didn't want to be Annika's in the ways that really mattered. That her worst fears were true. She'd finally let someone in past her defenses, and what she'd found had been lacking.

"What's going on in that busy, beautiful brain of yours, Nik?" Maia said, lying down to spoon Annika from behind, holding her bundled body over the covers. Despite the fact that it was the end of June and seventy-five degrees out, Annika found the weight of the blankets soothing, her sister's tight hold helping to ground her spinning thoughts.

"Do you think I'm too much?" Annika said haltingly, after a long moment. "Too flighty or irresponsible?"

"No," Maia said, simply and immediately.

"But you're always giving me a hard time, saying I need counseling—"

"You *do* need counseling," Maia cut in.

Annika glared at the white cotton of her pillowcase and said, "You think everyone needs counseling."

"Everyone *does* need counseling," Maia replied, and Annika rolled her eyes, even though her sister couldn't see them.

"I feel like you don't trust me to live my own life sometimes,"

Annika said quietly, and Maia sighed. "And don't say that this situation proves that."

"Oh my God, I wasn't going to," Maia said, annoyed. "But—"

"Oh, here we go," Annika grumbled.

"Holy shit, Niki, just let me speak," Maia said, swatting Annika on the butt.

"Hey!" Annika protested.

"Don't interrupt me," Maia said primly. "Listen, I love you and I want you to have a good, full life, okay? Sometimes, I think you get in your own way when it comes to that. Almost like, I don't know, you don't think you deserve it."

Annika shifted uncomfortably.

"Babe," Maia said, and she squeezed her sister tightly, pressing Annika's back into her slim chest, "you deserve the world. Even though I sometimes give you a hard time and we don't agree on, like, most things, I really do believe in you. You're an amazing goddess of the fabric arts, and I love you no matter what, you dumbass."

Now Annika was crying again, but for a completely different reason.

"I love you, too, Mai," she said, clenching her sister's arm to her chest as tears slipped down her cheeks and into her hair, "even if you are a nit-picking perfectionist pain in the ass."

Though she couldn't see Maia's face, she knew her sister was smiling.

"Now, do you want to eat the rest of the cake samples from the tasting and yell at the designers on *Project Runway*?" Maia asked.

"They just make such ridiculous design choices," Annika said, sniffling.

Maia hugged her tightly and murmured, "That's my girl."

CHAPTER THIRTY

True to her word, Maia had gone a week without speaking to Gabi, and Gabi had respected her boundary.

But exactly a week after their fight in Nashville, Gabi texted, sent a voice note, and called Maia, begging for her forgiveness and asking her to meet to talk it out. After keeping her text on read for three hours, Maia agreed to meet her for coffee the next morning at their favorite local coffee shop.

Gabi arrived at the converted gas station heartsick, exhausted, and looking it.

"You look like shit," Maia said in lieu of a greeting, and Gabi laughed until she felt something crack beneath her ribs, and tears fell from her eyes. Maia, an Eshet Chayil—a woman of valor—through and through and truest of friends, wrapped her arms around Gabi as they stood in line to order their coffees and waited for the well of her emotions to dry.

For all that Gabi and Annika gave her grief for her high-maintenance tastes, Maia had the biggest heart of almost anyone Gabi knew. In that moment, as she sobbed apologies on her oldest friend's shoulder, Gabi sent a blessing to the counselors who assigned them beds next to each other all those years ago.

They retrieved their coffees and a cinnamon bun to split and took seats at a sunny picnic table on the sidewalk. They sipped in silence, and Gabi's stomach twisted into knots with each passing moment. She watched Maia dig into the cinnamon bun, large and fluffy and oozing with cream cheese frosting, and resisted the urge to bite her nails.

Before the waiting became unbearable, Maia placed her fork on the side of the plate with a clink, smoothed down her ponytail, and folded her hands primly on the tabletop, ready to get down to business.

"I've heard Annika's version," she said. "Now I want to hear it all from you."

So Gabi told her.

Told her how she'd asked for Annika's help, but how, in hindsight, she'd really been into her all along. How it had gone from just sex to sleepovers and dinners and all-day text conversations. How Annika had somehow planted a seed in her heart that had taken full bloom before she knew it.

"You two really did fall in love," Maia murmured, taking a thoughtful sip of her coffee while Gabi picked half-heartedly at the remains of the cinnamon bun.

"How...how is she?" Gabi asked hesitantly.

Maia took a bite of cinnamon bun, then brushed her hands off deliberately.

"I'm not sure I'm at liberty to divulge that information," she said carefully.

Gabi snorted. "Okay, Maia Silberberg, Esquire."

Maia rolled her eyes and sighed.

"How do you think she's doing, babe?" she asked, crossing her fleece covered arms and leaning back on her bench, one eyebrow arched.

"About as well as I am?" Gabi guessed.

"Hmm," Maia said, and she tapped one coral manicured finger to her lips, "except you're the one who ended things because you were scared about how big your feelings for her were, and *she* was ready to dive into her feelings, for once, and you broke her heart. Oh, and you made her lie to me about it for months."

Gabi opened her mouth to argue, had to acknowledge the truth of her words, and groaned, laying her head against the rough wooden table instead.

"I know, girl, I know," Maia said as she stroked her hair sympathetically.

"Have I mentioned how fucking sorry I am about lying to you?" Gabi asked.

"At least twenty times in the last twenty-four hours," Maia said as Gabi turned her cheek against the table and peered up at her. "If I didn't think you were sincere, I wouldn't have come today."

"I don't deserve you, Mai," Gabi replied, feeling her ravaged heart ooze love for her oldest friend.

"I know," Mai said with a teasing grin so much like Annika's it was like a stab to her softest parts.

Weeks passed.

May turned to June, and Gabi's first Pride Month acknowledging her sexuality passed with little fanfare. She'd started wearing a rainbow heart pin on her scrubs at work next to her name tag, coming out to her colleagues in the most understated way she could imagine.

She and Rachel took Celia to a drag queen story hour at their local public library one weekend. Gabi had spent the morning crying her heart out to Rachel at her kitchen table, and Rach had decided Gabi needed some outside time.

After the reading, a cute single mom flirted with Gabi. Rachel shot her an encouraging look while Celia systematically took every book from the shelf at her feet and threw it on the floor. But while Gabi smiled and made small talk with the woman, her only thought was that she wasn't Annika.

When July arrived and summer with it, Gabi graduated from her residency and was hired by a small gynecology practice in South Portland, a goal she'd been working toward for the last twelve years.

For the first time in her adult life, her work schedule was reasonable. She figured, with little enthusiasm, now was as good a time as any to get back on the apps, since that was the whole reason she wasn't with Annika. She'd done very little dating research these past few months, besides exploring how many pints of ice cream one human woman could consume in a week.

But as she sat on her couch in her off hours and swiped, she found she had little appetite for it. There were women who came across her screen that looked lovely, who shared her interests and hobbies, who had funny responses to the prompts. But when her thumb would move to swipe right, there would be a pinch in her chest, and she would be overwhelmed with the absurd feeling that she was cheating on Annika by even contemplating matching with another woman.

Eventually, she thought to hell with it and messaged the first woman who matched with her and seemed somewhat normal to get drinks.

So now, on a weekday night in mid-July, Gabi was on a date.

She was on a date with a beautiful, interesting woman.

She was on a date with a beautiful, interesting woman who wasn't Annika.

And she fucking *hated* every minute of it.

Every time the woman smiled at her, she thought of Annika's teasing grin. The way she flashed it after she'd mocked her, before she kissed her, while she kept her on the edge of a pleasure so sharp it nearly hurt and made her beg for release.

Whenever her date laughed or sipped her drink or touched Gabi flirtatiously on the leg, knocked her knee into Gabi's as she faced her on their barstools, all Gabi could think was She's not Annika.

The worst thing was that she had no one but herself to blame for the stabbing pain in her chest as she walked home.

She saw Maia seated on the brick wall that lined the lawn in front of her building. She was dressed in jean shorts and a short-sleeve button-down, hair slicked back and sleek despite the humidity. Gabi's own hair was in a braided crown, the humidity too much for her curls.

Maia surveyed her outfit as she walked up the street, the orange and white printed short sleeve sundress she wore, unbuttoned to display a tasteful flash of cleavage, the low-heeled gold sandals that slapped against the asphalt, the small chunky gold hoops in her ears.

"How was it?" Maia asked.

She stood up to give Gabi a hug in greeting.

"It was fine. She was fine, I just felt..." Gabi said, trying to order the jumble of her thoughts.

"Nothing?" Maia supplied for her, and Gabi shook her head.

"You know when you put on a pair of jeans and before you even button them, you just know they won't fit, even though they're, like, really cute?" Gabi said. She turned to lead Maia into the building.

Maia laughed and nodded, said, "Uh-huh."

"It felt just like that," Gabi said.

"Yeah, it's hard to make it work when you already know that there's something out there that *does* fit incredibly well and makes your ass look fabulous," Maia said pointedly.

To Gabi's surprise, after her initial anger at being lied to had abated, Maia became wholeheartedly invested in Gabi and Annika rekindling their relationship. According to her, why wouldn't she want two people she loved to love each other?

"I'm just saying, in my professional opinion as someone who knows and loves you arguably too well, you're being a real knucklehead and need to get over yourself," Maia said as Gabi let her into her apartment.

"You really have a way with people, Mai," Gabi said wearily. "Those tech bros you work for are so lucky to have you."

Maia waved her hand dismissively and plopped her tote bag on the coffee table before falling back onto the couch.

"I'm spending all my extra empathy on keeping Jonnie's mom from having an aneurysm about the bridal shower," she said, body slumped on the couch cushions. "Plus, I think your hard head needs a little tough love to break through."

She knocked her fist lightly against Gabi's skull, and Gabi slapped her hand away.

"How are you feeling about seeing my dear sister next weekend at the shower?" Maia asked. "Is seeing her sweet bod all dressed up going to drive you wild?"

"Ew, gross, that's your sister," Gabi said, making a face.

"Hey, you're the one that's seen her naked," Maia returned with a shrug.

Gabi was already trying not to spend every waking moment thinking of Annika's naked body, and she didn't appreciate Maia bringing it up when she already felt like shit.

The truth was, she both dreaded the shower and was desperate for its arrival, if only because she'd finally be in the same space as Annika after two long months.

The next Sunday found her in her car, inspecting every angle of her face in the mirror. She had put in extra care with her makeup, the thin line of black on her upper lid crisp and clean, her lips a soft rose petal–pink that complemented the color of her strapless tea-length dress that was cut close to her body, her curls gelled and tamed within an inch of their lives. She wore simple teardrop freshwater pearl earrings that dangled an inch from her lobe and a matching gold necklace with one pearl charm that Matt had given her for their sixth anniversary.

Her mind could not be farther from her ex-boyfriend, though.

"Okay, Dr. Mendon," she said to her reflection, "when you see Annika, you will not freak out. You will be a normal adult and say hi to her, and then you will walk away. You will not spiral or ramble or cry. She is just a human woman you happen to love, but it's not a big deal. Who knows, maybe you won't even see her or have to interact with her at all."

Lie-filled pep talk complete, Gabi closed the sun visor mirror and exited the car, praying the combination of anxiety and the hot late July sun wouldn't ruin her makeup.

She opened the door to Jonnie's mother's house, a white colonial in Falmouth with black shutters and day lilies growing in clumps in the front yard, and ran right into Nora, Maia and Annika's mother.

"Gabi, how are you?" Nora said. She reached out and hugged Gabi. It might have been her imagination, but Gabi thought the hug was not as enthusiastic as it might have been in the past.

"Hi," said a familiar voice over Nora's shoulder, and Gabi looked up to meet Annika's eyes.

Looking at her was like jumping into the icy waters of the Casco Bay on a hot August day, the most painful relief she'd ever felt. Her eyes drank Annika in like they'd been gasping for the sight of her for the last two months.

She was even better than Gabi remembered, than the photos on her phone.

Her dark hair was loose around her shoulders in gentle waves, bangs a touch shorter than she remembered. There was a light shimmer of eyeshadow around her eyes, emphasizing the rich hue of their brown. Her eyelashes were darkened with mascara, lips a touch pinker than usual. She was dressed in a navy-blue linen vest that revealed a vee of tanned and freckled summer skin over her sternum and left her arms and shoulders bare, tattoos somehow more vivid against her skin than Gabi remembered. Matching wide-legged calf-length linen pants and light tan leather slides, finger and toenails painted teal for the summer. A stack of thin silver bangles on her untattooed wrist and slim silver rings on her fingers completed the look.

Deliciously, gloriously Annika.

Gabi felt her throat go dry and her stomach bottom out at the sight of her, her pulse pounding in every inch of her veins.

"H-hey," she managed to squeak out as she let go of Nora, who conspicuously seemed to vanish back into the house. She took a deep breath and squared her shoulders, faced Annika fully. "Cool outfit. Did you make that yourself?"

Gabi grimaced as the words left her mouth, thinking about Maia and Jonnie's engagement party all those months ago.

A shadow of her usual grin ghosted across Annika's lips as if she remembered their teasing and, okay, flirtatious conversation from that event.

"Thanks. Did you make yours?" Annika replied, eyes trailing across Gabi's body, taking in the clinging cut of the dress, the topography of her curves it emphasized. "You look nice," Annika concluded, voice neutral.

Gabi opened her mouth to say something more, but then Jonnie's mother clinked her glass and the twenty-five women assembled, aunts and cousins and friends of both mothers and the bride, turned their attention to her.

"If everyone could take their seats, please," she said, gesturing to the long banquet table that took up the length of their dining room.

"I'm sitting next to Maia in the middle and you're seated, um, next to me," Annika said, nearly shyly. She tucked her hair behind her ear and revealed even more silver jewelry through the lobes of her ears as she shifted on her feet.

"Do you want me to switch with one of the other bridesmaids? Because I totally can, Niki, if that would be better for you. I mean, not to presume that sitting next to me might be hard for you, you might be totally over everything that happened between us by now and want to just forget it ever happened and I'm being a total asshole and—"

"Gab," Annika said, resting her hand, as warm and rough fingered as Gabi remembered, on her biceps and squeezing lightly. Gabi shut her mouth immediately and grimaced again. "You don't need to switch with one of the other bridesmaids. I can handle sitting next to you for one meal."

She squeezed again, let go, and turned to head into the room. Gabi felt something in her sink. She hadn't addressed the part about being over Gabi.

If Annika had asked her to move, it would have meant she was still hurting, and if she was still hurting, she still cared about Gabi.

The fact that she might not, might have gotten over Gabi by now, sent a painful tremor of remorse flooding her system.

She settled on her chair next to Annika after giving Maia a huge hug and whispering mazel tov into her ear.

Maia cast a glance at her sister and then raised her perfectly filled brow in question to Gabi.

Gabi shrugged in response.

It was a tight fit around the table, and Gabi, body full and hips wide, found it nearly impossible to keep her arms or thighs from brushing Annika's during the meal. Each time her elbow, the tattooed one no less, brushed Gabi's arm, her thigh pressed to Gabi's, her foot accidentally touched Gabi's under the table, a thrill shot through Gabi, sparked in her veins like electricity.

She was so alert to Annika's presence, her heat and the clean citrus scent of her perfume, the soft fall of her hair as it brushed against her when she leaned forward to refill her glass of iced tea or pass a plate of sweet noodle kugel or spinach quiche along, that she could think of little else, let alone eat or engage with the conversation.

It was a dizzying mix of emotions. Longing to reach out and place her hand on Annika's toned thigh beneath the table, to feel the heat of her skin beneath the linen of her outfit.

Sadness at the knowledge that Annika, friendly and open and eager to please, would make polite conversation with her, play nice for her sister's sake, but the brightness she'd come to know, the quick mind and quicker wit, wouldn't be there.

Desire for her sparked in Gabi by the proximity of her body, the teasing glimpse of skin her outfit displayed, the plump shine of her lips as she licked a stray drop of iced tea from them.

It was too much for Gabi, the tidal wave of sensation she felt in Annika's presence.

She was trying to work out how she could extract herself from this situation when their hostess stood up and clinked her glass to announce the beginning of the games and presents portion of the event.

Gabi took this as her cue to slip out to the bathroom.

How had she fucked up this badly, letting Annika go?

Why had she insisted on needing more evidence, more time, when she'd known in her heart and her soul that she was head over heels in love with her? That she'd never felt this way for someone before?

Why was she such a coward, always choosing the easy way out?

With Matt, who she'd been with because it was simple, it had made sense, even if he'd never inspired even a fraction of the emotions she was feeling now.

With Annika, pretending it was just sexual exploration, just pure desire even as she watched her sleeping at night in her bed, traced the lines of her face with tender fingers, daydreamed about her at work.

Why couldn't she face her feelings until it was nearly too late?

Maia was right, she knew, that she'd run from what Annika had offered her because it scared her. Used the excuse of self-discovery as a shield from the truth.

That, at thirty-one, she didn't really know what love was and was terrified to let herself find out.

Despite her pep talk in the car, tears pricked her eyes as she sat on the floor in the bathroom and leaned against the door. She tipped her head back and blinked rapidly to try to dispel them, but they fell anyway.

She let them fall for a minute or two, let herself wallow in the misery of self-pity before she pulled herself together, for Maia.

She stood, looking at herself in the mirror as she gently blotted under her eyes and reapplied her lipstick, rearranging the fall of her curls as best she could.

Gabi opened the door to find someone standing in the narrow hallway, nearly knocking into them.

"Ah, sorry," she chirped, righting herself at the last second.

Only to look up and find Annika staring down at her.

Chapter Thirty-one

One look told Annika that Gabi had been crying in the bathroom, and it broke her heart wide open.

Her lovely round face was blotchy, and there was a smudge of mascara in the corner of her eye. Annika longed to reach forward to fix it with her thumb, to wrap Gabi in her arms and hold her close. The obvious pain on her face called to the softest, gooiest parts in Annika's heart.

She didn't know what had upset Gabi so much that she'd run to the bathroom, if it was Annika's presence or the reality of Maia's impending marriage or something else. She'd felt Gabi's discomfort radiating off her as they sat next to each other at the table, had noted how little she ate and how much less she spoke.

Annika didn't want to be this aware of the woman who stood before her. The one she'd accidentally sent her fragile heart to. The one who had returned it to her, box unopened and contents smashed to pieces. But, fuck, if she hadn't been tracking every move Gabi made since she'd walked through the front door. If her whole body hadn't relaxed at the sight of Gabi in her clingy dress that forcibly reminded Annika of the hours she'd spent cataloging every bare inch of her body.

The space between them felt like a yawning chasm, despite the fact that they were now barely a foot apart in the hallway.

God, how Annika had missed her. Just being this near her was enough to send her heart into overdrive, make her body demand to be pressed to Gabi's.

"Um," Annika said eloquently, "hey."

Gabi just stared at her, her eyes wide and bright with recent tears, the whites tinged pink from crying.

"I came to find you." Annika tried again, voice nearly cracking with tension, throat bone dry. "Marla wants us to help with the newlywed game."

"Oh," Gabi said, a hint of disappointment coloring her voice. "Yeah, okay."

Neither of them moved.

"Are you okay?" Annika blurted out and then cringed internally at the volume of her own question. "I just mean, um, it...maybe it's hard for you, knowing Maia's really getting married?"

Gabi gave her a skeptical look.

"That's not why I was crying," she replied, crossing her arms across her ample chest.

Why couldn't Gabi look bad, at least? It would be easier to see her if she looked even a fraction less gorgeous. If her hair was frizzy, or she had a pimple on her chin she couldn't cover up, or her dress wasn't the proper color for her skin tone. Or even better, if it was made from a polyester blend. But who was Annika kidding? Gabi would still look radiant to her even if all those things were true.

The dress Gabi'd chosen to wear today was the prettiest pink against her pale skin. The summer-weight cotton fabric clung to her serpentine curves, and her curls hung loosely around her shoulders.

"I have plenty of friends who are married," Gabi added.

"Right, right." Annika swallowed and nodded.

Did she want to know that Gabi had been crying because of her? Did she want Gabi to be distraught over her?

"Why were you crying, then?" her mouth said before her filter could catch up.

Gabi looked down at her feet.

Annika wanted to fist her curls roughly and tilt Gabi's head back, make her look at her and really see what Gabi had done to her. Wanted to push her against the wall and kiss her breathless, push up her skirt and touch her until she begged for release and then keep her there until she told her if it had been worth it, breaking her heart. To make Gabi tell her why she hadn't been enough to make her stay. Wanted to hold her so tight Gabi was grafted to Annika's soul so she couldn't slip away from her again.

"Because," Gabi said slowly, cheeks flushing, "I miss you, Niki."

Annika closed her eyes against the sight of her.

"And what does *that* mean, Gab?" Annika said, voice breaking as she held back tears, anger flaring in her chest, "That you miss my company? Miss us having sex?"

"I miss *you*, Niki. All of you," Gabi said quietly.

As much as she tried, Annika couldn't hold her own tears back, and they began rolling down her face. Here she was having an overwrought emotional showdown with Gabi, just like she'd sworn to herself she wouldn't do for Maia's sake.

She'd told herself while she got ready this morning that she'd get through the party, keep it light and breezy, stick to safe topics, and stay at least five feet away from Gabi, and then get home and collapse.

She knew Gabi took a step closer to her, though her eyes were still squeezed shut. Could feel the heat and proximity of her as Gabi lifted her hand to her face, cupped her cheek, and brushed at her tears with her thumb as they rolled silently down her cheek. She had cried more over this woman than she'd ever thought she could cry over someone, and yet still they came. As if she was trying to drown the hollow in her heart that Gabi had left, fill it up like a sandcastle moat on the beach at high tide, full when the water recedes.

"I missed the way your whole body lights up when you talk about your store, missed never knowing what I'd find when I opened the door to your apartment. Would you be making mozzarella or sewing a doll's dress for Vanessa's niece from leftover scraps from work or buzzing with some new piece of information you needed to tell me about in detail?" Gabi murmured.

Despite herself, Annika laughed.

"You really needed to know everything about the matriarchal social structure of orca whales," Annika replied tearfully, eyes still closed.

"It *was* highly interesting to learn that pods that are related share dialects," Gabi said tenderly, her other hand cupping Annika's face as Annika let out a watery chuckle, sighed, and opened her eyes.

"I can't believe you remember that," Annika said. She rested her forehead against Gabi's, gaze locked on Gabi's eyes.

"I remember everything, Nik," Gabi said, voice weighty with emotion.

She lifted her head, and Annika, weak fool that she was, let Gabi glide her lips over hers once, twice, savoring the sweetness of her as it mingled with the salt of her own tears.

"You hurt me," Annika said into the quiet between them when they'd pulled apart, "so bad. You made me feel like I wasn't enough."

A shudder went through Gabi's body, as if the sadness and hurt in Annika's voice was painful for her to hear.

"I know." Gabi sighed out. "I'm so, so sorry for doing that. You are enough, oh my God, you are *more* than enough."

"Did you find what you were looking for at least?" Annika asked as she pulled back from Gabi, out of her touch, and put space between them.

Gabi let her hands fall to her sides, defeated.

"Yes," Gabi said, gaze not leaving hers, fingers curled like she might still reach out for her.

Annika nodded. "That's good."

She stepped away from Gabi, pulled on the bottom of her vest to straighten it.

"We'd better get back, or Marla might have a stroke," she said, referring to Maia's future mother-in-law.

Annika turned to go, ready to leave Gabi behind her, to truly close this chapter forever and try to let her love for Gabi recede into a memory.

"Wait," Gabi said. Her hand shot out and grabbed Annika's wrist, her smaller fingers dry and warm against her skin.

Annika paused midmotion and looked down at her hand, her touch familiar. It brought to mind all those late nights talking on her couch, Annika playing absent-mindedly with Gabi's fingers. All the mornings she'd woken to find Gabi had reached for her hand in the night.

"I did end up going on dates with a few women," Gabi began.

"Gab, I *really* don't want to hear about that," Annika interjected, her muscles tensing, readying to flee.

"Just listen to me, please, Annika," Gabi pleaded, tugging slightly on her arm to keep her in place. "I went on a few dates, but I knew they wouldn't work out because I kept comparing them to you. To what you would have said or thought of them, to what you would have done in their place. I couldn't kiss any of them because it felt like I'd be cheating on you," Gabi said, speaking quickly, as if she wasn't sure how much time Annika would give her, and she needed to make the most of it.

"I love *you*, Niki, and I was a fucking *coward* for not taking what you were offering in Nashville. The truth is that it was never about finding myself or getting more queer experience. It was always about how scared I was of the way you make me feel, how big those feelings are, how terrifying it is to try and embrace them when I've been running from big and settling for just enough for a long time. But I've seen what it's like without you, and I'm not interested in that life anymore," Gabi finished, chest nearly heaving with the effort of speaking the words.

Annika stared at her in shock. "You...what?"

"I want you to be my girlfriend, you dork," Gabi said, giving her arm a yank in emphasis. "I want to go to sleep with you by my side and wake up with you every morning. I want to take you on a real fucking date, Niki. I want to go to the farmers market with you and make a big meal out of what we bought from some overly complicated recipe you found on social media. I want to run out to the store to get you the crucial ingredient you inevitably forgot to buy. I want to hold your hand as I walk down the street and dance with you at Maia's wedding and text you to remind you to eat lunch every afternoon because you don't take care of yourself, Nik, and you really need to look up from your work and remember to eat—"

Her rambling was cut off when Annika swooped down to kiss her, wrapped her in her arms, and pulled her close, pressing their bodies together.

Gabi let out a little yelp of surprise, and Annika laughed against her lips, kissed her harder.

"Of course I'll be your real, official girlfriend, you dumbass," Annika said, tears dripping down her face again. "You're not scared anymore?"

Gabi shrugged. "I mean, yeah, I'm still fucking terrified, but I figure what's life without a little terror?"

Annika grinned back at her and kissed her again, letting herself get lost in it.

"As much as I love that you two have *finally* seen the error of your ways," a familiar voice drawled from the doorway at the opposite end of the hall, "today is *still* about me, so if you wouldn't mind turning off your sex brains and turning on your maid of honor brains, I would much appreciate it."

Annika pulled back to look at Maia and glared.

"Sure thing, Mai," Gabi said, and Annika looked at her to see that she was grinning.

Maia rolled her eyes and walked back to the party.

Gabi went to follow her, but Annika wasn't quite ready for this moment to be over yet. She grabbed Gabi's hand and tugged her back toward her, pinning her to the wall with her body.

"Niki, we have to get back out there," Gabi said.

"She can wait one more minute. I need to kiss my girlfriend," Annika said, and she kissed Gabi with two months' worth of pent-up longing until both of them were panting and flushed.

"I really missed that," Gabi said as Annika stepped away from her.

"Yeah," Annika said, a smile, real and broad, spreading across her lips. "I did, too."

EPILOGUE

The Wedding

October

On a crisp Sunday afternoon in the middle of October, Maia Silberberg joined Jonnie Cohen under the chuppah, and the two were wed.

Wine was shared, rings were exchanged, the bride circled the groom seven times, and the groom smashed a glass beneath his leather dress shoes to cries of *Mazel tov!*

Many people cried, but no one cried harder than the bride's sister.

"I thought you hated all of this shit," Gabi whispered to Annika as they walked down the aisle after Jonnie and Maia.

Jonnie scooped Maia up into his arms, the voluminous skirts of her gown trailing behind them. She threw her arms around his neck, their eyes locked on each other like no one else existed in the world. Pure happiness burned from their gazes like beacons.

Gabi had her own arm linked through Annika's, the one dense with tattoos, and leaned into her as Annika dabbed at her eyes with the tissues she'd stashed in the pocket of her dress.

"I hate the wedding-industrial complex," Annika said, bending to murmur to her girlfriend, tears smearing tracks through her makeup. "I hate compulsory heterosexuality, and the hoops people jump through to stick to it. I *love* love. And I really, really love my sister."

Gabi grinned up at the tearful woman on her arm and craned her neck to kiss her as they followed Maia and Jonnie down the aisle.

"*I* love *you*," Gabi said, and she trailed her touch down Annika's arm to take her hand and intertwine their fingers.

Annika smiled down at her, light and love and happiness shining from her brown eyes.

"I love you, too, Gab," she replied.

They walked into the reception hall together, past the cake that had been paid for with part of the proceeds from Annika's wedding grinch jar.

Past Annika's parents, Nora's eyes as wet as her own.

"And to think, a year ago you were deep in your gay panic, and I was pretending I didn't have a huge crush on you," Annika said as she picked up a flute of champagne from a waiter's tray and took a sip.

"And now you're basically living with me and we're talking about adopting a dog," Gabi replied.

What a difference a year makes, Gabi thought, remembering that night at the climbing gym, the way her heart had raced when she'd locked eyes with Annika and realized the woman she'd been checking out was her best friend's little sister.

"Oh, how times have changed." Annika grinned, the corners of her eyes crinkling. Her long hair curled loosely around her bare shoulders, bangs shiny and just brushing her eyebrows. She'd made herself a simple strapless sheath dress that skimmed enticingly over her spare curves and flowed around her like water with her movements, and Gabi thought she was the most beautiful woman she'd ever seen.

She clinked her own glass of champagne against Annika's.

"We'd like to thank you all for coming today to celebrate our love with us," Maia said sometime later, standing from the little round table the bride and groom sat at beside their framed ketubah, wobbling slightly on her heels, clearly already tipsy. "I'd especially like to thank my Mohs, Dr. Gabi Mendon and my sister, Annika, who kept me sane these last few months. Annika, Gabi, you will no longer have to deal with me interrupting your date nights to panic about wedding catastrophes. I want to apologize, again, for that time I barged in without knocking when the DJ canceled. I promise, I didn't see anything."

All the guests laughed, including Gabi, who squeezed Annika's thigh under the table. Annika glared at her sister and flipped her off from her seat at the bridal party's table to the right of the bride and groom's.

"In all seriousness, I love you guys, and I think I more than made up for all the meshugas of the last year by being the reason you're together," Maia went on.

"I object," Annika called out, to laughter from the crowd.

Maia rolled her eyes. "Whatever, let's raise a glass to all the many people who helped Jonnie and me get here today. We love you all."

She raised her glass and drank, everyone in the hall echoing her movements.

"Now," she called, "let's party!"

Maia grabbed Jonnie, tugging him onto the dance floor with one hand and holding her skirts up with the other, the big bow that held up her train to her trim waist flopping with the swaying of her hips.

Gabi stood up, turned to face Annika, and offered her her hand.

Annika, grinning, took it.

❖

Annika thought that maybe she didn't hate weddings after all.

Not as she gazed adoringly into Gabi's face as she gazed adoringly back up at Annika while they danced together. Annika's right hand was clasped in Gabi's left, her left hand on Gabi's hip and Gabi's right hand on her shoulder.

"Have I told you how fucking gorgeous you look today?" Annika murmured to her, voice just audible over the music the band was playing.

"You might be a little biased, since you made the dress," Gabi replied, her cheeks turning that lovely shade of pink that bewitched Annika.

No matter how many times she complimented her, whether they were fully clothed or in the middle of sex, Gabi always blushed, and it never failed to make Annika's heart soar.

"Mm, I was talking more about the woman in the dress, actually," Annika quipped, and Gabi rolled her eyes.

Annika leaned forward and down a little, their height difference less pronounced with Gabi's four-inch platform heels and her flats, to whisper in Gabi's ear. "I can't wait to take it off you later."

Her breath ghosted across the sensitive skin of Gabi's neck before she placed a chaste kiss on Gabi's cheek and felt Gabi shiver against her body.

"You're a little mean," Gabi said, biting her lip as Annika wiped away the smear of her lipstick from her face.

"And you love it," Annika replied with a smile.

"God, I really do." She grinned back at her.

"Oh, aren't you two just so beautiful together," her mother said as she appeared at their side with Annika's father in tow.

"Mazel tov, Nora," Gabi said, turning away from Annika, her cheeks still splashed pink. "You look amazing today."

Annika had to admit she'd done a good job with her mother's dress, a high neck A-line dark blue silk gown with a gold-flecked accordion-pleated organza layer on top that floated loosely to the floor, the tie at the neck forming a bow that hung beneath her shoulder blades. Simple and elegant, just like her mother.

"Didn't Maia plan such a gorgeous event?" her mother cried, looking wondrously around the event hall. "I'm verklempt. She's got such an eye for detail."

"She certainly knows exactly what she wants," Annika replied smugly.

"Oh shush, Niki," her mother said, and she swatted her on the arm. "Be nice to your sister on her special day."

Annika rolled her eyes and saw Gabi looking down to hide the smile on her lips.

"You two aren't getting any ideas, are you?" her mom asked, eyebrows raised hopefully.

"What kind of ideas?" Annika said, eyes wide and innocent.

"Come on, Nora, leave them alone," her dad said, and he tugged her away to dance, shooting Annika a wink over his shoulder.

Annika looked down to the woman in her arms, the woman who had, somehow, caught her fickle, floundering heart.

"I don't think I'd mind spending the rest of my life with you, Dr. Gabi Mendon," Annika mused.

Gabi's eyes went wide, and before she could do more than open her mouth, Maia appeared in a cloud of tulle and silk.

"My Mohs," she cried affectionately, throwing her slim arms around them both and tugging them into her chest. "Come on, it's time to hora. I need you to help lift me in the chair."

She rushed back into the crowd as the first lines of "Havah Nagilah" came out of the speakers, and the guests crowded onto the dance floor.

Gabi gripped Annika's hand and held on tight, her feet kicking up as they got lost in the flow of people dancing.

And Annika gripped her hand right back, laughing as they went.

About the Author

Sarah G. Levine writes stories about women who look and act like real women finding love and figuring out life. Originally from a small seaside town in Massachusetts, she lives in Brooklyn, NY, with her wife where she tends to many houseplants and dreams of the ocean. You can reach her through her Instagram handle @sgl920, her TikTok @slev920, or her website sarahglevine-agsites.net.

Books Available From Bold Strokes Books

Feeling Lucky by Krystina Rivers. What happens when, despite suddenly having enough money to buy almost anything, Lucy and Tanner start to discover that maybe all they need is each other? (978-1-63679-876-9)

Iceberg by Gun Brooke. When Lady Arabella hires Zandra, she never expects to find love, especially not as a disaster looms on the horizon. (978-1-63679-908-7)

It Happened One Semester by Aurora Rey. After a Pride night hookup, can eager new Assistant Professor Hudson Greene and Dean of Advising Callie Shaw overcome the odds and ace falling in love? (978-1-63679-814-1)

It's Kind of a Bad Idea by Sarah G. Levine. What happens when an emotionally unavailable serial dater meets the one woman she can't help but fall for—who happens to be the one woman who told her not to? (978-1-63679-920-9)

Thankful for You by Tagan Shepard. Everyone deserves to find their person. Maybe Karen has finally found hers? (978-1-63679-884-4)

What Happens On Location by Nan Campbell. How can Helen produce a successful movie when its director is the woman responsible for the demise of her marriage? (978-1-63679-904-9)

When Love Comes Around by Radclyffe and Ronica Black. Can Maya Sanchez and Nolan Wright trust each other enough to build something real, or will the past tear them apart? (978-1-63679-930-8)

Anywhere with You by Margo Glynn. On a road trip through the Great American Southwest, two friends discover nature, hope, and each other. (978-1-63679-907-0)

Burning Bridges by Lesley Davis. Can Clancy and Jude crack the case of eight missing women—and the secrets of their own hearts? (978-1-63679-872-1)

Dreams Entangled by Sophia Kell Hagin. Amid self-doubt, secrets, a pandemic, fear of attack and attempted murder, Pirin and Gracie's attraction turns to love, and their lives will never be the same. (978-1-63679-892-9)

Echoes of Love by Catherine Lane. As Hazel's and Jo's paths intertwine, they're swept up in a whirlwind of long-buried secrets, sizzling chemistry, and memories that won't be denied. (978-1-63679-835-6)

The Fame Game by Ronica Black. Wild child Hollywood actress Luna Kirkman begins dating Hollywood's leading man, only to fall for his straitlaced sister instead. (978-1-63679-858-5)

Moonlight Obsession by Sheri Lewis Wohl. All it takes to stop a clever killer is moonlight, love, and a silver bullet. (978-1-63679-831-8)

My Boyfriend's Wife by Joy Argento. Amid betrayal and heartbreak, can two women discover a love that could heal their pasts and rewrite their futures? (978-1-63679-866-0)

Tapout by Nicole Disney. A struggling MMA fighter finds her edge in an underground ring, but as she falls for the magnetic and ambitious promoter behind the matches, their dangerous world threatens to destroy everything they've fought to rebuild. (978-1-63679-924-7)

An Extraordinary Passion by Kit Meredith. An autistic podcaster must decide whether to take a chance on her polyamorous guest and indulge their shared passion, despite her history. (978-1-63679-679-6)

Heart's Appraisal by Jo Hemmingwood. Andy and Hazel can't deny their attraction, but they'll never agree on the place they call home. (978-1-63679-856-1)

That's Amore by Georgia Beers. The romantic city of Rome should inspire Lily's passion for writing, if she can look away from Marina Troiani, her witty, smart, and unassumingly beautiful Italian tour guide. (978-1-63679-841-7)

Through Sky and Stars by Tessa Croft. Can Val and Nicole's love cross space and time to change the fate of humanity? (978-1-63679-862-2)